ORDINARY PEOPLE

"AN EXTRAORDINARY BOOK!"
Philadelphia Inquirer

"Judith Guest writes with great skill . . . she gets down on the page difficult feelings and complex states of mind, weaves a thread of humor through a fabric of tears, and time and time again rubs two characters together to produce sparks of insight."
Christian Science Monitor

"AN UNPRETENTIOUS, EXPERT PIECE OF POPULAR FICTION . . . GUEST HAS THE VALUABLE GIFT OF MAKING US LIKE HER CHARACTERS; SHE HAS THE RATHER RARER ABILITY TO MOVE A TOUGHENED REVIEWER TO TEARS."
Newsweek

"A GENUINE FIND . . . A LOVELY, HEART-WARMING FAMILY NOVEL IN WHICH 'ORDINARY PEOPLE,' UNDER PRESSURE, TURN OUT TO BE SOMETHING SPECIAL AFTER ALL."
Publishers Weekly

ORDINARY PEOPLE

ORDINARY PEOPLE

ORDINARY PEOPLE

Judith Guest

BALLANTINE BOOKS • NEW YORK

Acknowledgment is made to Norma Millay Ellis for the quotation from "Sonnet CLXXI" by Edna St. Vincent Millay, from *Collected Poems*, Harper & Row. Copyright 1954 by Norma Millay Ellis.

Library of Congress Catalog Card Number: 76-2368

ISBN 0-345-29132-8

This edition published by arrangement with
The Viking Press, Inc.

Manufactured in the United States of America

First Ballantine Books Edition: February 1977
Fifteenth Printing: March 1981

First Special Edition: August 1977
Second Special Edition: September 1980

First Canadian Printing: February 1977
Sixth Canadian Printing: March 1981

for Sharon and Con
and for my husband

all their words,
spoken and unspoken,
being worth remembering.

SONNET CLXXI

But what a shining animal is man,
Who knows, when pain subsides, that is not that,
For worse than that must follow—yet can write
Music, can laugh, play tennis, even plan.
                                        —*Edna St. Vincent Millay*

1

To have a reason to get up in the morning, it is necessary to possess a guiding principle. A belief of some kind. A bumper sticker, if you will. People in cars on busy freeways call to each other *Boycott Grapes,* comfort each other *Honk if You Love Jesus,* joke with each other *Be Kind to Animals—Kiss a Beaver.* They identify, they summarize, they antagonize with statements of faith: *I Have a Dream, Too —Law and Order; Jesus Saves at Chicago Fed; Rod McKuen for President.*

Lying on his back in bed, he gazes around the walls of his room, musing about what has happened to his collection of statements. They had been discreetly mounted on cardboard, and fastened up with push pins so as not to deface the walls. Gone now. Probably tossed out with the rest of the junk—all those eight-by-ten colorprints of the Cubs, White Sox, and Bears, junior-high mementos. Too bad. It would be comforting to have something to look up to. Instead, the walls are bare. They have been freshly painted. Pale blue. An anxious color. Anxiety is blue; failure, gray. He knows those shades. He told Crawford they would be back to sit on the end of his bed, paralyzing him, shaming him, but Crawford was not impressed.

Lay off. Quit riding yourself. Less pressure more humor go with the stuff that makes you laugh.

Right, of course. Right again. Always right: the thing that is missing here is a Sense of Humor. *Life Is a Goddamn Serious Big Deal*—he should have that printed up to put on his bumper—if he had a bumper, which he doesn't, not Conrad Jarrett the Anxious Failure dress this guy in blue and gray. A thousand-word book report due Wednesday in English Lit. The book has not been read. A test over the first six chapters in U.S. history. A surprise quiz in trig, long overdue.

He rolls onto his stomach, pulling the pillow tight around his head, blocking out the sharp arrows of sun that pierce through the window. Morning is not a good time for him. Too many details crowd his mind. Brush his teeth first? Wash his face? What pants should he wear? What shirt? The small seed of despair cracks open and sends experimental tendrils upward to the fragile skin of calm holding him together. *Are You on the Right Road?*

Crawford had tried to prepare him for this. "It's all right, Con, to feel anxious. Allow yourself a couple of bad days, now and then, will you?"

Sure. How bad? Razor-blade bad? He wanted to ask but he hadn't, because at that point his suitcase was packed and his father already on the way to pick him up and remarks like that only got you in trouble, pissed people off. Cancel the visa. Passport Revoked: they stamp it in red across your forehead. Uh uh. He'd had enough of that place. In the last months he had been able to spot the permanent residents every time. That unmistakable shuffling shoulders-bent walk. Mostly old men but some younger ones, too, in the dull, dusty-maroon bathrobes, sides flapping loosely, like the drooped wings of dying birds. Never. It was too damn small a world. Except that you always knew where you were. Mornings you talked first, then had O.T.—macramé, painting, woodworking, clay. Afternoons you could take a nap, go for a walk, work out in the gym—a well-equipped, exclusive YMCA—basketball, handball, racquetball, you name it. Evenings there were card games, small get-togethers in the corners of the lounge, Scrabble, backgammon. Leo told him once, "Stop worrying. You're okay. You can play Scrabble, that means you can concentrate. You're ready." He had laughed. "It means you can spell," he said. "That doesn't mean shit." "Well," Leo said, "it's nice to be good at something."

His father calls to him from the other end of the house. He thrashes to a sitting position, connected at once to sanity and order, calling back: "Yeah! I'm up!" and, miraculously, he *is* up and in the bathroom, taking a leak, washing his hands and face, brushing his teeth. Keep moving, keep busy, everything will fall into place, it always does.

He takes a quick look in the mirror. The news isn't good. His face, chalk-white, is plagued with a weird, constantly erupting rash. *This is not acne,* they assured him. What it *was,* they were never able to discover. Typical. He tries to be patient as he waits for his hair to grow out. He had hacked it up badly, cutting it himself the week before he left. "I didn't think they would let you have scissors," his grandmother said to him. "They shouldn't have," he answered her, oh, so casual, thereby relieving the listeners of shock and embarrassment while exhibiting his poise, his Sense of Humor, see folks? Everything's okay, he's here, wearing his jeans, boots, and jersey shirt, just like everybody else, all cured, nobody panic.

This house. Too big for three people. Straining, he can barely hear the early-morning sounds of his father and mother organizing things, synchronizing schedules at the other end of the hall. It doesn't matter. He doesn't need to hear, and they would certainly not be talking about anything important. They would not be talking, for instance, about him. They are people of good taste. They do not discuss a problem in the presence of the problem. And, besides, there is no problem. There is just Phase Two. Recovery. A moving forward.

From what? Toward what? He dresses himself (Progress!), looking out of the window, studying the lacy line of Russian olives that separates their property from the next-door neighbors'—what's their name? Nice couple, but no kids, they've lived there for years—dammit, dammit, that's the kind of stuff that scares you, not being able to remember names. He stares in concentration at the tall hedge of cedars hiding the house from the road. Cahill. Their name is Cahill. Okay, now relax.

But he cannot relax, because today is a Target Date. Tuesday, September 30. One month, to the day, that he has been home. *And what are you doing Jarrett? Asking weird questions like From what? Toward what?* Questions without answers. Undermining. A serious affliction. Worse than acne, worse, even, than an unidentifiable rash. So what the hell kind of cure was that? In the rec hall one night they showed a movie on insects, *The Something Chronicle. Hellstrom,* that was it. The May fly has a life-span of eighteen hours. It spends that entire time laying eggs for the next generation. May flies, the narrator explained, know the answer. Because they never even have to ask the question. Nice for the May flies.

There is a prickly sensation at the back of his throat. He turns away from the window, picking up his books from the desk. Then he puts them down again. No. Follow routines. First, the bed; then line up the towels in the bathroom; then pick up books; then eat breakfast; then go to school. Get the motions right. Motives will follow. That is Faith. Vainly, he has taken to reading bumper stickers again, but they belong to other people. They are not his statements. *I Am a Hockey Nut. Christ Is the Answer—What Was the Question?*

4

Vaguely he can recall a sense of calm, of peace, that he had laid claim to on leaving the hospital. There were one or two guiding principles to get him through the day. Some ambitious plans, also, for putting his life in order. But the details have somehow been lost. If there ever were any.

2

Razor in hand, he stands before the rectangular, gold-trimmed mirror, offering up a brief prayer: *Thanks. Appreciate all you've done so far. Keep up the* good *work,* while, beside him, his wife brushes her hair. Her face is soft in the morning, flushed, slightly rounded, younger than her thirty-nine years. Her stomach is flat almost as if she never had the babies. She raises her hands to the back of her neck, pinning her hair into a neat coil at the back of her head. Beautiful hair, the color of maple sugar. Or honey. Natural, too. The blue silk robe outlines her slender hips, her breasts.

"Did you call him?"

"Yeah, he's up."

She sighs. "I hate to play golf when it's cold. Why doesn't anybody in this league know enough to quit when the season's over? Leaves on all the fairways, your hands frozen—it's ridiculous."

He leans toward her; gives her a kiss on the neck. "I love you."

"I love you." She is looking at him in the mirror. "Will you talk to him this morning? About the clothes. He's got a closetful of decent things and he goes off every day looking like a bum, Cal."

6

"That's the style. Decency is out, chaos is in——" As her brows lift, he nods. "Okay, I'll talk to him."

"And the other thing, too."

"What other thing?"

"Stopping by Lazenbys' on the way home. Carole called again last week. It's such a little thing. . . ."

"I don't want to pressure him about that. He'll do it when he wants to. Carole understands."

She shrugs. "When people take an interest, it would seem courteous——"

"We all know he's courteous." He turns his attention to his beard. Every morning the same face, the same thoughts. A good time to take stock, though. Calvin Jarrett, forty-one, U.S. citizen, tax attorney, husband, father. Orphaned at the age of eleven. He has caught himself thinking about that lately, thinking of the Evangelical Home for Orphans and Old People, an H-shaped, red brick building on Detroit's northwest side, where he grew up. Wondering if after all these years it is still in existence. Strange that he has never bothered to check. An odd kind of orphanage: most of the kids had at least one living parent; some even had two. He had moved there when he was four, leaving the tiny apartment where he was born. His mother sent him gifts on his birthday, and at Christmas. Occasionally she visited him. Periodically she explained why he was living there, and not with her; there was no room for him in the apartment, no money; it was no neighborhood in which to bring up kids. She had a friend who knew people that were connected with the Home; just luck. The director had told him once that the Home was financed by "religious benefactors."

He was named Calvin, for his dead uncle; Jarrett had been his mother's maiden name. When she came to see him, she came alone. No one claiming to be his father had ever been in attendance; he had no memories of being any man's son. So, if anyone should

7

ask, he can always point out that he had no example to follow.

And what is fatherhood anyway? Talking to a kid about his clothes. Not applying pressure. Looking for signs. He knows what to look for now: loss of appetite, sleeplessness, poor school performance—all negative, so far. His son eats, he sleeps, he does his homework. He says he's happy. Another duty: asking silly questions. *Are you happy?* He has to ask, though; pretends that he is kidding, just kidding; Conrad replies in kind. Pointless. Would the answer have been any different, even if he had thought to ask, before? Good manners have nothing to do with communication, he must remember that. And being a father is more than trusting to luck. That, too. Nobody's role is simple, these days. Not even a kid's. It used to mean minding your manners, respecting those who were bigger than you, treating each day as a surprise package, waiting to be opened. Not any more. So what's changed? Not enough surprises? Too many, maybe.

He has had a vision all these months, of boys, with their heads next to stereo speakers feeding music into their ears, their long legs draped over chairs and sofas. Or their arms, stretched toward a basketball hoop in the side drive (he had sunk the posts in cement himself, when Conrad was eight, Jordan, nine; just after they bought the house). Where are all these kids? Joe Lazenby, Phil Truan, Don Genthe, Dick Van Buren —they are all seniors in high school this year. Is eighteen too old to play touch football on the lawn? Basketball in the side drive? Is it girls? Studies? Since he has been home, Conrad has gone once to the movies. Alone. "Didn't anybody else want to see it?" Cal had asked. "I don't know," he said. "I didn't ask."

Responsibility. That is fatherhood. You cannot afford to miss any signs, because that is how it happens: somebody holding too much inside, somebody else missing signs. *That doctor in Evanston. Make sure he calls him. It is for his own good.* Why? Because his own vision, that of the boys hanging around, isn't coming true? It has only been a month. All the other signs seem right. Stay calm. Keep it light. Try not to lean. A balance must be struck between pressure and concern.

Back when Conrad was in the hospital, back when the visits were limited to twice a month, he could afford to take responsibility for everything: the sections of gray peeling paint in the stair wells; small gobs of dirt swept into the corners of the steps; even a scar at the side of one orderly's mouth. Now that he is home again, things are different. The responsibilities seem enormous. Staggering. His job alone, nobody else's. Motherhood is different, somehow. And what about fathering girls? He must ask Ray Hanley sometime, how it feels. Is there more, or less responsibility? He couldn't take more. *Your mother wants me to tell you, you have a closetful of decent clothes.* He will smile. "Okay. You told me." But, in a minute, he will ask, "What's wrong with what I've got on?"

Nothing. Nothing I can see. Only I don't pass up any chances to discharge these fatherly duties, this is the age of perfection, kid. Everybody try their emotional and mental and physical damndest.

Strive, strive. Correct all defects. All those Saturday trips to the orthodontist, when they were in junior high. Both of his boys had inherited from him, that long, slightly hooked nose; from their mother, the small, determined lower jaw. On them it had required thirty-eight hundred dollars' worth of work, courtesy Peter Bachmann, D.D.S., M.S. "Hell, what's a little money?" he had raved. "Overhaul their whole damn jaws if necessary, this is the age of the perfect mouth!" But, secretly, he had been proud that he was able to afford such expenses. He was supporting his family, *his boys,* in style: whatever they needed, whatever they wanted, they got. He had arrived. He was

here. Not bad for the kid from the Evangelical Home.
And now? Where is he now?

Beth sets breakfast in front of Cal: eggs, bacon,
toast, milk, juice.

Conrad looks up. "Morning."

"Morning. You need a ride today?"

"No. Lazenby's picking me up at twenty after."

He treats this as a piece of good news. "Great!"
Said too heartily, he sees at once. Conrad looks away,
frowning.

"I've got to get dressed," Beth says. "I tee off at
nine." She hands him his coffee; crosses to the doorway; motes of dust flutter nervously in her wake. Conrad is studying. The book is propped against the butter dish.

"What is it, a quiz?"

"Book report."

"What book?"

He raises the cover. Cal reads, *Jude the Obscure.*

"How is it?"

"Obscure."

He sips his coffee. "No bacon and eggs this morning?"

He shakes his head. "I only wanted cereal."

He has lost twenty-five pounds in one year. Another year before his weight will return to normal, Dr.
Crawford predicted.

"You feel okay?"

"Yeah, fine. I just didn't want a big breakfast."

The bony angles need to be fleshed out.

"You ought to keep trying to put weight on," Cal
says.

"I am. I will. You don't have to be heavy to swim,
Dad."

Back to the book, and Cal studies the crisp, dry
rectangles on the tile floor. Patterns of sunlight. Familiar and orderly. "How's it going?" he asks.

Conrad looks up. "What?"

"How's it going? School. Swimming. Everything okay?"

"Yeah, fine. Same as yesterday."

"What does that mean?"

A faint smile. "It means you ask me that every day."

"Sorry." He smiles, too. "I like things neat."

Conrad laughs. He reaches out to flip the book closed. "Okay," he says, "let's talk."

"Can't help it," Cal says. "I regard it as a challenge, people reading at the table."

"Yeah."

"So, how come Lazenby's picking you up?"

"He's a friend of mine."

"I know that. I just wondered if it meant you'd be riding with him from now on."

"I don't have a formal commitment yet. I'm gonna have my secretary talk to his, though."

"Okay, okay." ·

"We should have the contract drawn up by the end of the week."

"Okay."

He does a familiar thing, then; shoves his hands into the back pockets of his jeans as he rocks backward in the chair. Conrad, after all. A good sign, despite the brutal haircut; the weary look about the eyes. The eyes bother him every day. He still believes in the picture he carries in his wallet of a boy with longish, dark hair and laugh lines about the mouth and eyes; no weary look there. This gaunt, thin figure that sits across from him, hair chopped bluntly at the neck, still grins; still kids, but the eyes are different. He cannot get used to it.

His old self. That is the image that must be dispelled. Another piece of advice from the all-powerful Dr. Crawford, Keeper of the Gate. "Don't expect him to be the same person he was before." But he does expect that. As does everyone. His mother, his grandmother, his grandfather—yesterday,

Cal's father-in-law had called him at the office: "I've got to admit, Cal, that it shocked me. He looked so—" and Cal felt him hunting for the painless adjectives "—tired out. Run down. I would think, for the kind of money you paid, they would have at least seen to it that he ate properly, and got enough sleep. And he was so quiet. Just not like his old self at all."

And who was that? The kid who got straight A's all through grade school and junior high? Who rode his two-wheeler sixteen times around the block on his sixth birthday, because somebody bet him he couldn't? Who took four firsts in the hundred-meter free style last year? *Last year.* No, he is not much like that kid. Whoever he was.

He says his piece about the clothes, and Conrad nods absently. "Okay. I just haven't thought about it much. I will, though."

What, no argument? No raising of the eyebrows, no hint of sarcasm in the reply? What kind of a sign is this? Surely not good. Okay, now is the time. Lean, if you have to.

"Another thing," he says. "That doctor in Evanston, what's his name? Berger? Have you called him yet?"

An immediate reaction. The look on his face is tight; closed. The chair legs come down. "No. I don't have time."

"I think we ought to stick to the plan—"

"I can't. I'm swimming every night until six. He didn't say I had to call him, Dad."

"No, I know." He waits while Conrad stares at the table. "I think maybe you ought to. Maybe he could see you on the weekends."

"I don't need to see anybody. I feel fine."

A strained silence. Conrad pushes the cereal bowl, lightly; left, then right.

"I want you to call him anyway," he says. "Call him today."

"I don't finish practice until dinner—"

12

"Call him at school. On your lunch hour."

An obedient boy. Polite. Obedient. Well mannered. Even in the hospital, with his fingernails bitten to bloody half-moons, the dark circles, bloody bruises under his eyes; always, always his behavior was proper, full of respect.

"Thanks for coming." Each time he would say that, as Cal readied himself to leave. The shirt he is wearing today—the way his shoulder blades shove out beneath the soft skin of jersey—it is a shirt he used to wear in the hospital. Growing up is a serious business. He, Cal, would not be young again, not for anything. And not without sponsors: a mother and father, good fortune, God.

3

He sits on the front porch steps, waiting for Lazenby. The air is crisp and cool, and he rubs his hands together, shivering in the thin denim jacket. He should go back inside; get a heavier one, but he doesn't want to risk it. Not that she will care, or say anything. But the hurdle has been jumped once today. Enough. He glances again at his watch. Almost eight-thirty. Lazenby has forgotten. He hopes for a moment that he has; then, prays he hasn't. She would have to drive him. She has a golf game; it will make her late. The wrong direction, across town the two of them alone in the car and he not wanting to screw up and say the wrong thing. *Haul ass Lazenby crissake don't make me stand here until she comes out.*

Abruptly he jumps up, walks to the end of the circular drive. Another thought nags at him, threatening to surface. He shrugs it off. Something unpleasant. Facing the house, he stares up at his bedroom window. In the early morning, the room is his enemy; there is danger in just being awake. Here, looking up, it is a refuge. He imagines himself safely inside; in bed, with the covers pulled up. Asleep. Unconscious.

The thought surfaces. His father has noticed. Whatever is wrong is now visible. That command: not, "Call the guy," but, "Call him *today*." Worrying.

There is something to worry about, as he has suspected. He did not want to have his suspicions confirmed. In cooler moments, the fear can be shoved back; thought of as overactive imagination, too much hot sauce. Now he has infected his father, and the gray disease is dangerous to both of them. His grandmother was eager to inform him: "Conrad, if you *knew* the strain that man was under these past months, the money was *nothing,* compared with the strain, my heart went out to him, I can't tell you."

Then, don't! he felt like screaming, squirming to pass through the remark, untouched. He wants to belong to this house again, needs to be part of these tall windows set low to the ground, walls half-hidden behind thick waxy rhododendron leaves, the cedar hedge in front, all of it—all elegance and good taste. Good taste is absorbed through the skin, like rays from the sun, in this elegant, tasteful section of Lake Forest, Illinois, a direct quote from a newspaper article. They had laughed when they read it and he laughs now, out loud. See? Haven't lost your sense of humor after all but your sense of identity is what seems to have been misplaced. No. Wrong. You don't lose what you never had.

Lazenby's red Mustang hurls itself into the driveway, and he tosses his books in the back seat; climbs in after them to sit beside Van Buren.

"We're late," Stillman says, "because Dickie's mom had to pack his lunch."

"Two minutes! Christ, you guys were already late when you got to my house!" Van Buren moves over to make room. "Hey, listen, I damn near killed myself over this poly-sci exam."

"Yeah, the guy wants a goddamn *personal analysis* of it all, I was up until two o'clock, trying to make sense out of the crap—"

"It helps," Lazenby drawls, "if you read the crap when it's assigned. Instead of inhaling it the night before the exam. Just a friendly hint."

"Tell me about it," Van Buren says.

Stillman sneers. "Get a sense of reality, will you, Lazenby? We swim our asses off every friggin' day. When are we supposed to study?"

Lazenby shrugs. "I swim. I study."

"Yeah, you're perfect." Stillman twists around in the front seat. "What're you reading, Jarrett? Is that Hardy? Junior English?"

Conrad nods. They are all seniors this year, except him. He had taken no finals last year. Not January, or June.

"You got all junior classes this year?" Stillman asks. "They didn't pass you on anything?"

Van Buren yawns. "They don't pass you on breathing in that dump if you haven't taken the final."

Lazenby says, "Kevin, will you quit screwing around with the dial, get something and leave it."

Stillman gives a mocking nod, turning up the volume on the radio. He continues to screw around with the dial. Conrad feels the slow, rolling pressure of panic building inside himself. The air in the back seat is being sucked out the windows by a huge and powerful vacuum. Relentless, it will soon crush the car like an eggshell. They cross the Chicago-Northwestern tracks and Stillman is immediately alert, on the lookout.

"Hey, there's Pratt," he says. "Lemme out. I need a jump."

A small, neat-looking redhead in a blue skirt and tan jacket is hurrying along the street, her books in her arms.

"Nice legs," Lazenby says.

"Nice ass." Stillman looking at him again; sees him glance out the window. "Huh, Jarrett? Hey, look. Jarrett's interested in something."

Lazenby says over his shoulder, "She's new. Just moved in last spring."

"She's new, she's blue, she needs a screw," Stillman sings.

Van Buren yawns again. "Christ, you're a god-damn comedian today, aren't you?"

He remembers this now, about Stillman; that it is too easy for him. He is too good-looking; girls have been falling into his lap since junior high, and he has done nothing to earn it, in fact, does not deserve it, spending his time as he does, in tossing off crude remarks about them and then grinning, as if he will be President someday. A diver on the swim team. In general, he has observed that divers tend to be crappy human beings. One of life's mysteries.

"Hey, a tongue twister," Stillman says. "Jarrett falls for Pratt's ass. How's that?"

Lazenby and Van Buren laugh. The remark has an indelible quality that makes Conrad's skin prickle. Stillman is an expert at that: he and Buck had phrases that would sing in the locker room for weeks. *No not today not today.* He wills his mind to slip over it, a blur of gold leaves and green grass sliding, sliding as they turn into the parking lot behind the school.

" 'Jarrett falls for Pratt's ass,' yeah, I like it." Stillman leers at him over the seat, gives him the Presidential grin. "What's the matter? Not funny?"

An undertone of faint hostility has crept into his voice. Conrad's stomach tightens. He needs no more enemies. He forces a laugh from the back of his throat; turns his attention outside the window *Forget it forget it he was never a friend* sends him a mental message *Screw you* he will not get it does not operate on the same frequency never will so fuck it.

"Conrad, what's your theory on Jude Fawley?"

"What?"

Miss Mellon smiles at him. "Do you think he was powerless in the grip of circumstances, or could he have helped himself?"

"I don't know," he stalls. "Powerless? I guess he thought he was."

17

"What's the difference?" Her attention on him now, full force. It will smother him. Too much interest brings out every ounce of reserve he has, makes him unable to think, to formulate answers, even to hear the questions. He looks blankly back at her.

"The guy was a jerk," somebody says. "All hung up on what was the *moral* thing to do. It didn't make any sense."

"That's too easy, Joel." And he breathes again, as her attention shifts. He knows, though, that she will corner him after class, and she does.

"I don't want you to feel pressured about this report," she says. "Do you want an extension?"

"No." Backing slowly out the door as she follows him. "I'll get it done."

"You're sure? There's no need to push yourself. . . ."

Wrong. There is a need. To regain his spot on the swim team, to get back into choir again, there are no choices at all, just endless motion. And no more mistakes. Like the ones he had made last year, when everything was sliding. He had made a lot of them, then. He had brought in some poems to her. That had been a big one. *"Why are you writing all this about violence and war? Aren't there other things you'd like to say, Conrad? This doesn't sound like you."* Now it's as if the whole thing were her fault. She is trying to make it up to him, and he wants no part of those memories. He doesn't know exactly what he wants from people except that he prefers indifference to concern. Easier to handle. *Please stop holding my goddamn hand,* he wants to say to her. She tears his pride to shreds.

Indifference? Or something more definite than that, strong waves of unfriendliness he can actually feel coming toward him, toward his seat at the back of the room in chemistry lab. Mr. Raymond doesn't like him any more. Why? They hardly knew each

18

other before. And Mr. Simmons, his college algebra/ trig teacher, is embarrassed; won't look at him at all. Well, tough. So what? They can all go to hell, he doesn't care. He has gotten what he wanted from all of them. They agreed to have him back in their classes this year, didn't they? "Maybe we ought to cut down on some of these extras, Conrad." At the meeting before school started, with the principal, Mr. Knight, his counselor, Mr. Hellwarth, his father. "Maybe take a straight English course, instead of English honors, and drop choir—" But, no, he had not wanted that, and then Faughnan, the choir director, had stepped in, told Knight that he was short on tenors, he needed Conrad for balance. Balance. Forester Singers were definitely the prestige group of the school. A Cappella Choir, selection by audition only. They have a reputation to maintain, and Faughnan has pull. If he needs Jarrett for balance, that's that.

Choir is the one time of day when he lets down his guard; there is peace in the strict concentration that Faughnan demands of all of them, in the sweet dissonance of voices in chorus. He has sung in here since he was a freshman. Faughnan is a serious student of music; also, a pefectionist of the sternest sort, who cares about nobody, about nothing other than the music. His shirt sleeves rolled to the elbows, his tie undone, he drives them. Every minute of every hour that is spent there, they work, and there is only one way to prove yourself. You sing, and sing, and sing. All else is unimportant.

"Nice job, tenors," Faughnan will say, once in a while, offhand. There are only six of them. He allows himself the smallest thrust of pride on those days. However, today is not one of those days. They sift down off the stands and he stops to retrieve his books from the back table. In front of him are two sopranos, one blonde and one redhead, whose hair hangs, silk-smoth and straight, almost to the middle of her back. No, not red: more of a peach color. The back of her head is three inches from his nose. He could touch it, if he wanted to.

"Hi, Con." The blonde has turned around; is looking directly into his face. He can't remember her name.

"Hi." His face flushes; burns. Beneath the roughened skin, he can feel the rash begin to prickle; stinging nettles against his face.

"Have you met Jeannine?"

"No."

"Jeannine Pratt, Conrad Jarrett."

"Nice to meet you." She smiles; puts out her hand. He stands there, stupidly confused. He still cannot remember the blonde's name and she acts like she knows him and this other one, the redhead blue eyes copper-colored freckles a blue skirt he suddenly remembers it is the girl he saw from the car: *Jarrett falls for Pratt's ass,* goddamn you, Stillman, anyway. He doesn't move doesn't speak stands helplessly waiting for inspiration, for release.

"I think you stand behind me," Jeannine says.

"You sing better than you talk," the blonde says, giggling, and he remembers. Gail Noonan is her name. Buck took her out once.

"Well—" she says, "we'll see you."

They turn away, and he walks blindly out the door behind them, down the hall toward history class. He thinks of a simple, spare melody, picking up the notes as they slide into his mind—"Rainy Day Man," an old James Taylor tune. That one is really old, goes all the way back to junior high. He hums it through to relax himself. He has escaped this time but even the smallest, most insignificant encounter is alive with complication and danger. He wishes himself, for a moment, back inside the hospital where things were predictable. Mercifully dull.

He yawns at swim practice, and Salan, the coach, catches him. "Maybe I oughta start a bed check on you guys again." He stares pointedly at him, calls him over after practice.

"Jarrett, you having fun out there?"

"Fun?"

"Yeah. You oughta be, you know." He sits, hands on his thighs, one thick ham hooked across the corner of the table. "The point is lost, if it's not fun any more." He inclines his head, wanting an answer. "Right?"

"I guess."

"You guess."

Salan wears a threadbare T-shirt and khakis, rolled above his ankles. He does not look like a man to be feared. Conrad, sick with fright, stands mutely, waiting for the ax to fall. *Doesn't matter doesn't matter I didn't really want to swim*, breathing in the heavy moisture-laden air, while behind him he can feel the steam rising lazily from the blue-glass surface of the pool.

"You on medication, Jarrett? Tranquilizers? Anything?"

"No."

Salan removes the stopwatch from around his neck. "Did I ask you before if they gave you shock out there?"

"Yeah."

"Yeah, what?"

"Yeah, you asked me before," he says. "Yeah, they did."

Salan shakes his head; clicks his tongue in disapproval. "I don't know," he says. "I'm no doctor, but I don't think I'd let them mess around with my head like that."

Conrad says nothing, does not look at Salan directly, looks instead at the low, brick wall behind the table. *It wasn't exactly an orgy of pleasure for me you dumb prick*. Salan is shaking his head.

"Your timing is lousy."

"I know."

"Look, I don't want to be—I'm not being too rough on you, am I? But I'm wondering if it's gonna be too much for you." He leans back, one arm around an upraised knee. "This is a team effort, Jarrett. I've got room for guys who are willing to work at it. Thing is, I can't figure out any more—if that's you or not."

He lets out his breath at last, but slowly, slowly *Keep it neutral don't beg.* "I'll work," he says. "I want to work."

"Okay, then. Better plan to stay after. We'll see if we can get your timing back. No, not today—" as he starts for the pool "—start tomorrow. Go take a shower now. And get to bed at a decent hour, will you? You kids stay up till all hours and don't take care of your bodies. . . ." His tongue clicks again, this time in dismissal, and Conrad heads for the locker room. He is shivering *Never hit it off with the guy not even before he is too brusque too all-knowing there is only one way to do everything only one main street.*

In the car on the way home, Lazenby says, "Salan's a damn, picky bastard. He drives me nuts."

"Everything drives you nuts," Stillman says. "The day is not complete without Lazenby telling everybody what a fucked-up state the world's in, right?" He turns around. "What d'you think, Jarrett? Danoff and Edge look pretty good, huh?"

Danoff and Edge are sophomores. They swim the free style. They have beaten him in practice every day for two weeks. There is a sudden, electrical silence. Lazenby says, "They're not that good, Kev."

"No? They look pretty damn good to me."

Lazenby drops him off and he lets himself in with his key. The house is dark. Silent and empty. He hangs his jacket carefully in the front closet and goes upstairs to his room. He sets his book down on his desk and stands, looking out the window from his tower of safety. Idly, he opens the desk drawer, sifting through a pile of papers: old stuff, schedules, letters, scraps of notes written long ago. Funny she has never cleaned out this drawer. He should do it, maybe sometime he will. Fingers ruffling, touching suddenly the glossy and slick surface of a photograph. He pulls it out looking quickly along the bottom of it in white letters FIRST PLACE MEDLEY RELAY TEAM. Lazenby. Buck. Himself in the middle. Arms around each other, grinning at the camera, all confidence *On the main street*. He snaps the drawer closed. It is like the hole in your mouth where a tooth was and you cannot keep your tongue from playing with it.

He goes out into the hall, just as his mother reaches the top of the stairs. She jumps, drawing in her breath sharply.

"Sorry," he says.

"I didn't think you were home yet."

"I just got in," he says. "How was your golf game?"

"Fine. Cold." Her hair is loose about her face. She lifts it in back, rubbing her neck. "Your father called. He'll be late. We're not eating until seven."

"Okay."

She heads toward her room. "I have an awful headache. I'm going to lie down awhile."

"Okay."

She is almost to her door and he calls after her, "I swam pretty well today. Salan wants me to stay later and work out. I might be starting in the fifty."

"Good." The door closes behind her, and he stands a moment in the hall, then goes back into his room. He shuts his door and leans against it, trembling. A dull, roaring sound in his ears as he doubles over, arms crossed, pressed against his waist. His stomach tightens, as if to ward off a blow.

4

The restaurant is dark; it has a heavy Mediterranean décor that Cal finds oppressive. It is not the kind of place he normally frequents. There is a lawyers' hangout, the Quik-Lunch, around the corner from the Plaza, but that would not suit Beth. This place is better for her. She had called him this morning; asked him to meet her here, her voice light, full of excitement and Good News. Well, great, we can all use some of that, can't we? And she looks like good news, seated across from him in a sleeveless knit suit, the color of straw, a V-neck bordered in orange, a thin gold chain around her neck. All elegance and self-possession. So beautiful in every detail that men and women both like to look at her. He has watched her enter enough rooms to know that, walking humbly and proudly behind her, a modest smile on his lips, *Yes, it's true, twenty-one years next spring we have been married.* He grins at the bartender, the envious customers. His description is accurate. Self-possessed is what she is; he emphatically does not own her, nor does he have control over her, nor can he understand or even predict with reliability her moods, her attitudes. She is a marvelous mystery to him; as complex, as interesting as she appeared to him on that first day he met her some twenty-two years ago on the tennis courts at the Beverly Racquet Club. Ray's father had a membership, and he was with Ray that day, working off the tensions of a hideous law exam. She was a good tennis player even then. She liked to play with men because the competition was better, she had told Ray, approaching him first. She had a friend who was good, also. Would they like to play doubles? Ray was all for it, he read possibilities into it; who cared if she could play at all? But she was good, and her friend was good, and the friend and Cal beat Beth and Ray easily, and afterward, he was never sure how it was arranged, Beth and Cal were paired off together, and Ray got the friend. They went out to dinner at the Chatterbox Café. God, what a storehouse of trivia he kept up there. The Chatterbox Café. It was an evening of unprecedented events. He had had a date with someone else that night. Midway through dinner he had excused himself, gone to the telephone, broken the date. He never had another with any girl except Beth.

"I was afraid if I had left early," he confessed to her later, "I wouldn't have made enough of an impression, and you wouldn't see me again."

"I was afraid, too," she said. "I thought you might be engaged or married and Lord, what a job it was going to be, getting you away from her. I knew when you aced Ray on that first serve I was going to marry you and that was all there was to it."

He laughs out loud, thinking about it, and Beth, sipping her drink, snaps her fingers at him.

"Where *are* you?"

"Nowhere. Right here. Just thinking. What have you got there?"

She has pulled an envelope from her purse, and the folded sheets of slick paper are suddenly before him: Athens, Rome, London, Dubrovnik. "They said it's late, but there are still openings. If we can let them know immediately."

"Let them know what?"

"I remember last year you said Yugoslavia, but, Cal, don't you think London would be fun? Like something out of Dickens. We've never done that. Christmas in London—"

"Listen," he says, "I don't think we should plan to go away for Christmas this year."

She looks at him over the rim of her glass. "We go away for Christmas every year."

Carefully he folds the sheets; places them in the center of the table. "I know. But not this year. The timing just isn't right."

"The timing isn't right," she says. "What does that mean?"

"You know what it means."

"Yes." She turns her head slightly away from him. Wearing her hair differently today; the sharp white line of her part at the side, wings of hair swept back and clipped at the top of her head. "Well. They said it would be better to leave in the middle of December and book a flight back after the first week in January."

"We can't go in the middle of December. He'd have to miss a week of school. And another week in January would be two weeks—"

"He could meet us there when school got out. He could fly back by himself. Mother and Dad would—"

"*No!*"

They sit in silence for a moment.

"I think you're wrong, Cal," she says. "I think it would be good for us all to go."

"No. Just—no."

The waiter appears with the menus.

"Never mind," she says, "I know what I want. The fish chowder and a green salad, Italian dressing. And some of your special bread. Coffee, too, please."

Cal orders a roast-beef sandwich and coffee. Leaning back in the chair, he tries to make out the dimensions of the room; he imagines it in the harsh, full light of day. Square and ugly. Better to keep it dark.

"Why don't you ask him if he wants to go? I think he will. Why wouldn't he?"

"I think," he says, "that was our mistake. Going to Florida last Christmas. If we hadn't done that—"

"It wouldn't have made any difference, you know that. Dr. Brandt told us—"

"Dr. Brandt told us he was depressed. Dr. Brandt is a G.P. What the hell did he know?" He sets his glass down, rapping it smartly against the table. He hasn't meant to. The sound is loud and it makes her jump.

"Are you blaming him, now? He gave him the physical, just as you asked. What more was he supposed to do?"

"I'm not blaming Brandt. I'm not blaming anyone. It wasn't anyone's fault, I know that."

"You don't believe that," she says. "You say it, but you don't believe it."

"I believe it," he says. "I'm not even talking about blame, I'm talking about being available. We were busy down there. Every goddamned minute. There wasn't time to talk."

"What was there to say? What do you think would have been said? Do you even think he knew at that point? And, if he did know, do you think he would have told us?"

"I don't know."

She shakes her head. "I don't think he would have told us."

The waiter brings their lunches, and they sit, silently, watching him serve. When he leaves the table, she looks down at her lap.

"I don't think it's a good idea for us to blame ourselves for what happened, Cal."

"Fine," he says curtly. "Don't, then. If that means a damn thing."

Her head sinks lower. She busies herself, buttering the pieces of bread in her hand.

"Beth," he says, "I'm sorry, honey. I'm sorry."

She looks up. "What's the matter?" she whispers. "Is something the matter?"

"No! Nothing's the matter."

"Then, why can't we go?" She leans toward him. "You know how good it feels to get away. All the wonderful places we've been, Spain, Portugal, Hawaii —I know it's a lot to ask, Cal, I know we have expenses—"

"It's not the money."

"—but I need it! I need to go! I need you to go with me."

"I want to go with you," he says. "We can go in the spring, maybe, any place you want."

She sits back, then, hands in her lap. "No." Her voice is flat. "If we don't go now, we won't go in the spring, either."

"That's silly," he says. "We will. I just think that now we should—this time we might try handling things differently."

"This time?"

He is upsetting her; upsetting himself, too. And he shouldn't drink at lunch, shouldn't have had two martinis, he is keyed up, now; nervous. This afternoon he will sit at his desk in a half-stupor, surrounded by a confusion of papers.

"Then, are we going to live like this? With it always hanging over our heads?"

There is a determined set to her chin that moves him, even when she uses it against him, even when it seems irrational and dangerous, accompanied by ideas he does not agree with. Thus, as she argued stubbornly with Ray over dinner that night that the Michigan *Daily* had no right to meddle in the financial affairs of campus sororities (her stand was based on rights of privacy, as he remembered it), he had fallen abruptly and thoroughly in love with her.

It was, on looking back, as good a reason as a tennis ace.

"Nothing is hanging over our heads," he says, as much to himself as to her. "Don't worry. Everything is all right."

She looks at him, reaching out to gather the colored sheets of paper into a neat pile, slipping them into the envelope. "Then, I don't understand you at all," she says.

He sits at his desk, working on the papers Ray has left there for him. At three-thirty he has a meeting with Sandlin. They will discuss a new angle on their annuities. A germ, Ray calls it. His ideas are always referred to as "germs"; his figure estimates are "in the ball park." Clichés. They jump out at you from everywhere, but you never see your own. Howard called again today, to talk about the Mercedes dealership opening up in Evanston. "Things are looking up, Cal. Light at the end of the tunnel. People buying expensive foreign cars again. Hell of a good sign, wouldn't you say?"

Yes, he had agreed with this spot analysis of U.S. economy, his mind automatically registering the old favorites. Where was *Out of the woods?* It was missing today.

He gets up to stretch and look out the window at the North Shore Channel; the fringes of Northwestern's campus; down below, Evanston proper. The offices of Hanley and Jarrett, Attorneys at Law, on the eighth floor of the State National Plaza, overlook the whole of southwest Evanston. He has always wished they were on the eastern side of the building, preferring to look out on frozen cliffs of water in winter, rather than dirty streets, dirtier cars; it is not a pleasant corner in the midst of the gray Chicago winter. Other than that, it is a good location. The atmosphere on the eighth floor seems cleaner; steadier. Years ago, when they were getting started, their one-room Chicago office was hot and crowded; their look-alike cramped apartments on the near north side were hotter and more crowded, yet. No more. Now Ray and Nancy live in Glencoe, and he takes the train in from his English Tudor castle, walking to the Plaza from the station. He tells Cal he is crazy to drive. The train is the only way, he says. But Cal prefers his car. It gives him control over his schedule, and, besides, riding the train has always made him nervous. He can't work, as he has seen some men do; he can barely read the paper. Riding the train gives him too much time to think, he has decided. Too much thinking can ruin you.

Ray knocks on the open door; sticks his head inside. "Got a minute to run this around before the meeting?"

"Sure. C'mon in."

"I just want to clue you in about Sandlin. Christ, I tell him twice a week he ought to go to law school. He thinks I'm kidding. I swear, he thinks he's the only account we have."

"You got the annuities straightened out?"

"Yeah, I think so. Have a look."

They go over the file together, Ray explaining the alternative tax consequences he has assembled, while Cal scans the stack of letters from G. Sandlin Corp., dating back over the past months.

"Looks okay to me. What's his problem?"

"No problem, really. He fancies himself this big wheeler-dealer and it frosts hell out of him that his transactions are not unique, that they have actually been performed many times before in the history of tax law."

"So what are we seeing him for?"

"Hell, I don't know—so he can tell his partners at lunch that he pointed out a few loopholes to those hot-shot lawyers up on eight. Do me a favor, will you? Get him to stop calling every day. You're good at that. Closing doors politely. If I tell him, he's going to get offended, but it's the goddamn, pathetic truth, if I had a buck for every time he calls me about junk, just niggling items, you know?"

"Okay, I'll try. Hey, listen, we can hold off on the Naylor account. I heard from them today. No tax court until January."

"Great." Ray sits back, puts his feet up on Cal's desk. "Beth looks terrific," he says. "God, she's tan. Must be playing a lot of golf, huh?"

"Yeah, she is."

"You two have a nice lunch?"

"Yeah, fine."

"Hey, we ought to have lunch sometime, partner. How about tomorrow?"

"Sure. I'll meet you at the Quik-lunch about eleven thirty. How's that?"

Ray laughs. "I meant you ought to take me to lunch."

"I know what you meant."

"Say, I heard you on the phone with Howard. Is Connie swimming this year?"

"Yeah, he is."

"You think that's a good idea? I mean, letting him get into all the stuff again? I don't know, if it were my kid—"

They look at each other, and Ray says, "Forget it. That was stupid. Forget it."

"No, that's okay," Cal says. "It wasn't my idea, anyway. He set it up himself, went in to talk to the coach about it. I didn't even know until he came home and said it was done."

He wants to ask, What the hell do you know about it, you with your two girls, one nineteen, away at college and everything roses, and how old is the other one? Seven? What is that, second grade. What do you know? But he doesn't. And he can't stay angry at Ray, who has been his friend since law school, nor at Howard, either; the concerned grandfather, the concerned father-in-law. All who are concerned only want to help.

Well, who can help. *Severe Depression Episodes: High Risk of Suicide* was the initial diagnosis on the commitment papers he signed last January. A seven word diagnosis. Is there a seven-word cure? *Is he cured?*

"Listen," Ray says, "I'll give you a couple of minutes to finish up."

"Okay." He pushes the papers around until Ray has left, then reaches into the bottom drawer of his desk for the Evanston telephone directory: Tyrone C. Berger, M.D. 651 Sherman Ave. So. Near the railroad station. Not the hottest of neighborhoods, but close to the Plaza. He can walk over to the office when he's through. They can ride home together. He had told Cal last night that he made an appointment. A good boy. Obedient. He does what he is told to do.

Another duty of fatherhood. Checking up. Signing commitment papers, and other papers, authorizing certain specified treatments. Protecting yourself from further grief, from any more facts of history that do not change; that cannot be changed. Like the loss of Jordan, his elder, his light-hearted son, the one who never worried, who believed they would all live forever. Two sons, Jordan and Conrad, born fourteen months apart. One now deceased. Another word from the commitment papers. Part of the background information he was required to furnish. Deceased. Too formal a word to have any meaning. A symbol without impression, without power to hurt, or to heal.

She was right. He lied to her at lunch. He does not believe himself to be innocent. It has to be his fault, because fault equals responsibility equals control equals eventual understanding. How things happened. Why they happened. So where is the fault? Is it in believing that the people you love are immortal? Untouchable? No, everyone believes that. Only no one knows it's what he believes—until it happens. Then comes the rage, the banging about the walls, crying what if, what if. Everyone is always so damned surprised, that is the horror of it.

The topic of London is not finished, he is sure, but merely held over for future discussion. Well, why not go? What difference will it make? If she's right, and it made no difference, last year was nobody's fault—nobody's fault. That is the truth. That is what makes it all so impossible to understand.

5

The building is shabby, and inside, the lobby is hot and dark. He glances at his watch; too dark in here to make out the numbers. The crisp and sunny day he has left outside has nearly blinded him. A directory on the far wall; he goes to it; scans the list of names. Eleven in all; seven with M.D. after them The top name on the list is the one he is looking for: T. C. BERGER M.D. 202. Would any of these guys be of use in an emergency? All specialists—podiatrists, optometrists, psychiatrists—but what if an accident were to happen in front of the building? Or a mugging? It looks like a great neighborhood for muggings.

Glancing at his watch again, he finds his eyes have adjusted to the dim light. Four o'clock. Exactly. *Well then get on it no backing out now* an idea he has toyed with all week not going just not showing up won't work. He is to meet his father at his office at five-fifteen. "Don't be late. I've got a meeting tonight. I'd like to get out of there as close to five as I can." Translated; "Don't let the guy upset you, show up when you're supposed to, it only takes ten minutes to walk from Sherman and Tenth to the Plaza, I have clocked it." No. Not fair. Not necessary to take everything so personally. He probably does have a meeting

tonight. Everything's all right, everything's fine, keep
it that way. On an even keel, as his grandfather would
say.

Stuck between the directory and the wall is a small
white business card:

I love you.
Is this okay?
            Jesus C.

The edges of it are furred; curved slightly inward.
As if it has been there a long time. He shakes his head,
making for the staircase; forces a growl from the back
of his throat. He is being strangled.

In the narrow hallway on the second floor, a single
light bulb burns, helpless against the invading gloom.
High, old-fashioned doors, with window of bubbled
glass in them; all dark on both sides of the hall, and
looking as if they haven't been used for years. Any
people in this building? Is this an emergency? Even a
podiatrist would do. Panic begins to settle in around
him.

At the end of the hall is a doorway with light behind
it. He goes to it. The letters, stuck to the opaque glass
with adhesive backing, spell out T C BERGER M D.
They slant upward, crooked rectangles, like a kid
would print them on unlined paper. He pushes experi-
mentally at the door, but it works on a heavy spring
mechanism. Even when he turns the knob, it doesn't
give. He pushes harder this time, and it opens. He
steps inside. The door closes sharply behind him.

He is in an entry, empty of people, longer than it
is deep, with a chair in it, a floor lamp, a small table
strewn with magazines, a green metal wastebasket.
Barely furnished, the room still seems cluttered. Opposite him is a doorway; an overturned chair blocks

it. From inside the other room mysterious, shuffling sounds are issuing. A scene of total disorder confronts him as he moves toward the door. Books, magazines, loose piles of paper are everywhere; empty plastic cups, pieces of clothing, a cardboard box, THE BAKERY lettered in script on its lid, all tossed together in the middle of the floor. Several ashtrays are dumped, upside down, on the rug. A gooseneck lamp lies, like a dead snake, beside them. In the midst of it, a man stands, bent over, his back to the doorway. As Conrad approaches, he turns. About him there is the look of a crafty monkey; dark skin, dark crinkly hair sprouting in tufts about his face, a body that hunches forward, an elongated question mark.

"Wait," he says, "don't tell me. Jarrett."

The eyes, a compelling and vivid blue, beam into whatever they touch. They touch Conrad's face now, and the effect is that of being in an intense blue spotlight.

He snaps his fingers. "Yeah. You look like somebody Crawford would send me. Somebody who's a match for my daring wit and inquiring mind."

Conrad, cool and polite, asks. "Am I seeing you? Or are you seeing me?"

He laughs, delighted. "That oughta be easy. This my office, or yours? No. No good. Lotsa guys in this business make house calls now. Let's see your appointment book." He steps over to the desk, rummaging fiercely for a minute; he comes up with a gray stenographer's notebook. "Here. Tuesday, four o'clock. Conrad Jarrett. Ah. I knew it." He grins, then.

Conrad is not easily charmed. Or fooled. Eccentricity. A favorite put-on of psychiatrists. He does not trust them. Too many oddballs floating around the hospital. Only Crawford had behaved as if he knew what he was doing. He bends to pick up the overturned chair.

"Bring that over here," Berger directs him. "Sit down."

He continues to prowl around the room, lifting books, setting them aside, retrieving papers from the floor, stacking up empty plastic cups. On further examination, he resembles a compact, slightly undersize gorilla. Conrad cannot take his eyes off him.

"I think I was ripped off this afternoon," he says. "Or else the cleaning lady did one hell of a job on me. Place didn't look this bad when I left. Somebody was after drugs, I guess. What a neighborhood. Nothing but placebos here. Use 'em myself for quick energy sometimes. Just sugar." He smiles, arms raised, palms turned up in an attitude of perplexity.

"You were robbed?"

"Looks like."

"You going to call somebody?"

"Who? You mean cops?" He shrugs. "What's missing? Maybe nothing. Maybe they even left something, who knows?" He moves to the small sink, half-hidden in the corner behind a huge pile of books. "You want some coffee? Listen, do me a favor, look on the desk there, see if you can find a data sheet —you know, name, age, date of birth, et cetera—fill it out for me, will you? Gotta keep records, the state says. Rules." He sighs. "Now what am I supposed to do with those poor bastards lying on the floor, I ask you?" He indicates the over-turned filing cabinet, its contents scattered. "Did you say yes or no?"

"What?"

"Coffee. Yes or no? Sit down, sit down."

"No. Thanks." Obediently he goes to the desk; searches through the papers on top of it until he comes up with a blank information card. He begins to fill it out. Berger empties the other chair of debris and drags it over to the desk.

"How long since you left the hospital?"

"A month and a half."

"Feeling depressed?"

"No."

"Onstage?"

"Pardon?"

"People nervous? Treat you like you're a dangerous man."

He shrugs. "Yeah, a little, I guess."

"And are you?"

"I don't know."

Berger grins, then. "You look sensible enough to me. At least, you looked sensibly disgusted when you walked in here. God, it is disgusting, isn't it? The second time this year. What do you think I oughta do about it?"

He is used to this technique; he looks for psychological design in the question. No. Too farfetched. Nobody would go to this much trouble just to set up a test for him.

He says, "I guess I'd just clean it up and forget about it."

"Yeah, you're right. Christ, what a gigantic pain in the tail though, huh?" The man sits back, fingers curved around his coffee cup, watching as Conrad finishes filling out the card. "Sure you don't want any coffee? I've got clean cups around here somewhere."

Conrad shakes his head; hands him the card.

He reads it quickly. "Good, strong print. Neat. Like an engineer. So. What're you doing here? You look like a healthy kid to me."

"What I'm doing here," Conrad says, "is that I had to come."

Berger nods. "Uh huh. Rules again. Authority reigns." He tosses the card onto the desk. "So, suppose you didn't have to come. What would you be here for?"

"I wouldn't."

He finds himself firmly enveloped in the piercing blue gaze; shifts uncomfortably in the chair.

"How long were you there?"

"Eight months."

"What did you do? O.D.? Make too much noise in the library?"

"No." Looks steadily at the bookcase in front of him; floor-to-ceiling, jammed with books. "I tried to off myself."

Berger picks up the card again; studies it as he blows his coffee. "What with? Pills? Gillette Super-Blue?"

He sees the way to handle this guy. Keep it light. A joker. Slide out from under without damage. "It was a Platinum-Plus," he says.

The eyes are fixed upon him thoughtfully. They hold him still. "So how does it feel to be home? Everybody glad to see you?"

"Yes. Sure."

"Your friends, everything okay with them?"

"Fine."

"It says here, no sisters, no brothers. Right?"

"Right," he says. *Don't squirm don't panic release is inevitable. Soon soon.*

Berger leans back in the chair, hands behind his head. It is hard to figure his age. He could be twenty-five. He could be forty. "So, what d'you want to work on?" he asks.

"Pardon?"

"Well, you're here. It's your money, so to speak. What d'you want to change?"

He thinks, then, of his father; of their struggle to keep between them a screen of calm and order. "I'd like to be more in control, I guess. So people can quit worrying about me."

"So, who's worrying about you?"

"My father, mostly. This is his idea."

"How about your mother? Isn't she worried?"

"No."

"How come?"

"She's—I don't know, she's not a worrier."

"No? What does she do, then?"

"Do?"

"Yeah, what's her general policy toward you? You get along with her all right?"

"Yeah, fine." He is abruptly uncomfortable. An endless grilling process, like it was in the hospital. He forgot how it tightened him up; how much he used to hate it.

"You've got a funny look on your face," Berger says. "What're you thinking?"

"I'm thinking," he says, "if you're a friend of Crawford's you're probably okay, but I don't like this already. Look, what do you know about me? Have you talked to Crawford?"

"No." The blue high-beams have switched to low. The smile is benign. "He told me your name, that's all. Told me to look for you."

"Okay, I'll tell you some things." He turns his head slightly, taking in the narrow window at the left of the bookcase. Sunlight streams in from the slot, cutting a bright path across the carpeting. "I had a brother. He's dead. It was an accident on the lake. We were sailing. He drowned."

"When?"

"Summer before last."

Staring now at the bookcase, he tries to make out the titles of the books from where he is sitting. He cannot. They are too far away.

"I suppose you and Crawford talked about it," Berger says.

"Every day."

"And you don't like to talk about it."

He shrugs. "It doesn't change anything."

A pigeon, dull-gray, lights on the cement window sill. It pecks inquiringly at the window for a moment; then flies off.

"Okay," Berger says. "Anything else?"

"No," he says. "Yeah. About friends. I don't have any. I got sort of out of touch before I left."

"Oh?"

He does not respond to this technique; the comment in the form of a question. He had cured Crawford of it by telling him it was impossible to concentrate on

40

what a person was saying if you were listening for his voice to go up at the end of the sentence.

"Well, okay," Berger says. "I'd better tell you. I'm not big on control. I prefer things fluid. In motion. But it's your money."

"So to speak."

"So to speak, yeah." Berger laughs, reaching for his notebook. "How's Tuesdays and Fridays?"

"Twice a week?"

He shrugs. "Control is a tough nut."

"I've got swim practice every night."

"Hmm. That's a problem. So, how do we solve it?"

A long, uncomfortable silence. He is tired and irritated. And again, there are no choices; it only looks as if there are.

"I guess I skip practice and come here twice a week," he says.

"Okeydoke."

It is over, and Berger walks him to the door. "The schedule," he says, "is based on patient ratings. A scale of one to ten. The higher I rate, the fewer times you gotta come. Example: You rate me ten, you only have to see me once a week."

Conrad laughs. "That's crazy."

"Hey, I'm the doctor." Berger grins at him. "You're the patient."

The worst, the first session has been gotten through. And the guy is not bad; at least he is loose. The exchange about the razor blades reminded him of something good about the hospital; nobody hid anything there. People kidded you about all kinds of stuff and it was all right; it even helped to stay the flood of shame and guilt. Remembering that day at lunch when Stan Carmichael rose from his chair pointing his finger in stern accusation: "Profane and unholy boy! Sinner against God and Man, father and mother—" Robbie prompted him "—and the Holy Ghost, Stan—" and he ranted on "—and the Holy

Ghost! Fall on your knees! Repent of evil! Ask forgiveness for your profane and evil ways, Conrad Keith Jarrett!" and he had nodded, eating on, while Robbie leaned across the table, and asked, "Stan, may I have your gingerbread? Just if you're not going to eat it, buddy." And Stan broke off his ravings to snarl petulantly, "Goddamn it, Rob, you're a leech, you scrounge off my plate at every meal, it's disgusting!"

So, how do you stay open, when nobody mentions anything, when everybody is careful *not* to mention it? *Ah, shit, Jarrett, what do you want? Want people to say, "Gee, we're glad you didn't die?"* Poor taste, poor taste.

He is suddenly aware of the people on the street, hurrying by, intent upon their business. See? No one's accusing. They don't even seem repelled. As a matter of fact, they don't even notice. So. No need to be affected by them, either, right? Still, as they pass him, he carefully averts his gaze.

6

Cherry comes in, coatless, breathless, late from her lunch hour again. She gives Cal the practiced, wide-eyed smile. "What are you looking for, Mr. Jarrett? If it's Braddock, that's on Mr. Hanley's desk. I'll get it for you."

"That's all right." He nods curtly. "I'm looking for the Sandlin account. I had it the other day."

"Oh, just a sec, I know right where that is. I'll bring it in to you, okay?"

And again, the smile. A tall, big-boned girl who wears too much make-up, and her skirts too short. He has noticed lately that women aren't wearing their skirts short. It must be out of style again, and now it looks cheap. Or else he is getting old. And the secretaries get younger every year. Cherry is nineteen. Lord, was he ever that young? Cherry. Now, who the hell would give a daughter that silly name? Nobody would. It's a fake, like the smile. He goes into his office and stands at the window, waiting for the file, staring out at the flat, red-brick complex of buildings to the west. Evanston Township High School. Strange how institutional buildings resemble one another. He can spot them a mile off. That one looks much like the Evangelical Home.

He glances at his calendar. Wednesday, November fifth. Get with Ray this afternoon about Braddock. Call George Sandlin's broker. Call Burns and Rousch, set up a meeting for the nineteenth. Duties, services, advice. A good thing you do not have to know who you are, Jarrett, in order to perform, because today there is a minimum of information available on that subject.

He hates fighting, and last night they had fought —over London.

"I think you're being unreasonable," she said, "not even daring to ask him about it. Why don't you just admit that it's you who doesn't want to go?"

"You ask him, then! What am I? The official interpreter here? You see him every day, don't you? Show him the travel folders, give him the pitch."

"I don't see him any more than you do," she said coolly. "What are you afraid of? It's a question. It requires a yes or a no. You certainly ask him enough other questions—How did he sleep? How does he feel? How did I sleep? How do I feel?"

"Okay," he said. "How *did* you sleep? How *do* you feel?"

"That's not *it!*" she said. "If we could all just relax a little! If things could just be normal again. I don't want you to start asking *me* the questions, I want you to just stop!"

Well, okay. Fair enough. If she knew, though, that it is not only of Conrad but of himself that he is asking questions now; basic, hopeless questions that mock him, finger him as a joker, a bumbler, a poor dope. *Who the hell are you?* as he walks down the street, and who can step in time to that music for more than thirty seconds? He ducks into a drugstore for respite, buys himself a cigar. *Who the hell are you?* follows him inside, leaning on the glass counter, waiting. Maybe everybody does it, that is the thought he hangs on to, like a drunk at a friendly lamppost.

Who in the world knows who he is all the time? It is not a question to ask a guy over a sandwich at the Quik-Lunch. If you must ponder it, then do it alone at isolated periods with long intervals in between, so as not to drive yourself bats.

I'm the kind of man who—he has heard this phrase a million times, at parties, in bars, in the course of normal conversation, *I'm the kind of man who*—instinctively he listens; tries to apply any familiar terms to himself, but without success.

Arnold Bacon. There was a man who knew who he was. Years since he has thought about him. In 1967, Ray noticed his obit in the *Tribune* ". . . nationally known tax attorney dies at seventy-two. . . . Tragic loss to the profession, ABA president says. . . ."

He was seventeen years old when he first met Arnold Bacon. Seventeen, a senior in high school, his plans for the future not extending past the next afternoon, and Bacon had come up to him at, of all places, a Christmas Tea in the lounge of the Evangelical Home. "Well, young man, what are you planning to do with the rest of your life?" He had laughed politely, looking for a neat and pleasant exit to the conversation, but Bacon was serious. "I've looked at your grades," he said. "You're smart. You know the importance of a good education. You ever thought about going into law?"

He had thought about being a Soldier of Fortune, after reading *The Three Musketeers*. Or a fireman. A professional athlete. He was a good tennis player, he was well coordinated. He learned games quickly. Those vague and wistful occupations faded out of the picture after that December afternoon. He did more than think about the law. He applied and was accepted to prelaw at Wayne University; he took a part-time job clerking in Bacon's office; he graduated from Wayne and was accepted into law .school at the University of Michigan, backed by Bacon's influential recommendation, he later found out from one of the deans.

A lucky accident. Bacon took him on; decided to be his mentor; told him what courses to take and which ones to stay away from; which scholarships to apply for; which professors he must not miss. He came to his aid financially whenever it was necessary. It was the closest thing to a father-son relationship—it *was* a father-son relationship, he thought. Bacon had one daughter; no sons. Bacon's daughter might have made a smashing lawyer; but women lawyers were rarer, then, and suspect. And he had this reverence, this vast, eclipsing love for the law that had to be coalesced. He needed a student, an apprentice. He needed to know that he was leaving his baby protected.

Bacon had not approved of law students who married while they were in school. Diffusion of energy, he called it. And so, of course, everything had changed, after Beth. Bacon was a man of strong views. He had principles. Integrity. He knew who he was and where he stood on certain—what he considered—inviolable issues. Bacon had been Cal's first actual experience with loss.

When he was eleven, he learned the association of that word with death. The director of the Evangelical Home had called him in to tell him of his "loss." His mother had "passed away"—another term he was more familiar with, having heard it used frequently in connection with the elderly, wraithlike beings who inhabited the east wing of the Home, coming and going very quickly. He remembered the feeling of awe that possessed him that day. He was aware that an event of some magnitude had happened *to him*. Someone close to him had passed away and it was his loss, and his alone. For a short time he became a figure of some importance to his peers. And he was invited to the director's office for cocoa and sermons on *Love and Loss,* and *How a Christian Deals with Grief.* The only difference he perceived was that he no longer had any visitor or presents on his birthday, or at Christmas. Well, that wasn't true, really. He had presents, they just weren't from anyone he knew. But he did not, at the time, understand the meaning of loss. And of grief. He still had not experienced those words at all.

He had grieved over Arnold, though. Not when he died, it was too late, then; years since he had seen him. But when he discovered that it had been a business venture, after all, that had felt like grief. It *was* grief. He and Beth had, together, repaid the money. It was, as Bacon pointed out to him, a financial obligation. It took five years, but it was not a hardship. Beth had her own money; he had a good scholarship, and they hardly felt the monthly bill. But Arnold's indifference, after the marriage—that had hurt him so much. It had undermined him, taken away something that he hadn't even realized he possessed; he had regarded it so lightly, so casually.

Cherry swings into the room with her smile, to put the papers on his desk. Seductively, that is how she does it. She works hard at it. Too hard. She has a good telephone voice. That's about it. Can't take dictation worth a damn, and she won't file. He wonders where she found this one; she must have had to do some hunting for it. Her boy friend goes to Northwestern, gets out of class at five o'clock each day, she has informed them. She is firm about leaving the office at exactly that time. Her habit of sneaking error-spotted letters on the desk for his signature, as she gives him the look of wide-eyed innocence, drives him crazy. What would Bacon have to say about a secretary like this? "Calvin, you get what you deserve."

I'm the kind of man who—hasn't the least idea what kind of man I am. There. Some definition. He is no closer than he was back in the director's office, back when he listened to the sermons, his mind wan-

47

dering, not even aware, then, that he was searching.

So, how does a Christian deal with grief? There is no dealing; he knows that much. There is simply the stubborn, mindless hanging on until it is over. Until you are through it. But something has happened in the process. The old definitions, the neat, knowing pigeonholes have disappeared. Or else they no longer apply.

His eyes move again to the calendar. Wednesday, November fifth. Of course. Obvious. All the painful self-examination; the unanswered questions. At least he knows what is wrong today. Today is Jordan's birthday. Today he would have been nineteen.

7

Karen smiles at him. Deep dimples in her cheeks. He had forgotten that about her, had forgotten how she lowers her head when she is embarrassed or nervous. Nervous now as she sits down across from him in the narrow booth. It makes him feel protective. She doesn't have to be afraid of him.

"Hi. How are you?"

"Fine. And you?"

He grins; shrugs his shoulders. "Not bad. Light, scattered paranoia increasing to moderate during the day." He means merely to jog her memory, but she frowns and looks away. He has offended her. "Hey, I'm only kidding. I'm fine. Really."

She leans awkwardly to the side, shrugging out of her coat; folds it neatly beside her on the seat. She has gained weight since the hospital. It looks good on her. She used to wear her hair long and straight. She would tuck it behind her ears while she talked. Now it is short, curling softly about her face. Dark feathers that brush against her cheeks.

"I like your hair that way."

"Thank you." She touches it. She touches and straightens her coat again. They look at each other. Slowly sinking in the awkwardness of the moment.

He didn't want that to happen. They were good friends at the hospital. They still are. No reason to be uncomfortable, is there?

She asks, "When did you come home?"

"End of August." A place where they were both safe. They talked for hours on the stone bench outside the rec-room door. Sometimes Leo would come and sit with them, cracking jokes, finding out they were alive. Surely she must remember.

"It's great to see you," he says.

"Good to see you." Again she ducks her head. "I can't stay too long. I've got a meeting at school. Our drama club is doing *A Thousand Clowns*—the Herb Gardner play—do you know it? We're going wild trying to get it together. I'm secretary this year, that's probably why we're so disorganized—"

He says bluntly, "Well, don't let me hold you up, then."

All that time to get here so he can have a Coke in this drugstore because it is near her house in Skokie, and she sits there as if she is being held prisoner. What a stupid idea. Sorry he thought of it, sorry he called her at all.

"I came because you asked me to," she says quietly.

And sorry again for being rude, and for exposing himself and his goddamn needs again. *Jarrett when will you grow up?*

"You kids gonna order or what?"

The counterman doubles as the waiter when things are slow, as they are on this Saturday morning. He eyes them with hostile boredom.

"I'll have a Coke," Conrad says.

"Just black coffee for me." Karen gives him a pleasant smile. Nothing doing. He scribbles off a bill and slaps it down on the table with a grunt of annoyance. Not the type to be won over so easily. Have to come up with something better. A million-dollar order, maybe. Conrad pulls his eyebrows together, mocking him, and Karen giggles. She bites her lip, looking down at the table. There, that's better.

He says, "I'm sorry. I didn't mean that."

"It's okay. I didn't mean to sound so rah-rah either. And I really did want to see you. Only I was sort of afraid. You seemed so down, over the phone."

"I'm not down," he says quickly. "Hey, everything's going great. I'm back in school, I'm swimming—"

"Oh, really? I'm glad."

"Well, we haven't had any meets yet. I could end up on the bench all year."

"Oh, no, you'll do fine, I'm sure."

The man returns. He is small and undernourished-looking. Sour. In silence, Conrad slides out of the booth to pay him. He looks at the coins suspiciously; turns away without a word.

Conrad shakes his head. "Hostile."

She giggles. "Definitely a low-self-image day." And they relax. She, the seasoned veteran, out six months to his three, asks, "Are you seeing anybody?"

"A doctor? Yeah, are you?"

She shakes her head and, obscurely, he feels ashamed. Another black mark against him.

"Dr. Crawford gave me a name," she says, "and I went for a while, but then I finally decided it wasn't doing me any good. I mean, he wasn't telling me anything I couldn't figure out for myself. Really, the only one who can help you is you. Well, you and God." She stops, but it is only to take a breath. "Anyway, that's what Dad says, and I know he's right. It's what they told us in the hospital, too, didn't they? That you have to learn to help yourself, and this guy was over in Elk Grove Village and expensive as hell." She looks at him and smiles. "That isn't why I stopped going, though. And I don't mean that there isn't any value in it, if you need it, I mean, for some people it could be just the right thing—" She looks to him for help, afraid that she has wounded him.

51

To reassure her, he says, "Well, I don't know how long I'll keep it up, either. I got shoved into it, sort of. My father—I don't think he's got that much confidence in me. He's pretty nervous about it all. Anyway I only go to get my mind flushed out. After an hour with this guy, you're not too sure about him, but you know you're okay."

Berger, and his visits with him, have gotten to be something that he looks forward to; a chance to feel better twice a week, even if the feeling doesn't have much carry-over yet. Now, on top of the shame, is disgust with himself for his slandering words. Not just Berger, but his father, too. *Christ Jarrett but you're a two-faced bastard.*

She says, "Things were so different in the hospital. People were, you know, turned on all the time. And you just can't live like that You can't live with all that emotion floating around, looking for a place to land. It's too exhausting. It takes so much energy, just to get through a day, even without all that soul-searching we used to do—"

"Hey," he says. "Remember Crawford, how he was always telling you to go with the things that made you laugh? Yesterday I heard a guy on the radio talking about how to take care of your trees. If you water after five, be sure to water only every other root. 'In other words,' he says, 'the U.S. Department of Agriculture requests that you use alternate roots after five o'clock.' "

She is laughing at him at last. "Con, you made that up!"

"No, the guy said it, I swear. I laughed for five minutes. It made me feel good. To know the nuts still have a chance to take over the world."

In the hospital, he was the only one who could make her laugh. His heart swells with pleasure and gratitude. Calmly, so as not to alarm her, he says, "You know, losing a whole year out of your life is turning out to be sort of a disadvantage, don't you think?"

"I don't think about it," she says. "You shouldn't either. Just keep going, get into things, forget about that. Try to be less intense."

Well, that's what he was asking for, wasn't it? Then why do the words irritate him so? With an imaginary pencil he writes in the palm of his hand. "Just a minute, 'less intense,' let me get this all down, gee, you sure do make it sound simple, Dr. Aldrich."

She frowns and looks away. "It isn't simple. And I'm not saying everything's perfect. But at least I try."

"I'm trying," he says. He makes a face, teasing her. "Don't I act like I'm trying?"

"I don't know. I don't really know you, Con."

This hurts. And then she looks at her watch, and this hurts, too. "I'm late. I've got to go."

"So, okay. Go." He spreads his hands, palms down on the table.

She hesitates. "Listen, call me again. I'd like to see you. Really. I mean it. Will you?"

"Sure." Call me, I'd like to see you. But just not real soon. *I might be crazy but I'm not dumb. I read.*

She gathers her coat about her shoulders. "The thing is," she says, "we should both be careful about who we see. It isn't good for either of us to get down."

"I'm not down!" It is definitely *not* the thing to be. More calmly, he repeats it. "I'm not down."

"Well, it's contagious, you know that." Her voice is flat, accusing. "We can't risk it."

"Okay."

Nothing more to say. He glances across the aisle at the rack of paperbacks, reading the titles in despair: *What to Wear and How to Wear It; How to Make the Most of What You've Got; Twenty-five Ways to Better Love-Making.* Oh, God, he did not come here to drain strength away from her he would not do that to anyone least of all her. They are friends aren't they?

She gets to her feet. "I'm sorry. I wish I could stay longer. You look great, Con. You really do."

"Yeah, thanks. You too."

"And you will call me?"

"Yeah, sure."

And then she is gone. He sits awhile longer, palming the empty Coke glass back and forth between his hands. He had thought, this morning, that he would ask her to one of the swim meets. How stupid even to think that she would go for that. Dull stuff anyway, compared to *A Thousand Clowns. Ah come on Jarrett don't be a shit she is a nice girl and she is right it's a dangerous business how would you like it if some screwed-up bastard kept coming around asking you for help asking you to make him feel Necessary?*

There is a sign over the door: NO LOITERING. The counterman/waiter keeps glancing over, getting ready to catch him in the act. He carefully folds his straw into a small rectangle and drops it into his glass. Getting to his feet, he puts on his jacket. *Okay Karen we'll see you around who needs you anyway who the fuck needs anybody?*

8

This Saturday he has repaired a broken doorknob, watched Michigan beat Navy on television, played two sets of tennis with Al Cahill, his next-door neighbor. A familiar and comforting pattern of triviality; the things that move time. First, sitting in the den with his feet up, a glass of beer beside him; then the tennis. He was even pleased about the doorknob; it gave the day that tiny period of purpose, and protected his soul from the sin of idleness.

He pours himself a scotch and water. This first drink of a Saturday evening, made for himself, and drunk in his own company, is another pleasure. Later on, he may become bored and drink too much. Or else he will enjoy himself, relax, and drink too much. Another familiar pattern. He has noted this about himself lately: that he drinks too much when they go out. Because drinking helps. It has gotten him through many evenings, either deadening the pain or raising him above it to where small events seem pleasurable and worth recording. It isn't likely that this will happen tonight. Tonight will not be memorable. He will have to take care not to get blitzed.

Waiting for Beth, he wanders into the den. Conrad lounges on the couch in levis and a T-shirt, hands in his pockets, legs stuck out in front of him, his boot heels digging into the carpet.

"Your basic teen-ager," Cal observes.

Conrad eyes the gray slacks, black turtleneck, gray plaid sportcoat. "Your basic suburban lawyer."

He sits down beside him on the couch. "What're you watching?"

"Dunno. Just got here."

From the television set comes the fervent announcement: "Watch the *Pete Pepper Show!* Share the joys of family living!"

"Who the hell is Pete Pepper?" he asks.

Conrad laughs. "You got me."

"Where were you today? I needed a tennis partner."

"Over in Skokie."

"Oh? Doing what?"

"Seeing somebody I know."

"Anybody I know?"

"No."

Period. A long way to go for friendship. All the way to Skokie. What happened to the people closer to home?

"What're you doing tonight?"

"Studying. Got a history mid-term on Tuesday."

Mid-terms already. He hopes Con is not uptight about the tests. Should he tell him not to worry? No, he will think it means something. Will think he, Cal, is worried. "How's Joe?" he asks. "You see much of him?"

"Every morning on the way to school. At practice. On the way home."

Not an answer, really, but it is conversation. Cal wants to keep it flowing between them. How to do this? Sometimes it is so difficult, feeling his way with this mysterious stranger, his son. He asks, "Why don't you call him and see what he's doing tonight?"

"I think I ought to study."

"Can't you study tomorrow?"

"Yeah, I'm planning on it." His eyes have not left the set. "It's a mid-term, Dad."

"Okay, I guess it takes time to get back in the swing of it again, huh?"

Conrad looks over at him and grins. "You been hanging around with Grandfather again?"

Cal laughs. He will be eighteen in January, but he looks younger than that, and vulnerable; yet older at the same time. Tired. His face is drawn. He has an urge to shield him, but how? There is no way. No way at all. He wants to give him a present of some kind, something to keep the currents of sound moving between them. He says, "Your mother and I were talk-ing about going to London sometime."

"Not for Christmas?" There is an odd look on his face that Cal cannot identify. Fear? Anger? It is gone before he can be sure.

"We haven't decided when," he says. "I thought maybe in the spring. No, this Christmas I thought we'd just stay around here."

"Yeah, that'd be fine. Unless—if everybody else wants to go for Christmas, I'll go, that's okay. I don't want to spoil things. I mean, if she wants to go, I'll go."

Beth is in the doorway. "I'm ready, Cal."

"Okay. In a second."

"We're late." She moves down the hallway to get her coat.

He is on his feet, but he doesn't want to leave yet. Conrad is looking up at him. There is nothing to worry about; he knows that. He has to get over this feeling of panic every time he leaves him alone in the house. He's a big boy. He will be eighteen years old in Janu-ary. Remember it.

"We'll be over at the Murrays', did I tell you that?"

"No. Fine."

"The number's in the book. Philip Murray, on Anhinga Boulevard."

"Okay." And he knows what Conrad is thinking: What would I need to call you for?

In the car, she says to him, "I told you he'd go if you asked him."

"He doesn't want to, though."

She shrugs. "Well, it's too late now, anyway."

She gave up on this, suddenly and simply. It was not like her. He hasn't realized until this minute that it has been several weeks since the subject of London was mentioned. Now he feels at once relief and guilt. "We'll go in the spring," he says, "I promise."

She doesn't answer.

"Who's going to be there tonight?" Testing. Her tone when she answers will tell him if she is angry.

"Well, the Murrays. It's their house." She slides over next to him. Happily grateful, he squeezes her hand. Wonderful, unpredictable girl. "And Mac and Ann Kline, Ed and Marty Genthe. And us."

"Why us? We hardly know the Murrays."

"That's why. That's why you have people over, darling. To get to know them better."

He does not want to know Phil Murray any better. He has played golf with him three times. He knows him well enough. The first time, he was told Phil's reasons for joining the golf club. "I'm an insurance salesman, Cal. A damn good one, too." He had laughed and said that he had all the insurance he needed. "That's what you think." Phil grinned at him. On discovering what Cal did for a living, he spent the rest of the round telling jokes about crooked lawyers. During the second round, Cal confirmed his earlier suspicion that he cheated on the golf course, saw his ball land with a thud in the trap; when they arrived at the shot, it hung, miraculously, on the lush green edge. Worse, Phil was fakily delighted. "Hey, what a break! That was close, huh?" Cal thought he was the only one who noticed, but afterward, in the locker room, Mac Kline shook his head, "Who does he think he's kidding?"

and at lunch someone cracked a joke about the best traps being the ones with the thickest lips."

He says, "Let's go to the movies, instead."

"Don't be negative." She squeezes his hand.

"Then, let's not stay too late."

She is looking at herself in the rear-view mirror. "Already? You don't usually say that until we pull in the driveway. Anyway, you've never even been to their house before. How do you know you won't have fun?"

"I can read my mind. It says, Stay home tonight, read *The Rise and Fall of the Third Reich*, do something constructive with your life."

"Everybody has to eat," she says.

They live only blocks away, in a wide, square-pillared house at the top of a gentle slope known as Anhinga Hill. The contractor, a Floridian transplant, named the streets after a host of Everglades birds—Bittern, Egret, Cormorant, Anhinga. Their own, Heron Drive. Eight basic designs of houses; twenty-four elevations. Each one carefully, artfully different. The subdivision has won prizes. Neatness, originality, aptness-of-thought.

"Here they are!" Sara Murray sweeps them inside. "How's that? Three blocks away, and the last ones to arrive! It's positively insulting. Here are the coats, darling." She ushers them into the large, elegantly furnished living room, done in shades of champagne and white. As is the hostess. A long, silky gown with a deep neckline. She is a tiny woman; nearly a head shorter than Beth. "Ed, move over, will you? Make room for Beth."

"Come here, you gorgeous thing," Ed Gentile says, reaching up to take Beth's hand and pull her down beside him on the couch.

"Edward, Edward," she says, laughing. "Control yourself!"

Gracious as always, but Cal knows she doesn't like this. She is wearing a white-knit pantsuit, a long-sleeved black blouse, her hair tied back from her face with a black silk scarf. She *does* look gorgeous.

"Cal, what would you like?" Phil asks. "Scotch?"

"Yes, please. Just a short one."

"Short on water?" Phil laughs. "Short on scotch?"

"Hey, c'mon, it's a party," Ed says. "Hey, somebody, how about a Dewar's ad on this guy? What's the latest book you've read, Cal?"

"How about *The Rise and Fall of the Third Reich*, the first hundred pages," Beth says. "Four times. Will that do?"

Cal says, "Not funny."

"How about a quote?"

He thinks a minute. " 'The only way to deal with absurdity is to recognize it.' How's that?"

"Pretty good. That yours?"

"Hell, no. You think anybody uses his own quotes in those things? Who talks like that?"

Sara comes in from the kitchen, a tray of cocktail snacks in her hands, all gracefully arranged in rows: sausages and mushrooms in tiny fluted pastry shells; crusty little pillows bulging with some unidentified, gooey filling; hot puffs of cheese-flavored dough. She passes the tray around. "Come on, take lots."

"Cal, you playing in the Lawyers' Invitational next spring?" Mac Kline drifts over to where he is standing, beside the mantel.

"I don't know. I'm not sure I posted enough scores this year to qualify."

"You ever won that thing?" Ed asks.

"Are you kidding? Too many lawyers play golf."

"Too many lawyers play golf is right," Phil says. "Try to get on that course on a Thursday afternoon. Hey, that reminds me—" and he is off on another crooked-lawyer joke.

Sara jockeys in between Cal and Mac with the tray. Her breasts swell provocatively from the V of the gown. He studies the tray in stern concentration. To raise his eyes a mere three inches would be

Ordinary People

to give her what she wants; she would like to catch
him sneaking a look, he can feel it, and he would
do it, too, if it were not for a frenetic-butterfly
manner that she radiates. It grates on his nerves. She
has an endless supply of nervous energy. Tiny
women are often like this, he thinks. They never run
down. They overwhelm him, make him feel lumpish
and stupid. Too large. He glances at his wife, who
is not that type at all. She is cool and quiet and
relaxed at parties. He would prefer sitting next to
her, talking to her. That is often the case with him.
He likes women, but not nervous women. He has
tried to like Sara and, at times, he has almost suc-
ceeded. So long as he doesn't have to see her often.
No, he would not like to be married to a damned
butterfly.

"I saw Conrad the other day," Marty Genthe
says. "Uptown. It's nice that someone that age still
believes in courtesy. Most of Donald's friends remember my face, but they can't be bothered putting
a name to it. It's just, 'Oh, hi there.' "

And suddenly, everyone is listening.

"How is he doing?" Ann asks. "I heard the boys
say he's swimming."

"He's fine," Beth says. There is something final
and forbidding about the answer, but Sara doesn't
hear it. They are still newcomers here, and she
wants to be polite. Inquiring after people's children
is accepted form everywhere.

She asks, "Has he been sick?"

"He was sick for a while," Beth says, "He's fine,
now."

"Another drink, Cal?"

"Yes, sure. Is there time before dinner?" He
crosses to the bar, the skin on the backs of his hands
tightening, as if from an electric shock.

He sits between Ann Kline and Marty Genthe at
the table, with Sara across from him.

61

"Sara, what a meal!" Marty says, "This is a tough act to follow, dear."

"Oh, no," she protests, "it's just plain food. I can't cook fancy, honestly. No, Beth is the artist in that department, I don't know how she does it!"

"The cheese sauce is great," Ed says, "Marty, get that recipe, will you?"

After the main course comes strawberry mousse; it is flawless. Then the children are served up. They enter the living room on cue, to say their good nights. A command performance for all. The guests are politely impressed. Cal cannot help being touched at their grave good manners. All four of them are beautiful children, having surpassed their models. No mere reproductions, but stunning originals. Their handsome, dark-eyed fourteen-year-old daughter supervises her younger brother and sister, while the eldest boy stands, shy and solemn, in the background. He reminds Cal of Conrad at that age. So earnest, so polite. Adults and children beam awkwardly at one another until Sara's motherly pride is satisfied, and they are dismissed.

"Good-looking children," Cal says.

"Thank you." She beams him a grateful smile.

In knots of two and three, they sit in the living room. Beth and Mac are in one corner, consulting earnestly about books, he is sure. Mac Kline is an English professor at Lake Forest College, who loves to talk about his subject. Beth would talk books to a deaf person, needing nothing more than an encouraging nod, now and then. He catches her eye and she smiles at him. Across the room, Ann and Phil and Ed are horsing around, Ed giving a lecture on the perfect tennis serve to Ann and Phil, the inept, giggling pupils. Cal sits on the couch between Sara and Marty, feeling pleasantly high, and full.

"Great dinner," he tells Sara. "Thank you."

Ordinary People

"When are we going to play some bridge, Cal?" Marty asks.

"Yeah, we ought to do that."

He has an arm around each of them, and has to disengage one from Sara to sip his drink.

"I mean, now that you two are social, again," Marty says. "How are things, really? Going all right?"

Marty is looking at him. A brittle, attractive redhead, she lost out on beauty through the accident of a razor-planed, imperious nose. One New Year's Eve, he remembers kissing her. A long, warm embrace. He was drunk. No one said anything about it afterward, not Ed, or Beth. He was surprised. He had felt guilty and embarrassed; he would have said something, he was sure, if it had been Ed and Beth.

"Yes,-pretty well," he says. "Only I miss the kids who used to hang around. What's Don doing these days? I haven't seen him in a while."

"Oh, the same old things, Girls. Swimming. You know how boys are, they don't tell you anything unless you back them into a corner and *bulldoze* it out of them." She laughs. "To tell you the truth, Donald says Conrad isn't very—isn't as friendly as he used to be. I suppose he feels a little, I don't know, self-conscious—"

"About what?" Sara asks. "I'm sorry, maybe it's none of my business."

"No, it's nothing," Cal says. He is suddenly uncomfortable. The drinks have made him fuzzy. He shouldn't have said that, about the boys not coming around. It sounded as if he were annoyed; put her on the defensive.

"Donald says he doesn't come to practice on Tuesdays and Fridays."

"No. There's a doctor in Evanston. He sees him twice a week."

"You mean he's still having problems?"

"Not exactly. It's somebody to talk to," he says

lamely. He looks down into his glass. This was not the direction he had intended the conversation to take. Sara is laughing loudly and elaborately at the antics of her husband, across the room, having decided not to get into this, after all. A wise decision. He wishes he had done the same.

"Cal, we've got to go," Beth calls across to him. "It's late."

"Hey, what d'you mean? Party's just getting off the ground!" Phil protests as they move toward the hall. "Okay, you'll be sorry! We'll talk about you!"

Somehow they are into their coats and out the door, and the night is cool and silent all around them, cool-ness against his cheeks, and silence as he opens the car door for her, closes it, walks around behind the car, gets in under the wheel.

"Do you want me to drive?" she asks.

He glances at her, surprised. "I'm not drunk," he says. "Do you think I'm drunk?"

"I don't know, are you?"

So she had heard it. "No," he says. "No, I am not, I promise." Seeking to lead her away from it, he laughs. "The thing you can't forgive about Phil Murray is that he's a goddamn, crashing bore. One more crooked-lawyer joke and I start in on my pesky-insurance-salesman routine—"

"I want to tell you something," she says. "You drink too much at parties."

"Okay."

"She pumped you," she says. "And you let her do it. You let her drag that stuff out of you, and in front of someone who doesn't even know us."

"My sentiments exactly." He nods, hoping to head her off, hoping she is not really angry, because he doesn't feel drunk tonight, just good and high; he would like to keep feeling good a while longer. He reaches over and pats her knee with clumsy affection. "Why did you tell her he was seeing a psychia-trist?"

Ordinary People

"Look, some people consider that a status sym-bol," he says, "right up there with going to Europe."

"I don't. And I thought your blurting it out like that was in the worst possible taste."

"I'm sorry."

"Not to mention a violation of privacy."

"Whose privacy?" he asks. "Whose privacy did I violate?"

She does not answer.

The light is on in Conrad's room. He is asleep, lying on his back, his mouth open and relaxed. He sweats heavily in his sleep. His hair is damp, cling-ing slickly to his forehead, curling against his neck. A book lies face-down and open on the bed. *U.S. History: Constitution to Present Day.* Cal picks up the book and closes it quietly. He sets it on the night stand. Reaching for the switch on the lamp, he looks at Conrad. His left arm is shoved underneath the pillow. His right is out-stretched; the hand with its strong, square fingers curved protectively over the palm is motionless. Still biting his nails. A nervous habit. So what? Lots of people do it; he himself used to do it when he was that age.

He looks, really looks, this time at the thin, vertical scar that extends up the inside of the arm, above the palm. More than two inches long, ridged, a gray-pink line. "He meant business," the intern told him in the ambulance. "Horizontal cuts, the blood clots. It takes a lot longer. You were damn lucky to catch him."

High achievers, Dr. Crawford told him, set them-selves impossible standards. They have this need to perform well, to look good; they suffer excessive guilt over failure. He had groped to understand. "But what has he failed at? He's never failed at any-thing!"

Conrad's head moves on the pillow, and Cal snaps off the light, not allowing himself to look again at the scar, not wanting to be guilty of any more

Ordinary People

violations of privacy. Listen, he prays, let the exams be easy. Don't let him feel he is failing.

Beth is awake, waiting for him, her hair loose about her shoulders. She reaches up to put her arms around him, all tawny, smooth skin, those gray eyes with thick lashes, silent and insistent. She leads to-night, and he follows, moving swiftly down that dark river, everything floating, melting, perfect, and com-plete. Afterward, she slides away from him, and her hair, soft and furry against his shoulder, smells sweet and fresh, like wood fern. He buries his face in it, still hungry. "Let me hold you awhile."

But she is tired. She curls away from him; pushes him gently from her, in sleep. He rolls to his back, hands under his head, staring upward. Other Saturday nights, lying, waiting after sex, for the comforting sound of a car door slamming, and whispers of laugh-ter under the windows. And earlier, at the beginning of the evenings, the endless jokes, the hassles over clothes *Hey, that's my sweater! The hell it is, posses-sion is—hey, Dad, what's possession? Possession is gonna get your head broke—now give it to me! And* sounds of a struggle and fiendish, sadistic laughter *Take it, fag, it's a fag sweater, you'll look great in it* and more laughter *You oughta know!*

He will not be able to sleep tonight for hours; an-other side effect of drinking too much. It condemns him to wakefulness. Without expectation of anything —of a car, of whispers or laughter. Resigned, he keeps watch and continues to listen.

6

A surprise quiz in trig. He takes his seat, the mimeo-graphed sheet in his hand, his stomach pulling nerv-ously. He wills himself not to panic. *I know this stuff.
I know it.*

Across the aisle from him sits Suzanne Mosely. They have known each other since grade school. What is she doing in here? She must have flunked it, too, last year. He watches as her pudgy fingers grip the pencil. Her brow is furrowed; her mouth pinched. It makes him ashamed of his own fear. She has always had trouble in math, could take it from now until the world ends and it won't help. He looks up. Mr. Simmons is staring at him. Guiltily he looks down at his paper.

Given: reduction formulas

$$\sin \theta = - \sin (-\theta)$$
$$\cos \theta = \cos (-\theta)$$

Stay calm. It will come don't think about anything else just the problem easy does it confidence.

Halfway through the test his pencil point snaps. He straightens up; lets out his breath with a sigh. Not hard. It is not as hard as he thought it would be. His back is tense, and he rubs it, stretching. He goes

Ordinary People

to get another pencil from the box on Simmons' desk. No pencil-sharpening during a quiz, that is one of the unbreakable rules.

Simmons looks up. "Everything okay, Jarrett?"

He nods, returning to his seat. Out of the corner of his eye he can see Suzanne's paper. Cross-outs everywhere. The poor kid. He knows what that feels like. What did she take this course for anyway?

There are five minutes left in the hour when he hands in his paper. He leaves the room, taking up a spot against the lockers as he waits for the bell to ring. Down the hall, the smoking lounge overflows with people let out of class early. He does not go down there. He has nothing to say to anyone. Suzanne comes out and leans against the wall. Her head is bent over her books. She is wearing a dark skirt, a brown sweater that's too tight. God, she's so fat. Has she always been that fat? He doesn't remember it. Hunched over, huddled against the wall, her hair stiff, like brown cotton candy. A lion's mane around her face. Pretty. She was pretty in junior high.

She is staring at him now, and he straightens up *Shit she is crying* The tears are spilling down her cheeks. He stands there helpless, watching.

"What are *you* looking at?"

She clutches her books against her breasts as he moves toward her.

"Hey, it's only a stupid test."

She glares at him. "You can say that. You passed it. My dad's going to kill me. God, why am I so *dumb!* I work and work at it and it's all a jumble. . . ."

"It's just crap," he says. "Tangents, cotangents, when are you ever going to use them? It doesn't matter."

The bell rings and she jumps. She turns away from him and he has to run to catch up with her. "Listen, if you want some help—"

She stops in the middle of the hall to stare at him.

"I'll help you. I can explain it, if you want. In study hall. Or after school some night."

"Why would you want to do that?" she asks, her eyes narrowing. "No. No thanks, it's all right."

The crowd sweeps them along in its flow, and a voice cuts across the hall: "Hey, Jarrett!" He looks over. Stillman grins at him. Suzanne has gone on ahead and Conrad stands a moment, looking after her, feeling relieved, and yet oddly hurt.

In the locker room that afternoon, Stillman lies in wait. "Hey, Jarrett, she busy Saturday? Hey, Lemme know if she's easy, will you?"

"Who?" Van Buren asks.

"Hey, c'mon, Jarrett, I'll let you know about Pratt, if you let me know about Mosely."

"Mosely?" Van Buren echoes, *"Mosely?"*

He slams his locker closed and their laughter follows him up the stairway to the pool. *Pricks. To hell with them forever.*

In bed he waits for sleep. He cannot get under until he has reviewed the day, counted up his losses. He must learn more control, cannot allow himsef the luxury of anger. He has seen it happen before. Guys become easy targets for the Stillmans of the world. *Next time laugh when he needles you.*

What about the test? Did he pass it? He thinks so but something else—what had he said to Suzanne? *It doesn't matter* and suddenly it clicks into place: why Simmons had kept such an eye on him all through the hour. Oh God, that was the class. Last year. A quiz being returned. Across his paper in red pencil *Incomplete. See Me.* He had stared at it all through the hour while the rest of the class discussed and made corrections. No use listening, none of it meant anything to him. He sat there, his eyes slowly filling with tears, trying to blink them back but they would not stop, and Simmons bending over his desk, asking

Jarrett, are you sick? Nodding, stumbling up the aisle, facing the blackboard as Simmons wrote out a hall pass. An electric wall of silence behind them. Out of the classroom, heading not toward the nurse's office, but toward the double exit doors. Into the parking lot to find a car that was unlocked. Him on the floor in the back seat, crying, leaning out to be sick in the snow. He had left school that day, walked around uptown, looking in windows at the Christmas displays. When it was time he went home. And the next day, the last before Christmas vacation, his homeroom teacher had called him up to the desk.

"I got a skip notice on you this morning. What happened?"

"Nothing. I didn't feel like going to class."

"Were you sick?"

"No."

The teacher had looked at him. "Okay. Let's forget it. We'll talk about it after the holidays."

The holidays. Christmas in Florida. Lying on the bed at the Sonesta Beach in his bathing suit, staring at a mosquito above his head, its tiny body pressed against the rough plaster ceiling, spreading a half-inch gray shadow on the stark white. The only memory he has of that period. That, and the ceaseless, remorseless blue of ocean.

Brightness surrounds him. No shadows but it must be night the sand is stiff and cold squeaks under his feet a breeze bends the spiky beach grass double to the sand.

He walks. The moon is above him and to his left. Miles and miles the sand stretches in front of him a cool smooth highway and the mouth of the tunnel appears a metal cylinder curving ten feet over his head the lower rim buried in the sand.

He enters it. Brightly lit inside its walls a polished silver-gray like the inside of a galvanized pail girders forming the rib cage that supports its walls. A sharp right-turn ahead obscures his view when he turns the corner there is disappointment the tunnel continues on no end in sight only the dimensions have shrunk. He can touch the walls now the ceiling too smooth and cold against his hands. The backs of his legs ache. He kneels down to rest sifting the fine sand from the tunnel floor through his fingers it blows away from him taking the shape of the wind like pictures in a fairy-tale book but there is no wind in the tunnel and no wires where does the light come from?

He stands discovering that the dimensions have shrunk again and now he must move forward on his hands and knees but even then his head brushes the ceiling the light is less bright and he cannot see clearly just shadows on the sand and ahead of him another turn he moves eagerly toward it.

A makeshift rectangular chute beyond the turn the sides are shored with two by fours. He is perplexed vaguely angry what crumby workmanship how will he maneuver here he must crawl on his stomach scraping piles of sand toward himself he is too tired for this game would like to quit but still he keeps going wriggling past the first set of shorings before he rests again. He puts his head down and the cool sand feels pleasant and grainy under his cheek. When he raises his head he sees nothing. Only darkness. He is convulsed with panic begins to work himself backward and his feet strike the wall of the tunnel he shifts his position and tries again solid wall no matter where he moves his head wedged against the ceiling his chin touching the tunnel floor Oh God he is sealed in this metal tomb and the walls press upon him from all sides he cannot breathe cannot move must must twisting violently onto his back he screams.

It wakes him. He can hear the echo of it inside his head. Did he scream out loud? He listens for some sound in the house, for someone pounding out of bed and down the hall toward his room. Nothing.

71

The blood tingles in his veins, hot and then cold. His heart is pounding painfully.

He sits up; turns on the light, but slowly, slowly. No sudden movements. He feels as if he could shatter into a million pieces if he is jarred.

"I don't hold much stock in dreams," Berger says. "In fact, I don't hold stock. Of any kind."

He is annoyed. "What the hell kind of psychiatrist are you? They all believe in dreams."

"Do they? Goddamn, I'm always outa step. Do me a favor, will you? Lie down. On the floor, that's it. I want to try something."

"Christ! You're nuts, you know that?" Still, he obeys, lowering himself to the carpet and stretching out, ankles crossed, hands behind his head.

"Change of perspective," Berger says. He likewise lowers himself. "Steadies the blood."

"Steadies the blood," he scoffs. "This is stupid. Besides, I lie down all the time at home. It doesn't help. Maybe I need some kind of tranquilizer."

"Tranquilizer?"

"Yeah. What d'you think?"

"I think," Berger says, "that you come in here looking like something out of *The Body Snatchers*. It is not my impression that you are in need of a tranquilizer."

"I feel nervous all the time. I can't sleep."

"Maybe your schedule's too heavy. You're trying to do too much. Maybe you oughta drop a course or two."

"No."

"No. Why not?"

"Because. I'm behind already."

"Behind what? The Great Schedule in the Sky? The Golden Gradebook? What?"

"God, you're preaching again. And your ceiling's dirty."

"So, sue me. Listen, kiddo, I lied. I believe in

dreams, and I especially believe in yours, they're fascinating as hell. Only sometimes I like you to tell me about what happens to you when you're awake, okay? Something is bugging you, something is making you nervous. Now what is it?"

He sits up; reaches for his coffee. "Okay, I know what it is. I don't want to swim any more. I look horrible, my timing is for shit. He's got two guys who are better than me swimming the fifty, and, anyway, I don't give a damn about those guys, they're a bunch of boring jocks. And I can't *stand* him, he's a tight-ass son of a bitch——" He breaks off, clamping his teeth over the rest of the words, gripping his knees, his stomach in knots.

"Well," Berger says, after a moment. "Well, why don't you quit, then?"

"I can't. It'd look so stupid. I go to him and beg for one more chance. Then, I swim for two months and quit again. Can't you see how stupid that would look?"

"Forget how it looks. How does it feel?"

He shakes his head. "No. That's what happened last year. It's the same damn thing I did last year."

"Forget last year. You think you're the same person you were last year?"

He shrugs, lying down again, staring upward at the ceiling.

"So, tell me about the coach," Berger says. "How come he's a tight-ass son of a bitch?"

He smiles faintly. "I don't know. He's a jerk. He says to me—this is typical—'Jarrett, I had a friend who was hospitalized for this same thing, five years ago. Been in and out of institutions ever since.' Now what the hell am I supposed to say to that?"

"What did you say?"

"I told him I wasn't planning on going back. He says, 'No, I don't suppose you are.'"

"Sometimes," Berger says, "people say stupid things. They feel like they gotta say something, you know?"

"Sometimes people say stupid things, because they're stupid."

A wooden clock on the wall behind his head ticks away loudly, and it is relaxing to lie here with this placid man beside him, talking of anger and of change, without being irrevocably committed to it. He could go to sleep here; right now he is yawning, pleasantly tired, but it is five o'clock, time to go home.

"This problem, kiddo," Berger says, "it's real, you know. A good, healthy problem needs a good, healthy solution. Point of separation. Between the sicks and the wells. Real problems, real solutions, you get it?"

He rolls onto his stomach, his head buried in his arms. "Sounds like a chapter heading to me."

Berger sighs. "I hope to hell you're writing this stuff down. It'll be a shame if it's lost to the future generations."

"I've got it taped up over the back of the john."

10

Laughter drifts upstairs from the locker room, loud and raucous. From the top of the stairs, he can hear Stillman, his voice raw with complaint: "Lazenby, Jesus, why you so nervous about making a commitment, just yes or no!"

"It costs money, that's why. For three bucks, I like to know what I'm seeing."

"Hell, it's a goddamn French sex film, what more do you have to know?"

More laughter, and he starts down the stairs, rubbing his head with a towel.

Lazenby says, "Okay. How about if I ask Jarrett?"

And he stops; loops the towel around his neck, listening.

"You ever think about doing anything without Jarrett?"

"What's that mean?"

"Means what it says. I just wondered."

Genthe says, "Hey, what's with him anyway? How come he gets all the extra practice time? Hell, I could look better if I had extra practice time—"

"Genthe, you couldn't look better if you were a girl," Truan jeers. "That's the goddamned truth."

75

He stands outside the open door, smoothing his hand lightly along the polished wood frame, slowly, slowly.

Lazenby says, "I just thought we'd ask him, Kevin."

"You know what happens when you hang around with flakes," Stillman says. "You get flaky."

"Man, d'you mind?" Lazenby asks mildly. "He's a friend of mine."

"He's a flake."

"You oughta get off his back, Kevin," Van Buren says. "The guy's got enough problems."

"He sure has."

More laughter and he does not wait to hear the rest, but turns abruptly, heading back up the stairs. Nothing touches him on the way, not even the air in the hallway. Salan is sitting where he left him, his head still bent over the clipboard. He listens, his mouth a taut line, as Conrad explains. That it is something he has been thinking about for a long time, and he is sure, now, he knows he is doing the right thing.

At last, he says, "Jarrett, you gotta be kidding me. I don't get it. I excuse you from practice twice a week so you can see some shrink. I work with you every damn night *at your convenience*, now what the hell more am I supposed to be doing for you?"

"Nothing." *Shrink. Hate that word coarse ignorant just the kind of word you'd expect from stupid bastard like Salan will not get mad control is all just someday come down here tell him what he can do with his goddamn ignorant opinions.*

"A bright kid like you," Salan continues, "with everything going for him. I don't get it. Why do you want to keep messing up your life?"

He says carefully, "I don't think it'll mess up my life if I stop swimming." *Stay calm stay calm this is not a spastic leap this is a well-thought-out sane and sensible decision. A real solution to a real problem.*

Salan says flatly, "Okay. This is it. You're a big

kid now, and actions have consequences. I'm not taking you back again. You remember that."

Fucking swell I'll remember all right. Aloud he says, "No, sir. I won't ask you to, sir."

The locker room is empty. He showers, dresses, packs his athletic bag, making sure all his stuff is cleaned out of the locker. Stalling, but he knows it's no good, Lazenby will wait for him. He doesn't want to ride home with them, doesn't want to see them again, but it would look stupid, letting them sit there, sneaking out the back door, and why the hell should he walk? Why should he freeze his ass off because they are jerks and pricks?

He heads for the car. The smell of snow is in the air. Early this year. It is still a week before Thanksgiving. Truan, Van Buren, and Stillman are in the back seat. He gets in front, setting his bag on the floor. Lazenby asks if he is interested in going to the show tonight. He declines. He has to study.

"You oughta lay off studying, Jarrett," Stillman says. "Screws up your mind. Keep all the channels clear up there for heavy thought."

They laugh. To his ears, the sound is forced; false.

"We'll be back by eleven," Lazenby says.

"No. I can't."

"Who says?" Stillman asks. "Your mom?"

He ignores that, not answering. The ride seems long. Even though he is the first to be dropped off.

"I'll see you tomorrow," Lazenby says. "About eight-twenty."

"I've got to go early tomorrow," he says. "I'll get a ride with my dad."

"How early? I can go a little early—"

"No, that's okay. I'll see you there."

Let them find out from Salan that he is finished with them. He gets out and closes the door without looking back.

His father stops at the door of his room that night. The ritual stop. "How's it going?"

"Okay. Fine." He returns the ritual answer. It is not a lie, really; just the safest thing to say for now. He does not want to discuss it tonight. A small thing, after all. To mention it is to make too much of it, and there will be flak—"Why? Did something happen? Is anything the matter?"—and he isn't ready for it. Not yet. He has done it, maybe for the wrong reasons, but it was the right thing to do. There is no problem improving your timing, or perfecting a stroke, if the desire is there, but you cannot fire up, cannot manufacture desire, when there is no spark at all to build on. This was not a mistake, what happened today. It is not to be looked at as a failure.

Summers ago when they all took the trip to Maine and climbed Cadillac Mountain, looking in every direction—nothing to see but water except for the thin strip of land, an arm and a fist, holding the mountain and the park to the state of Maine. They tried to look beyond the water to the east and Portugal; to the north, the Hebrides, Iceland; to the south, the Antilles and farther, South America and the Antarctic Peninsula. *Impressive,* they tossed out the adjectives, *Majestic. Awesome.* And then somebody said *excessive,* and they all laughed. That was it. Everything seems excessive, now, and too intense, too important. Karen is right, learn to relax, don't think so much, just *be.*

Night is fast replacing morning as the worst time of day for him. The way it used to be in the months after the accident. He wasn't sleeping much. And suddenly, he wasn't sleeping at all, he was unable to close his eyes, his body was tense, his brain seethed from night until morning. He would set his alarm at eleven and crawl into bed, praying, and he would lie there and lie there until at last he would hear the warning click as the radio turned itself on and it was morning again. His father would come down the hall, to make sure he was awake. *Awake.* And he was never able to tell them, he would get up, get dressed, eat his breakfast, go to school, just as if his ass wasn't dragging on the goddamn ground, he was so tired, so tired. He told Crawford once that was why he had done it— he had to get some sleep.

But things are not that bad. Not yet. There are still methods that work, and he rolls onto his face, hands between his legs. They used to kid each other about it. Sixty seconds or you haven't got it, well, he can beat that record anytime. Banging the bed. Or the shower. That is his specialty.

11

Ray sticks his head inside Cal's office. "Nobody knows," he says, "the trouble she's seen."

"What's up?"

"It seems our secretary is minus a boy friend. At least that's what I get from the stuff going out over the telephone wires. She's got her own personal Ann Landers on the other end, I guess. Lord, I wish she'd blow her nose!"

"You're a hard-hearted bastard," Cal says.

"Yeah, she'll find out how hard-hearted if she doesn't get some of this mail out. Not that I'd presume to compare it with the tragedy of the century that's going on out there."

"Somebody who's going through a romantic crisis shouldn't be expected to get the mail out."

"Hey, whose side are you on?" Ray comes in; shuts the door behind him. "You through with that pension plan yet?"

"Not yet."

"Hey, buddy, what have *you* been doing all morning?"

"Hey, buddy, don't get on my back. I'm not Cherry."

Ray laughs. "See? What she's doing to me? Making me into a browbeater and a nagger, with my own partner, Jesus!"

An endless parade of secretaries. He has seen them interviewed, instructed, hired, used, and lost, forever and ever, on into eternity. They have been doing it for seven years. It has been that long since they have had a good legal secretary. Since Lynn Searles.

Poor Cherry. People are like icebergs; one-seventh visible and operative, and the rest just so much protoplasmic energy, seething around under there, looking for a target to funnel toward. Too bad she picked the wrong target. Yet it's hard to imagine that giddy, empty girl with any hidden energies; how did she summon up that much feeling for anybody? *Watch it—your immunity is showing.* That is it, of course. He has become immune to the sufferings of others. *I don't give a damn. Let them hurt.* The things which hurt instruct—Benjamin Franklin. That was one of Arnold's favorites. Not true, though. The things which hurt don't always instruct. Sometimes they merely hurt. *Ask me. Ask Nancy Hanley.* Instruct sounds like such a positive word, but he doubts whether Ray's wife, even now, would believe in that saying. In any case, he would not ask her. A long time ago, and water over the dam.

Lynn Searles. What made him think of her? Stern, straight-thinking Lynn, who always looked right into your eyes when she spoke to you, as if she could see behind them and into your head. He wonders, idly, what she is doing now. He wonders if Ray knows; if he knows where she is. Another question he would not ask. What was that? Water over the dam? Con is right, he will have to watch it, he is getting to think more like Howard every day.

He runs into Carole Lazenby downstairs in the Plaza. Hatless, wearing a tweed pantsuit, her large-boned, square figure looks farmlike, out of place here, among the coeds and snazzy secretaries parading the streets of Evanston at noontime. And because she looks so real and so alive, he is absurdly glad to see her; asks her to go to lunch with him on the spot.

"Gee, nobody's asked me to lunch in ages! I wonder if I'll know how to act!"

She offers to take him to the University Sandwich Shop, where she commands a discount with her student I.D.

"What are you taking?" he asks.

She laughs, self-consciously. "It's called Search for Identity."

Funny, he would never have picked her out as a woman with identity problems. He tells her so, but she just laughs.

"Oh, come on. Everybody has them, Cal. Looking forty in the face is what scared me. Maybe if I was your wife, I could handle it better."

"Why?"

"Why?" She laughs again. "Oh, I don't know. I guess because she doesn't look it."

A pleasant lunch. He has forgotten how easy she is to talk to, how genuine. She asks about Con, and that makes it easy for him to inquire after Joe, to mention how he misses seeing him around the house, as he used to.

"Yes, they don't spend much time together, do they? Well, you tell Connie that I miss him. Tell him to stop over some time soon. Beth, too. How is she? I only see her at bridge once a month, and we never seem to get a chance to talk."

"She's busy, too," Cal says. "She's chairing the tennis tournament at Onwentsia next spring. She spends a lot of time over there."

"I admire her organization," Carole says. "She's such a perfectionist. And yet she never lets herself get trapped into things she doesn't want to do.

82

Now, there's an art. I'm just beginning to learn the trick myself. I hope it's not too late!"

He walks Carole to the corner; sends his greetings to John, and to Katy, their daughter.

"We'll get together," he promises.

On the way back to work he thinks, She never lets herself get trapped. Not strictly true. He can remember a period of their lives when she felt distinctly trapped. When Jordan was two years old, with Connie toddling around after him at ten months, both of them spreading havoc in that tiny northside apartment. *Those first five years just passed in a blur!* he has heard her say gaily at parties. But he remembers them, and remembers the scenes: her figure, tense with fury as she scrubbed the fingermarks from the walls; she bursting suddenly into tears because of a toy left out of place, or a spoonful of food thrown onto the floor from the high chair. And it did not pay him to become exasperated with her. Once he had done so, had shouted at her to forget the damned cleaning schedule for once. She had flown into a rage, railed at him, and flung herself across the bed, in hysterics. Everything had to be perfect, never mind the impossible hardship it worked on her, on them all; never mind the utter lack of meaning in such perfection, weighed as it was against the endless repetition of days, weeks, months. They learned, all of them, that certain things drove her to the point of madness: dirt tracked in on a freshly scrubbed floor; water-spotted shower stalls; articles of clothing left out of place. And, he had to admit, he liked a clean house; he liked the order she brought into his life, perfectionist that she was.

And so had he been, after a fashion. No more. Not since the summer before last and an unexpected July storm on Lake Michigan. He had left off being a perfectionist then, when he discovered that not promptly kept appointments, not a house circumspectly clean, not membership in Onwentsia, or the Lake Forest Golf and Country Club, or the Lawyers' Club, not power, or knowledge, or good-ness—not *anything*—cleared you through the terrify-ing office of chance; that it is chance and not perfection that rules the world.

"I saw Nancy Hanley today. Having lunch at the Deerpath."

"Oh?" He keeps one eye on the newspaper be-fore his face: *Welfare Fraud Investigated.*

"She said Ray's been putting on weight."

"He has?"

"He has?" she teases. "Darling, Ray Hanley. Your partner."

"Oh, yeah, him." Grinning, he puts down the paper. "I hadn't noticed. Yeah, I guess he has been."

"Twenty pounds. That's a lot not to notice."

"That much? How did she happen to tell you that?"

Beth shrugs. "Just conversation. She said she's been trying to get him to see a doctor. It's just since he quit smoking. She looks terrific, by the way. Have you seen her lately?"

"No. That's what Ray said about you."

"Well, she's thin. As thin as I've ever seen her, and she's done something to her hair. A rinse, I think—"

. . . officials in the downtown office say as much as $300,000 may have been misdirected by the fraudulent claims. . . .

"—asked her how she stays so thin. She said, 'Worry, and a bad marriage—' "

"What?"

She smiles. "Just checking. To see if you were listening. Would you like a drink before dinner?"

"No, thanks." He glances at his watch. "Is Con home yet?"

"Not yet."

"It's six-thirty."

"He's been later the past couple of weeks."

"I've got an idea," he says. "Why don't you come down tomorrow, and take a look at that car with me? We can have lunch."

"I can't tomorrow."

"I ought to put the order in soon, to get delivery before Christmas."

"Then, do it," she says. "Do what you like. I'm not good at picking out cars anyway."

"You don't sound terrifically sold on the idea."

"I'm sold. I think it's a nice idea."

"Well, it would give him some independence. He wouldn't have to rely on us for rides."

"Fine. We can make it a combination Christmas and birthday present. You decide. I'll leave it up to to you."

If it was up to him, he would give him everything —sun and moon, eternal happiness, serene and uncomplicated, *Here, will this fix it?* But nothing needs fixing, does it? Things do seem better, more relaxed, just since Thanksgiving. No, even before that. Is that illusion or reality?

Illusion or reality. Seven years ago, he had had a conversation on that very subject with Nancy Hanley. At the Law Club Christmas Dance, sitting on the upper deck of the Chicago Yacht Club. Nancy had leaned over and said to him, "Tell Beth for me how lucky she is, will you?"

"Why?"

"To have you. And never to have been disillusioned."

He had laughed, embarrassed, knowing where it was leading. He had emphatically not wanted to go into it, had never wanted to take sides in the thing, but Nancy was not about to let him off the hook.

"People make mistakes, Nance."

A mirthless laugh. "Yes, they do."

Carefully, because he had no desire to disturb the truce that had been so recently effected between them, he had said, "Don't you think people are entitled to a few mistakes in a lifetime?"

"No," she said. "What people are entitled to are their illusions, and frankly, I preferred my illusions about him. I would have preferred it if he had screwed her until he was sick of it and gotten rid of her without my ever having found out about it at all."

"I can't believe that," he told her. "Illusions are for fairy tales. Your marriage is stronger now—"

"Don't bet on it. And if you ever do a survey, you'll find that people prefer illusion to reality, ten to one. Twenty, even. Any odds you want to give, I'll cover."

Worry and a bad marriage. Beth was joking. She said she had been joking. It had been seven years since Ray's affair with Lynn. Seven years since Nancy had packed up the girls and gone to her parents in Oklahoma, and Ray, wild with grief, had come charging into the office to tell him.

"How could I have been so stupid, Cal? How could I have been so selfish, thinking I had it so tough, having to come home to a squalling baby every night? She's gone, Cal! She left me! What the hell am I going to do without her?"

Well, things change; people change. Lynn had left, and Nancy had come back, and they had moved out of their apartment and bought the big house in Glencoe. And surely Nancy is not the type of woman to live with somebody she doesn't love "for the sake of the children." No illusion there. They are still married; therefore, they are happy. But he sees the point she had been making. Depending upon the reality one must face, one may prefer to opt for illusion.

He wants so much to believe that all is well. But, then if it is, why does he keep taking pulses, and looking for signs?

The front door opens. He hears the familiar sounds, of his feet scuffing the doormat, of the hangers clanging against each other in the closet as he hangs up his jacket.

"Hi. You're late tonight."

"Am I?" He looks at his watch. "Yeah, a little. Hey, it's snowing."

"Is it? Must have just started."

"Yeah, it looks nice." He sits down, and Cal hands him the sports section. "You finished? Thanks."

"How's it going?"

"Fine. Great. He gave back the trig quiz today. I got an A on it."

"Great. Terrific."

"Well," he says and shrugs, "it was just a quiz."

But a gift. To have offered it is to show that it must have value for the giver, also.

"That your first A this semester?"

He looks up from the paper. "Yeah. I'm getting back in the swing of things, huh?" He grins.

So truth is in a certain feeling of permanence that presses around the moment. They are ordinary people, after all. For a time they had entered the world of the newspaper statistic; a world where any measure you took to feel better was temporary, at best, but that is over. This is permanent. It must be.

Beth comes in from the kitchen. "Dinner's ready."

Conrad puts the paper down. "I'm coming. Just have to wash my hands."

"Didn't you just take a shower?"

He grins again. "Forgot to wash my hands."

Cal laughs. "Tricky."

12

At first he was afraid that the hours after school would drag, but they do not. He fills them with studying, at school, or in town, at the library. The old building is comfortable and secluded and dark, with its narrow stained-glass windows and soft leather chairs. He can stay there until five-thirty and make it home on time. Or else he walks, keeping an eye on his watch, checking the time. Down Deerpath, past the Presbyterian church to the north campus of Lake Forest where he can sit on a park bench and watch the birds. Nuthatches, creepers, chickadees, grosbeaks (he bought himself a bird book, and is learning to identify them) go sedately and earnestly about their business, which is eating. He carries envelopes of sunflower seeds in his jacket pockets. He has his own Life List.

This month he has another activity. Christmas shopping. He wanders through the stores of the U-shaped, outdoor mall admiring the piles of merchandise in the windows—sweaters, shirts, gloves, scarves, jewelry, sports equipment, shoes—the monotonous beauty of wealth. Crystal wine goblets on red velvet. Onyx chess sets. Japanese cameras. Golf clubs. Books. Undaunted, the traditional Christmas scene-stealers—carolers, coaches and horses, shepherds, angels, wise men, kings—do battle in the same windows, with the tainted goods that surround them. *Good for you. Fight the good fight*. He is not daunted, either. Christmas means gifts, and he puts his money down with the rest; says, "Have a nice Christmas," when he is handed his packages. "You, too," they say.

Before class one morning, Lazenby corners him at his locker. "What happened? Salan says you quit."

He nods curtly.

"Why?"

The halls are teeming with people. Mild frenzy. Two minutes before the final bell.

"I felt like it," he says. "It was a bore."

"Some reason."

He doesn't answer; busies himself with rummaging in his locker for his chemistry book. Lazenby leans an elbow against the wall. "Con, is something the matter?"

"What d'you mean?"

"I don't know." He shrugs his shoulders, looking worried. Big, blond, sincere-type. When he was in the hospital, Lazenby wrote him his only letter, told him the scores of the Cubs and White Sox games; at the bottom of the page, "I miss you, man." He had read it a million times before he finally threw it away.

"Listen, don't worry," Conrad says. "Everything's fine."

"I don't know, man. You've been acting funny lately."

It trips the lever on the thing he meant *not* to say.

"Laze, take my advice. You hang around with flakes, you get flaky."

"Shit, I knew that was it. Well, why you pissed at me?"

"I'm not pissed!"

"Ah, Connie. I *know* you." He tries a grin. "Look,

89

I'm sorry. I'd be pissed, too, but you shouldn't have quit—"

"That's not why! Man, I said it was a fucking bore." He slams his locker closed, giving the lock a savage twist as he walks away. Lazenby falls into step beside him.

"Wait a minute, listen, will ya? I talked to Salan and he says—"

"Well, quit talking to people!" he snaps. "Leave me alone!"

The bell rings shrilly over their heads. They stare at each other.

"Ah, shit," Lazenby says. "The hell with you."

A hollow feeling in the pit of his stomach, as if he has been punched—*Never mind screw him screw them all they were Buck's friends anyway*—he walks on to class, feeling nothing.

"So, what does your dad say about it?" Berger asks.

He sighs. "I haven't told him yet."

"How come?"

"I don't know. The timing isn't right. He sweats everything so much. He'll just worry about it."

"So you haven't told anybody? Your mother?"

"My mother? No. Listen, my mother and I do not connect, I told you that before."

"So, does that bother you?"

"No. Why should it?"

Berger shrugs. "I don't know. Some people it might bother, that's all."

"My mother is a very private person," he says. "We don't ride the same bus. Who does? What do you have in common with your mother? Surface junk—brush your teeth, clean your room, get good grades. My mother—" He stops. Careful, careful. "People have a right to be the way they are," he says.

"Noble thought," Berger says. "So how's it going? You feeling better since you're not swimming?"

"I guess." He picks, with his thumbnail, at the wooden arm of the chair.

"Sleeping better?"

"I jack off a lot. It helps."

Berger grins. "So what else is new?"

He slides down to the end of his spine, his legs stretched in front of him, staring at the floor. Over his shoulder, the clock ticks loudly.

"Come on, kiddo," Berger prods gently. "Something's on your mind today."

"Nothing's new, nothing's on my mind. I don't think anything. I don't feel anything." Abruptly he sits up. "I oughta go home."

Berger nods. "Maybe so. What is it that you don't feel, huh? Anger? Sadness? Any of the twenty-eight flavors?"

A tiny seed opens slowly inside his mind. In the hospital the seed would grow and begin to produce thick, shiny leaves with fibrous veins running through them. More leaves to come. Like tiny, curled up fists they will hit at him. He tightens his grip on the arms of the chair. The wood is sticky and wet under his hands. He wets his lips nervously. "What time is it?"

"Lots of time," Berger says. The eyes are fixed on him, a tender and compelling blue. "Hey. Remember the contract we got? You wanted to have more control. You see any connection here, between control and this—what'll we call it—lack of feeling?"

He closes his eyes. A jungle in there, inside his head. He opens them quickly. "I didn't say I never feel things. I feel things."

"When?"

"Sometimes."

"You gonna give me the famine, wars, violence-in-the-streets business again?"

He doesn't answer.

"Come on, kiddo, I'm doing all the work here. I thought you told me you didn't like to play games."

"I don't. I'm not. I don't know what you want."

91

"Then, I'll tell you. I want you to leave 'I don't know' out there on the table with the magazines, okay?"

"And what if I don't have an answer? You want me to make one up."

"Yeah, that'd be nice. Make me one up right now, about how you've turned yourself inside out and the overwhelming evidence is that there are no feelings in there no-how."

"I said I have feelings."

Berger sighs. "Now you have 'em, now you don't. Get it together, Jarrett."

"Why are you hassling me? Why are you trying to get me mad?"

"Are you mad?"

"No!"

Berger sits back in the chair. "Now that," he says, "is a lie. You are mad as hell. You don't like to be pushed. So why don't you do something?"

"What?"

"Geez, I don't know! Tell me to fuck off, go to hell, something!"

"Fuck off," he says. "Go to hell."

Berger laughs. "Glory, what feeling. When's the last time you got really mad?"

He says, carefully, "When it comes, there's always too much of it. I don't know how to handle it."

"Sure, I know," Berger says. "It's a closet full of junk. You open the door and everything falls out."

"No," he says. "There's a guy in the closet. I don't even know him, that's the problem."

"Only way you're ever gonna get to know him," Berger says, "is to let him out now and then. Along with the boots, and tennis rackets, stale bread, whatever you got stored up there. You go through it, you sort it out, you throw some of it away. Then you stack up the rest, nice and neat. Next time it won't be such a big deal."

"I don't have the energy," he says.

"Kiddo, you got any idea how much energy it takes to hold the door closed like you do? That's power. Your own personal power and nobody else's."

"Sometimes," he says, "when you let yourself feel, all you feel is lousy."

Berger nods. "Maybe you gotta feel lousy sometimes, in order to feel better. A little advice, kiddo, about feeling. Don't think too much about it. And don't expect it always to tickle."

On another shopping trip after school, with his head somewhere else, he sidesteps a puddle, nearly walking into someone coming the other way.

"Oh," she says. "Hi. How're you?"

Embarrassed, he mumbles an apology; then looks at her. It is Jeannine.

"What're you doing up here?" she asks. "I thought the swim team practiced until six."

"They do," he says.

"I thought you were swimming."

"I used to," he says. "I don't any more."

"Oh. Don't you swim as well as you sing?"

"What?"

She laughs. "Just kidding. I'm getting to know your voice now. You're the tenor who stays on pitch."

He takes it as a reprimand. She should not be able to hear him above the others. "I'll sing softer tomorrow."

"No. You know, you ought to be doing the solo in that Russian thing. You have much better tone than Ron."

The voice of authority. He knows about her; that she has applied for a music scholarship to the University of Michigan, that she takes private voice lessons, that Faughnan is in love with her ability. He has stood in the back of the auditorium after class, listening to her practice, while Miriam Gleason accompanies her on the piano and Faughnan stands next to her, stopping her in the middle of a phrase, instructing her. She nods her head, gravely; goes back and repeats, all the time looking as if she *is* the music itself, and she is small and grave and beautiful; her hair shimmers under the stage lights; her eyelashes are light-gold crescents.

"You want to have a Coke?" he blurts out suddenly.

She hesitates. "Sure. Fine."

They walk along the street together and she fills the spaces easily with words while he, amazed and dumbstruck at what he has just done, struggles with the overwhelming problems confronting him: where will he take her? what will they talk about?

"—kind of music that I like. He's the most *classical-minded* teacher, don't you think?"

Not Pasquesi's. It is always crowded after school; filled with people that he knows, and yet, doesn't know any more. The windows are opaque with the steam of bodies. Just walking by the place reinforces his sense of separation.

"There's a place up around the corner," he says.

"Fine. It's nearer to my house. I have to be home by four-thirty. My brother doesn't have a key."

She looks up at him. Clear, blue eyes. Like someone else's. With a start, he recognizes them. Berger's eyes. Weird.

Inside the small, nearly empty coffee shop (it is *not* an in-place, obviously), she loosens her coat; slips out of it. She is wearing a gold-and-yellow-striped sweater, a gold chain around her neck. He cannot look directly at her, focuses his eyes slightly to the left of her face.

"Well," she says, "I'm doing all the talking. What kinds of music do *you* like?"

He shrugs. "I don't know. Modern jazz. Folk rock. Whatever's around, I guess."

"You don't like classical?"

"I'm not too familiar with it."

"Do you know baroque? Telemann? Ortiz?"

"No. Tell me about them. Telemann and who?"

She looks down at her hands, flushing. "What a dull conversation. I'm sure there must be things you'd like to talk about."

He laughs, reaching into his back pocket. "Sure. I carry a list around with me. Here. Pick a subject."

She looks up, then, and smiles at him. "Why is this always so hard? The first time you talk to somebody—"

He calculates quickly. The first time. A second time. Other times—and the tension within him dissolves. They talk: about movies, about books, about his classes, her classes, what she likes, what they both don't like, about being new to a school and having to start over, making friends. . . .

She glances at her watch. "Oh, I've got to go. He has fits if I'm late."

He walks her to the railroad tracks, where they stand and talk some more. It is snowing again, and she buttons her coat up to the neck, tucking her hair inside the collar.

"I told my mother to give him his own key. She works until six, and she doesn't like to leave the house open all day. He's eleven, but he's sort of a scatterbrain. She's afraid he'll just lose it. Do you have brothers and sisters?"

"No," he says. "No, I don't."

She makes a face. "You're lucky. Anyway, thanks for the Coke. And thanks for walking me."

The huge, airy flakes sizzle away to nothing on his suède jacket.

He watches her as she runs across the street. On the other side, she waves to him. He waves back and heads down Western, against the snow, keeping his head bent, staying close to the buildings. He would like to run, only the street is crowded with people. They would stare at him, wondering what the hell he was doing, was he trying to stir up trouble? So many people in the world, so few behavior tracks, you can't even run any more without attracting attention to yourself, and he turns his head as he passes the window of a travel agency. He stops: goes back to get a closer look.

In the window a model airplane sleek and silver-green shearing off between two papier-mâché mountain peaks. Held up by a thin shaft of wire from below somewhere. Fastened to its body. Behind it a travel poster: *Ski the Laurentians!*

He narrows his eyes sees the path again clean and clear and dizzyingly steep Buck sweeping around the curve and disappearing the wind screams in his ears he blindly follows staying up staying up nearly to the end when the smallest of moguls flips him he has let it cross his mind that the slope is too hard for him dangerous as hell skiing beyond yourself it is how you break a leg or get killed. And Buck bending anxiously over him: "Hey, buddy, you okay? Talk to me!" When he can breathe when he knows that nothing is lost or broken he wheezes feebly, "I missed the goddamned turn!" and Buck sits down beside him laughing. "You were Killy himself coming around, what happened?"

"I missed the goddamned turn, that's what happened!"

He hangs on now, pressing his hand lightly against the wall, below the window, waiting for the familiar arrow of pain. Only there is none. An oddly pleasant swell of memory, a wave of warmth flooding over him, sliding back, slowly. It is a first.

He looks around: the street behind him, the shoppers, the dull-gray parking meters near the edge of the sidewalk. Everything in place; as it was before. Obscured at once by his awareness of it, the moment blurs. He cannot reach beyond it. He does not need to. At peace with himself, he walks home through the falling snow.

13

The Christmas-tree lot has a sign over it: FIRS BY LENNIE. From two loudspeakers mounted on the pay booth, canned music blares forth "Oh, Come, All Ye Faithful," and Cal clenches his gloveless hands together against the cold, stamping his feet.

"How's this one?"

The man lifts a tree from its hole, shaking the snow from its branches.

"No. Not tall enough," Conrad says.

The man looks at Cal. "Tall as you are, sonny," he says, dropping the tree back into its hole. "You want taller? I got taller, over here. Come on."

He is built like a lumberjack (Lennie himself?), with a red-and-black-checked lumberjack shirt tucked into mud-colored overalls, his forehead and ears banded by a purple knit ski-shield. They follow him, Cal stepping carefully on the path of bark and pine needles, trying to keep the mud off of his shoes. He eyes the lot man's thick rubber boots with longing.

"How about this?"

"No," Conrad says. "Too scrawny."

The man gives Cal a faintly patronizing smile, showing him what he thinks of fathers who let their sons run things. He points out a huge blue spruce, dense and full. "Okay, how's that one?"

"That's terrific," Conrad says. "Hey, that's it."

Cal issues a feeble protest: "Con, it's twelve feet tall!"

"You guys live in a church, or what?"

Conrad is busy surveying it from all sides, a smile on his face.

Cal reaches for his wallet. "Okay, how much?"

"Twenty bucks."

He whistles. "Thought this was a buyer's market."

"Not this year." The lot man is cheerful, forgiving. "Pay at the booth. Me and sonny here'll tie it on your car. You guys be sure and let me know when the services are, ya hear?"

Weightless with joy he watches while his son assumes the burden of this small decision. At dinner tonight, Conrad had told him of his plans for the kind of Christmas they should have this year. "Just greens and pine cones, nothing fancy. Lights on the tree, but no ornaments. Popcorn, cranberries, maybe a few candy canes, how does that sound to you?"

"Sounds great," Cal had said. A few deft strokes and the picture had been painted, as easily, as confidently as Con had scanned the menu and ordered: "Hamburger. Onion rings. Chocolate malt. Banana cream pie."

Just last summer, Cal had sat with him at a lunch counter near the hospital. He had stared at the single-sheet bill of fare, enclosed in plastic. After ten minutes, he had passed it over to Cal with a weary sigh. "You order, okay? I can't decide."

They drive through Evanston, decked out in all its Christmas finery: fake garlands of pine, wrapped around lampposts and colored lights strung across the intersections. It does not have the air of fantasy, of fairyland, that covers Lake Forest. It is too big a city for that; its streets are too dirty, its buildings too coarsely utilitarian. Yet, there is a confidence and completeness about this town that Cal loves.

Too many places he has been seem tainted with that anxious atmosphere of unreality; a one-sidedness of conception. Too perfect to be believed. Aspen. Indianwood. Florida. Exotic and comfortless, like movie sets.

"I tried to let you pick it out," Conrad says. "We would have ended up with the worst one on the lot. You always want to buy some tree you feel sorry for."

"Never mind, *sonny*," Cal says. "When we're stringing popcorn and cranberries till our fingers fall off, you remember who did the picking."

Heat curls about their ankles, as thick as water.

It goes up easily, fitting easily under the cathedral ceiling in the family room, dominating the space before the window. Crisp, bluegreen lace splashes across the snow-white of the draperies.

"I think it's silly," Beth had said that morning. "We've got a perfectly good artificial one in the basement. The needles will absolutely *imbed* themselves in that white shag, Cal."

"It's probably flat and limp as hell. We haven't used it for five years—do you realize it's been that long since we've had a tree? We're always on our way to somewhere a week before Christmas."

She had shrugged, turning away. "Do what you want."

She had had a meeting tonight anyway, so when Conrad met him at the office after his session Cal had suggested dinner out instead of the TV dinners waiting for them at home, and the tree-shopping expedition. Now he lies on his back as he gives the screws in the stand a final tightening. Conrad holds on to the trunk.

"Some of the lights have burned out. I'll pick up

some extra bulbs on my way home tomorrow," Conrad says.

The front door opens and a gust of cold air greets them. Moments later, she joins them.

"How do you like it?" Cal asks. He looks up through the branches at her: a splash of orange skirt and paler orange blouse. Those graceful, pretty legs.

"I like it," she says. "It's lovely."

He feels a sudden rush of love for her; gets to his feet, floating and weightless again. "How was your meeting?"

"It was interesting," she says. She goes to the bar at the opposite end of the room. "I think I want a drink. How about you?"

"Sure. Here, I'll make them."

"We've got popcorn and cranberries to string," Conrad says to her. "You want to help?"

She looks at him for a long moment. "Of course."

"So what happened that was so interesting?" Cal hands her the glass. Scotch she likes in the evening, short, and no ice.

She swirls the oily liquid, looking down into it. "Not what happened," she says. "What I heard."

"From whom?"

"From Carole Lazenby."

Something is wrong. The lunch that day? He should have told her, probably, but he hadn't thought anything about it. Just a lunch. Nothing to tell.

"It's not my news," she says, "it's Conrad's. Maybe he should tell it."

"Tell what?" Cal asks.

Conrad is looking at her warily.

"It was rather embarrassing," she says, not looking at either of them. "Carole thought I knew. After all, why wouldn't I know? It happened over a month ago."

"*What* happened?" he asks.

"Dad," Conrad says, "I quit the swim team."

"Quit? Why?" And then it hits him: the nights he sat waiting for six-thirty, the newspaper in front of him, unconcerned. He knew exactly where his kid was. At practice. Riding home with Joe in the car. *A month ago*. And another picture, of Mr. Knight and Mr. Hellwarth at the meeting. They suggest that he call the counselor's office on Fridays, for a "progress report." "Just so we stay on top of things, Mr. Jarrett." He had rejected that plan immediately. No, it was too much like spying. *A month ago*.

"Where have you been every night?" he asks.

"Nowhere," Conrad says. "Around. The library, mostly."

"I don't get it," he says flatly. "Why didn't you tell us?"

"I was going to. I've been meaning to—"

"I'm sure you would have told us before the first meet," Beth says. "When is it, next Thursday?"

"I'm sure I would have told you," Conrad says, "if I thought you gave a damn!"

And the wellspring of anger erupts, engulfing them all.

"What the hell does that mean?" Cal demands.

"Never mind," she says. "It's meant for me. Isn't it? I wish I knew, Conrad, why it is still so important for you to try to hurt me!"

"Hurt you? Me hurt you! Listen, you're the one who's trying to hurt me!"

"And how did I do that? By making you look like a fool in front of a roomful of people? Did you have to sit there, getting those looks? Poor Mrs. Jarrett, oh the poor woman, she has no idea what her son is up to, he lies and lies and she believes every word of it—"

"I didn't lie—"

"You did! You lied every night that you came into this house at six-thirty. What do you mean, you didn't lie?" She presses her hands tight to her head. "I can't stand this, I really can't! If it's starting all over again, the lying and the disappearing for hours, the covering up—I won't stand it!"

"Don't then!" he snarls. "Go to Europe, why don't you? Go to hell!"

"Con—"

But he backs away from Cal's hand, "Listen, don't give me that, the only reason you care, the only reason you give a *fuck* about it is because someone else knew about it first! You never wanted to know anything I was doing, or anything I *wasn't* doing; you just wanted me to leave you alone! Well, I left you alone, didn't I? I could have told you lots of things! Like, up at the hospital there were rats! Big ones, up on three, with the hopeless nuts! But that's okay; see, I was down on two. with the heads and the unsuccessfuls—"

"Con, shut up, stop it—"

"Damn it!" he says. "Tell *her* to stop it! You never tell her a *goddamn thing!* Listen, I know why she never came out there, not once! *I know!* Hell, she was going to goddamn *Spain* and goddamn *Portugal,* why should she care if I was hung up by the *goddamn balls* out there—"

"Christ! That's enough!"

He takes a swift, sobbing breath, fixing them both with a look of utter fury. And then he is gone, his feet pounding up the stairs. Moments later, the shattering slam of his bedroom door.

Beth has her back to Cal, her hands clutching at her head. "I won't, I won't!"

He goes to her; puts his arms around her. Her body is stiff. She is trembling, but she does not relax against him.

"What happened?" he asks. "What the hell happened?"

"I don't know!"

"Somebody'd better go up there."

"Go!" she says. "Go ahead, that's the pattern, isn't it? Let him walk all over us, then go up there and apologize to him!"

"I'm not going up to apologize."

"Yes, you are! You always do! You've been apologizing to him ever since he came home!"

"Ah, Beth, crissake, lay off, will you? I feel like I've been at a goddamn tennis match tonight! Back and forth, back and forth—"

"Don't talk to me like that!" She twists violently away from him. "Don't talk to me like he talks to you!"

He grabs her, holds her, his cheek colliding with her skull, hard. "I'm sorry," he murmurs. "I'm sorry let's not fight. . . ." He rocks her in his arms, gently, and her hands are up between them clenched into fists on his chest. She lets him hold her, but only for a moment.

"Let's go upstairs," he says.

"No. You go. He wants you. He wants somebody who's going to accept everything he does. Without question, without criticism . . ."

"And you think that's what I do?"

"I know it is!"

"I think," he says cautiously, "that there might have been a better way to handle this."

"Oh, I'm sure of it." Her voice is bitter. "For openers, he could have come to us and told us the truth."

"No, I meant tonight."

"I know what you meant! You see? Everything he does is all right! Perfectly understandable! And everything I do is—is mixed up, and wrong, and could have been handled a better way!"

"That's not true! That's not what I'm trying to say!"

His nerves are raw. His eyes feel as if they have sunk back into his head, pulling the flesh down. "Beth. Please. Let's just go upstairs!"

"No. I will not be pushed!" she says. She moves away from him to stand before the window, looking out. Calmly she says, "I will not be *manipulated.*"

He stands, looking over her head at the black window, then at the tree with its strings of lights dangling loose from the branches. Disjointed. Unfinished. "All right," he says. "I'm going."

She does not turn around, nor does she make a sign that she has heard him.

Conrad lies face down on the bed, his body outlined in the light from the hall. One hand covers the back of his neck; the other is limp at his side. Cal moves to the nightstand and snaps on the light.

"I want to talk to you."

"I need to sleep," he groans. His voice is muffled in the pillow. "Let me sleep."

"In a minute."

He pulls the chair over from the desk and sits beside the bed. Outside the window, heavy flakes of snow splatter and stick fast to the glass, sliding down to make miniature hills and valleys at the lower edge of the sill. "First. I give a damn," he says, "about everything you do."

Conrad's head jerks on the pillow. He rolls onto his back, shielding his eyes with his arm. "I didn't mean that," he says. "I didn't mean any of it, I'm sorry. Please. Don't be mad."

"I'm not mad," Cal says. "I'm just trying to figure out what happened down there."

"I don't know what happened! I don't know! I'm sorry about everything! I—look, can't we talk about it tomorrow, Dad, please! I feel lousy tonight, everything is shit—Listen, I didn't mean to say any of that, you tell her, will you? Tell her I'm sorry."

"Why don't you tell her?"

"No! God, I can't, I can't talk to her!"

Abruptly he sits up, clasping his arms about his knees. His eyes are dry. There is a red crease along his cheek. He wipes his mouth nervously, staring at the window. "Because it won't make any difference."

"What do you mean?"

"It won't change anything. It won't change the way she feels about me."

"The way she—Con, she was upset tonight. She was angry—"

"No, I don't mean tonight."

"What, then?"

But he shakes his head. "No. I can't. Everything's jello and pudding with you, Dad. I can't—you don't see things—"

"What things?"

He continues to stare out the window at the snow, rocking slightly, back and forth, his arms clenched around his knees.

"What things?" Cal asks gently. "I want you to tell me."

His eyes flick over to Cal's face; instantly flick away. "All right, then. She hates me. There's nothing I can do about it." His voice is curt and flat—without hope.

Something terribly wrong. He stares out the window, now, too, thinking of last year and Mr. Knight calling him at the office with the grade reports: "Something terribly wrong, here, Mr. Jarrett, a straight-A student dropping to D's and E's in three months' time. Most of the papers are not completed. Tests with half of the answer spaces blank, tests not handed in at all. . . ." Cal had asked him, "Why didn't you tell me you were in trouble?" Conrad said, "I'm not in trouble. I'm passing, aren't I? D is passing." And he had tried to be gentle, knowing that something was terribly wrong. "It's not a matter of passing, Con. Going from A to D like this, it doesn't make sense." And they had looked at each other over the words. *What makes sense?*

"Conrad," he says, "that's ridiculous. Your mother does not hate you—"

"*Okay.* All right, you're right, I just—Please, let me go to bed, now."

He jumps up and goes to the closet, stripping off his shirt.

"What do you think of this Dr. Berger?" Cal asks.

He tries to keep his voice calm, neutral. "Do you think he's helping you?"

"Dad, don't blame it on Berger! It isn't his fault." He stands, facing the closet door. He does not undress any further, and Cal knows he is waiting for him to leave. The snow, piled high against the windows, seals them inside its softness, its silence.

14

Afterward. The hammer blows of guilt and remorse. He has no weapons with which to fight them off. No words of comfort, none of Berger's advice applies. He has slandered her, to her face and behind her back. He has pushed everyone away who tries to help. If he could apologize. If he only could but they are no longer at home to him and it is not their fault. All his fault. All connections with him result in failure. Loss. Evil.

At school it is the same. Everywhere he looks, there is competence and good health. Only he, Conrad Jarrett, outcast, quitter, *fuck-up,* stands outside the circle of safety, separated from everyone by this aching void of loneliness; but no matter, he deserves it. He does not speak to anyone. He does not dare to look his classmates in the eye. He does not want to contaminate, does not wish to find further evidence of his lack of worth.

Music is his only escape. It makes the weight of his crimes bearable. The melody harmony rhythm a visible structure as it winds through his mind. He can concentrate completely in here as they practice obscure French carols for the Christmas concert, and Faughnan, pushing all the time, ignoring all protests—"Tenors! Too heavy on the 'Everlasting!' And save the 's' for 'sting,' will you? Don't be cute. Sopranos! Screeching again, what am I gonna do with you girls? Everybody! Watch, for pete's sake, watch!"

So he watches. He never takes his eyes off Faughnan the whole hour as the music fills out the corners of his mind. It is where all danger resides. Not the same as listening to his records at home. That is dangerous, also. Flipping through album covers gives an eerie feeling of time past, like last year's calendar, carrying too much of the weight of Before. There is no possibility of a return to that period when he believed in the summer lyrics of John Denver, the easy philosophies. Seals and Crofts, Traffic, The Guess Who. And television. Merely bright patterns of color that jump around on the screen and do not soothe or settle his brain. He wonders what it would look like inside his brain. All brown and dusty from disuse.

"Well," Berger says, biting a corner of his thumbnail. "Quite a recitation. So, how come you're such a rotten kid?"

He sits in the chair, staring at his hands. He has dreaded this session, knowing that they would end up talking about it, knowing that he no longer has control in here. Press a button; out it comes. "I don't know," he says dully.

"Ah, come on. Sure you do."

He gives him a fierce look. "I don't know! Look, if you think you do, why don't *you* tell *me,* and we'll quit going around in circles!"

"That's what happens when you bury this junk, kiddo. It keeps resurfacing. Won't leave you alone."

"Crap," he says. "I went off the deep end, that's all. Jesus, now I sound like my grandfather. The deep end! I just shouldn't have done it, it was stupid, it didn't make any sense."

"Nope." Berger shakes his head. "There's sense here. Proportion, that's the problem. The stuff came out too strong, and now you won't let yourself buy any of it. The feelings are real enough. Trust that guy in the closet, will you?"

As an answer, he slides, resting the end of his spine on the seat of the chair, his legs outstretched. He stares at his boots, at the lower edge of Berger's desk, at the grainy patches of color in the rug.

"Listen, Tuesday you felt great, didn't you? You went out for dinner, you bought a Christmas tree, everything's okeydoke, am I right?"

"You're the doctor."

Berger grins. "Hey. The doctor thinks the patient has a bad habit. He takes refuge. He throws out one-liners, like 'You're the doctor.' So, when does he start talking in French, huh? I never took French. I wouldn't understand a word of that. That what you want? See, kiddo, this problem is very specific. It is not necessary to pull the whole world in on top of you, it is only necessary to finish with Tuesday night. Everything's fine until you up and have this fight with your mother. Then, everything's lousy. A equals B." He leans back in his chair, also, his hands behind his head. "So, have you tried to talk it out with her?"

"Jesus, no."

"Why not?"

"I can't."

"You sure?"

"Yeah, I'm sure!"

"Have you tried?"

He doesn't answer.

"Tough to be sure if you haven't tried."

"Listen, you don't know her. She—it's impossible. Not that I blame her—I don't blame her. I mean, she's got reasons. After all the shit I've pulled—"

"What shit have you pulled?"

He looked down at his hands.

"Come on," Berger coaxes. "You oughta be able to come up with at least one example, huh?"

"Okay," he says. "All right. Once I tried to kill myself, how's that?"

"That," Berger says, "is an old turkey. I am talking about what have you done lately."

"Lately! Listen, if you—listen! I am never going to be forgiven for that, *never!* You can't get it out, you know! All that blood on her rug and her goddamn towels—everything had to be pitched! Even the goddamn *tile* in the bathroom had to be regrouted. Christ, she fired a *goddamn maid* because she couldn't dust the living room right, and if you think she's ever going to forgive me—"

He stops, staring at Berger, whose eyebrows are raised in mild surprise, his body sitting motionless in the chair. The wave of anger recedes slowly, leaving a tightness, a burning sensation in his chest. With an effort, he pulls air into his lungs, clenching his fists on his thighs, breathing slowly. He gets up from the chair, moves to the window, and stares down at the curls of slush in the street; at the cars creeping by behind a curtain of gray winter rain.

Behind him he hears Berger get up; pour himself another cup of coffee. He turns his head to watch him. "I think I just figured something out," he says.

"What's that?" Berger asks.

"Who it is who can't forgive who."

Reclining on an elbow on the floor, Berger doodles on a scratch pad with his silver pen. Conrad sits beside him, his back against the wall, knees up, holding a cup of coffee in his hands. "Jesus, am I tired," he says.

"Yeah, well, that's a helluva big secret you've been keeping on yourself," Berger says.

"So what do I do now?"

"Well, you've done it, haven't you? Revelation. She's not perfect. Recognize her limitations."

"You mean, like she can't love me."

"Like she can't love you enough. Like she loves you as much as she's *able*. Perspective, kiddo, remember? Maybe she's afraid, maybe it's hard for her to give love."

"No," he says. "It isn't. She loves my father, I know that." He closes his eyes. "She loved my brother, too. It's just me."

"Ah, now we're back to the old rotten-kid routine. She doesn't love you because you're unlovable. So where does that leave your dad? Doesn't he know what a rotten kid you are?"

"That's different. He feels responsible. Besides, he loves everybody."

"Oh, I get it, the guy's got no taste. He loves you, but he's wrong. See, kiddo, you keep asking the same old questions, but you only listen for the one answer. Give yourself a break, why don't you? Let yourself off the hook."

"What d'you mean?"

"I mean, there's somebody else you gotta forgive."

"You mean me? What for? For the other night, you mean? For trying to off myself?"

The eyes have pinned him to the wall. A hard blue light.

He shifts uncomfortably. "I haven't done anything else," he says. "I haven't."

The beams switch to low, and Berger smiles benignly. "Okay. You haven't."

He gets to his feet and finishes the last of his coffee. "This stuff's rotten, you know that?"

"Damn right. Otherwise, I'd be up to my ass in patients. Listen, be aware, kiddo. People don't change on command from other people. You oughta know that, having already given her the ultimate command a year ago."

A hair trigger of release, waiting to be sprung. No more, no more, he is too tired. "That isn't why I did it," he says.

"No? Why, then?"

Nearly time. Nearly five o'clock, and he is exhausted. Even his bones ache. "I don't know," he says.

"The body doesn't lie," Berger says. "You remember that. So all you gotta do is keep in touch."

15

"Now, this is what I call a real Christmas," says Howard. "Snowing to beat the band, a turkey in the oven, a real live tree—a lot better than having dinner in some hotel in Florida, right?"

Beth smiles at him.

"Anyone care for a drink?" Cal asks.

"I would," says Ellen. "A small glass of wine, if you have it, Cal." She is sitting next to Beth on the couch. They look more like sisters than mother and daughter. Ellen's hair is thick and silvery, cut short, and waved expertly to flatter the thin, aging face. Her body is slim and firm. It is easy to see where Beth gets her looks. "Where's Connie?"

"Upstairs. He's coming. Howard, scotch?"

"Fine."

"Beth?"

"No, thanks. Not right now."

"Beth's got a dinner to put on," Howard booms. "We can't have the hostess dipping into the sauce too early, can we?"

No comparing this with Florida. Last Christmas there had been the arranging of hotel reservations and flight schedules and tickets for the Orange Bowl. Last Christmas they had played golf and gone deep-

sea fishing and tanned themselves beside the aqua-
marine blue of the swimming pool at the Sonesta
Beach, looking at other people from the distance of
delirium. They were going through the motions of a
family on vacation. And each day opened to a scene
more beautiful than the last: palm fronds, like
upside-down green bowls under an upside-down blue
bowl of sky. Lagoons full of lazy jumping fish. White
sand that clung to their bodies like confectioner's
sugar. Australian pine trees and sea grape. Lord, how
he had hated it. Like medicine you took, knowing
that it had no power to heal. A relief to come back to
the cold and gray reality of a Chicago winter.

"Hi. Merry Christmas."

"Same to you, dear!" Ellen holds out her arms and
Conrad goes to her; he bends his head obediently for
a kiss. He is dressed up today—tan slacks and a tan,
bulky-knit pullover, his boots polished—a concession
to his mother? He looks healthy. His cheeks are
flushed. The ugly rash is nearly gone.

"You did a great job on this tree," Howard says. "I
hear it was all your idea. How long did it take you?"

Conrad grins. "About a month of Sundays." Something is different about him lately. The smile is a good
kid-grin, with his eyes into it. He looks handsome,
that's it, with those long, thick eyelashes, like a girl's.
The build is all boy, though—all angles, elbows, and
knees.

Howard rubs his palms together briskly. "Let's get
this show on the road, folks!"

They exchange glances, he and Conrad; then they
look away. Cal is reminded of the game they used to
play: Grandfather Trivia. "What does he say after a
horseshoe ringer?" "That's one for the good guys!"
"What time does he get up in the morning?" "At
the crack o'dawn!" "When will he eat liver?" "When
hell freezes over!" Jordan had invented it, with his
eye for detail, his unmerciful memory. And another
game. Nicknames. He had nicknames for everyone;

new ones each week. His grandfather, the Kid, his grandmother, the Girl Friend. "Here comes the Kid in the Mercedes, he's got the Girl Friend with him!"

A blessing. That you do not know at the moment of impact how far-reaching the shock waves will be. He is at once achingly aware of the force of Jordan's absence. Only a year and a half. Still, it is a long time to discover that you are still in shock, still in the infant stages of recovery.

Surrounded by gifts, Conrad, anxious giver, seeks reassurance.

"You really like it, Grandmother?"

She holds up the candle, apple-shaped and scented with apple, for all to admire. "Like it? I love it, it smells delicious."

"And the gloves fit okay?"

"Perfect," says Howard.

"Like a glove," Cal says. His mood is buoyant, expectant. Patiently he listens, hanging on to his own excitement, as Conrad explains about the golf book he has bought for him; it is guaranteed to cut six strokes from his game. "Then, I'd better not catch you reading it before me!" he warns him happily.

For his mother, Conrad has picked out a bracelet of silver; fragile, delicate links that loop over and under each other, like figure-eights on a glassy pond.

"I hope you like it," he says.

"It's beautiful," she says. "It's lovely. Thank you."

They are polite and careful with each other these days. The mood of the house is subdued and calm. A truce of some kind has been effected. Cal, the fumbling, uncertain negotiator, has stayed out of it. A cooling-off period must be observed. It is not his way at all; he is all for plunging in, taking people by the shoulders, shaking them into submission, into daylight. But he cannot bully either of them, he has discovered. They are alike in this way. All healing is done from the outside in.

"Hey, isn't there another present down there?" Howard asks.

Conrad leans over, searching among shirts and sweaters, a navy ski-vest, a pen-and-pencil set; he comes up with a small package, wrapped in silver paper.

"No card. Who's it from?"

Cal says, "It's from your mother and me."

He opens it. Glittering on the nest of white cotton, is a key ring, with two keys on it.

Howard nudges Cal in the ribs. He has been like a kid with this, calling Cal on the telephone, checking on the details—How would they present it? Where will they keep it over the long Christmas weekend? He drove to the dealership with Cal to pick it up; has kept it in his garage for nearly a week. Now he cannot hide the smile on his face. "Well? Why don't you go look in the driveway?"

They all go to the door. The green LeMans with its white vinyl top is parked at a jaunty angle in the drive. Howard has wired a huge red bow to the door handle.

"Sneaky, huh?" he crows. "Dad, I think we fooled him good this time. He looks like we could knock him over with a feather about now!"

True. He stands next to Cal on the porch, as they all admire the car, glittering under a light coat of fresh snow. His expression is totally blank and unreadable, but Cal reads anyway: I don't think he likes it.

"How about the color?" Howard asks. "You like it?"

"They had it in a pale gold," Cal says. "You might have liked that better."

"No. This is great." He looks at Cal, then, a smile pasted on his face. He seemed dazed. "I like it a lot. Thanks. It's—I just didn't expect it, that's all."

"Got your license on you?" Howard asks. "Take it for a spin."

"No," he says. Then, "Yeah, okay. I think I will.

Thanks. Thank you both, it's beautiful, really. It's terrific."

And he gets in; it starts up smoothly. It glides smoothly out of the driveway, and Cal, resisting the urge to call, "Take it easy!" or any other of those good-luck charms, thinks, He will be careful. He will take it easy, even though he has not driven in nearly a year, because he is a good driver. He will take care because of that, and not because of anything that I yell at him.

"Well," says Howard. "What a surprise, huh? I don't think he quite knew what to make of it."

Beth and Ellen have already gone inside. The wind has lifted suddenly. It pierces Cal's shirt; makes him feel shrunken, and old.

"I think he liked it, though," Howard says. "A kid's first car. Always a big deal, right?"

"Right," Cal says.

"Yeah, I remember when you gave him that two-wheeler. God, he loved that thing, didn't he? Rode it around the block all day. When was that?" He holds the door for Cal. "Kids. They sure do grow up in a hurry, don't they?"

And so it had gone wrong. The neat, even pieces of the day have somehow slipped awry. Disengaged. He sits alone on the couch, his head back, his feet on the coffee table. He has driven Howard and Ellen home, and Conrad is upstairs in bed, asleep. Beth has cleared the dessert plates from the table and is busy with them in the kitchen. He stares out of the window at the snow, at the fuzzy jewels of reflection from the Christmas-tree lights. Colored stars in a white sky.

Something was missing *something terribly wrong,* but it was not just the car. It was the whole day. *Well, what do you expect? We are a family, aren't we? And a family turns inward toward itself in grief, it does not go in separate directions, pulling itself apart. Like hell it doesn't. Grief is ugly. It is isolating. It is not some-*

thing to be shared with others, it is something to be afraid of, to get rid of, and fast. Get those months, days, hours, minutes out of the way, it can't be quick enough.

He gets up to make himself a drink at the bar and Beth comes in from the kitchen. She looks tired; her face set, her mind occupied elsewhere. We should have gone to London, he thinks. Aloud, he asks, "Would you like anything?"

"No. I'm tired. I think I'll just go to bed."

And, knowing that he shouldn't, knowing somehow that it will only disarrange the contours of the day more thoroughly, still he says it: "I guess he didn't like the car."

She is silent.

"Did he?"

"I think," she says, "you worry too much about him."

"Yeah." And I think that you don't worry enough, but let it go, call it a very merry rugged Christmas Day, and let it go.

"And you expect too much. From all of us."

He takes a healthy swallow of his drink. "Uh huh. That sounds like the beginning of a lecture. What's it for? I thought I behaved myself pretty well today."

"You want us all to perform for you," she says. "Make the day go right for you—"

"Well, I'm willing to do my share. I'll sing and dance and tell crooked-lawyer jokes—it won't be my fault if it falls apart."

"Or mine, either! Or Dad's or Mother's! You didn't have to close up on them that way, just because your surprise didn't work out the way you planned it."

"I didn't close up. What're you talking about?"

"Yes, you did. You moped and pouted around here, as if your whole day was spoiled over that one thing."

Okay, I moped, I pouted. All right. I give up. Uncle. He leans his elbows on the bar, his back to her.

"I'm tired of you getting your feelings hurt, Cal,

because you refuse to see things as they really are."

"And how are things?" he asks, turning around. "How are they really?"

She is so lovely, so lovely. That white skin and the pale, lavender silk of the dress, the honeyed hair, loose about her face. What are we fighting about?

"He's not your little boy," she says. "He'll be eighteen years old next month. For some reason, you want to think he needs your constant concern and protection. You worry over his every reaction. He smiles and you smile. He frowns and you baby him—"

"Okay, I'm concerned! Sometimes I worry! I'm *interested*, damn it! Are you interested?"

"Oh, I hate you," she says. "Sometimes I really hate you when you get that look on your face. Why couldn't you see this was the way it would work out if we stayed here this year?"

"At last!" he says. "Down to basics! Listen, if my day was spoiled, it was because I had that hanging over my head, so I'm sorry, okay? I'm sorry I didn't take you to London!"

"Are you sorry about giving him a car he didn't want, and doesn't need? Sorry about spending thousands of dollars, just to make something happen that I could have told you would never happen?"

They look at each other, and he wants to say, But that's not it, don't you see? At least, not all of it. And he knows as she turns away from him, going back to the kitchen, and moments later, there is the familiar and purposeful hum of the dishwasher, that the day has not gone the way she planned it, either. They are both disappointed. They are both grieving. And he thinks about going upstairs; thinks about passing Conrad's door, going down the hall to their bedroom, where they will silently undress, and separately grieve. *And what about tomorrow then? And all the tomorrows to come? Why can't we talk about it? Why can't we ever talk about it?*

16

He has concluded, on this crisp and sunny day in January, that what his life lacks is Organization. Goals. Standing at his desk, his foot on the chair, he gazes out of his bedroom window, pondering, making rapid notes.

1. *Finals*

Essential that he pass. Above all else. Only two weeks left in the semester. One last push and study like hell.

2. *Exercise*

Not enough in the last months. In fact, nothing, except for gym. His skis, lying dusty and neglected at the back of his closet, reproach him each morning. Someday after school he will drive to Wilmot, take a lesson, maybe. Grab a sandwich, ski some more. Be home by eleven. No. Not something to do alone pointless unless you have somebody to do it with. In the warming room afterward scanning the crowd for a familiar face. No.

3. *Friends*

He is definitely in need. The worst thing about the hospital. An absolute lack of privacy. People crowding you, pressuring you, examining and reassuring. Never alone. Now. Excess turns virtue into vice. He finds each day as he looks around him that he is achingly lonely. Goes over the list again: Lazenby. Truan. Van Buren. Genthe. No. He is not ready for them and anyway they are all seniors now, thinking about graduation and not interested in their old buddy, Jarrett. Besides, their old buddy, Jarrett, no longer exists. He is extinct. Someone else, now. Needing new friends. But how?

4. *Job* (?)

Doing what? Yard work? (It is January, kiddo.) Volunteer work? Not too likely, somebody needing him. Oh, yeah? Why the hell not? There are plenty of things he could do for other people. Maybe the placement office could give him some suggestions, or he could call organizations, the Red Cross, the Foundation for the Blind, put some thought into it, some imagination.

He sits down, suddenly, looking out of his window again at the tall cedars, the bare gray limbs of maples and olive trees, at Heather, the Cahills' big, black Lab, nosing under bushes, scratching herself a spot in the snow to crouch. Everything as usual; fuzzy and slightly out of focus, no, wait a minute, wait a minute, it is not out of focus. It is clear and sharp, distinct, in place. His whole life is in place and it spreads out around him, steady and full of purpose. A mystic source of energy, flooding his body, his mind, all at once. Joy. He wants to go off in every direction at the same time. Swiftly he notes:

5. *Guitar*
6. *Books*
7. *Girls*

A million years ago, when they were both sixteen, he and Lazenby discussed the topic daily; compared notes on their Experience. They concluded that they had none. For him, nothing has changed. He remembers Bernard Renaldi, a kid in his freshman comp class, relating his triumph: he had kissed a hundred girls on New Year's Eve. The sheer volume of it had staggered their minds. So, how many girls has C. Jarrett kissed? How many girls has he even spoken to in the past year and a half? Karen. Suzanne Mosley. A girl who occasionally sits at his table in A lunch. He doesn't even know her name. And Jeannine. Eighteen years old in two weeks. Two weeks, ye gods, and what does he *know?*

Never mind. Worry about it later. For now, he is too filled with this good feeling, too filled with *himself*, to care, and he jumps up, goes to the closet, looking for his guitar—it's back there somewhere—but can he still play it? Sure, it's like riding a bicycle, you don't forget. And tomorrow he will go to the library for books on what? Anything. Everything. He wants to learn everything, know everything.

Lists. Buck used to find the scraps of notes on his desk; those stern, written commands to himself to shape up. He would cop them and they would show up, folded inside his napkin at dinner, or taped to the mirror in the bathroom. "The Great Listmaker is at it again, folks!" he would tease him. Reverting to old ways—does that signify a moving backward, or forward? The natural, sane ticking inside him eliminates all need of an answer.

Standing in an aisle in the library, he can feel the eyes on him. He turns his head to look. A pretty, dark-haired woman. Staring at him. Guiltily, he looks away. Should he know her? Someone's mother, maybe? One of his friends? No, too young. Well dressed, nice figure, nice legs. He takes another look, and she is watching him, her head tilted in an attitude of appraisal.

He moves to the next aisle, as embarrassment and anger work within him, giving way then, to the familiar cloak of shame that settles about his shoulders. A freak. A one-man side show, carrying the mysterious label; off-brand. What *is* this about him?

Still. People shouldn't do that. Stick somebody like

a bug on the head of a pin and stare like that. And he shouldn't do it to himself, either. It is disgusting. Also, boring.

He takes down a book and blindly reads until the words begin grouping together, forming small patterns of reason, of sense. The feeling of joy exists, he knows it now. It must exist outside the sterile medium of his bedroom, too. It has to be wider than the dimensions of his window, and never mind all the people who pigeonhole other people with their cracks, their amused, superior smiles.

He checks out his books. The librarian slips his plastic credit card into the machine. Even the library is run like a department store now. The whole world is one, big Department Store, one big Computer, but never mind. They still might need some people. *So ask!* The librarian is small and wispy. Her washed-out blue eyes will not pierce or injure him. Yet he stumbles over the speech he has been preparing all week. ". . . interested in working here . . . wondered about . . . possibilities of employment . . .?" She smiles. Oh, yes, they do take on part-time help occasionally. However, they are fully staffed right now, but if he would like to fill out an application? Yes, he would like to. She gets him a form, and he begins to fill it out at the counter, but she waves him away. That's all right, just bring it with you sometime when you come.

So much for 4. *A Job. Ah Jarrett attaboy just like you to give it all up after one try how about the volunteer work how about the placement office all the things you were going to do? And how about lacks?* 1. *Experience.* 2. *Financial Need.* 3. *Confidence.* 4. *You Name It.* He shifts his books to fit under his arm, zipping his jacket against the wind *Face it kiddo things are not gonna be that easy so grow up.*

A blue Karmann Ghia is parked in the lot, beside his car. Bent over, half-in and half-out of it, is the woman from the library stacks. He recognizes the legs, the blue skirt that matches her car. The open car door is blocking his path. He stands, waiting for her, his face wooden. He will stare her down this time.

She glances over her shoulder. "Oh, sorry." Then, she straightens up. He has caught her off-guard, but she is still more poised than he, and this close he can see her face: small, delicate features, the casual elegance of a painter or a dancer, a beautiful pointed nose. She smooths her hair back from her face. "I embarrassed you in there, didn't I? I'm sorry." She shrugs her shoulders. "You're very good-looking. But I'm sure you already know that."

She closes the door on the passenger side, moving around him, around her car, to get in on the driver's side. The car starts up and she backs out, carefully, in no hurry at all. She waits in the drive for the traffic to clear, then pulls out into the street and disappears.

He stands, looking after her, his books still under his arm, while a feeling of total displacement sweeps over him. Mechanically he opens the door; tosses his books on the seat; gets in. *You're very good-looking.* Observing meticulously all traffic signs, all other cars on the road, all pedestrians, being careful, missing no turns. He arrives home safe and intact, and parks in the circular drive so that his father can put his car in the garage. He enters the house through the door in the garage. His mother's car is still missing. There is no one home but him. He goes straight upstairs to his bedroom, without taking off his jacket; drops his books on the bed; goes into the bathroom and turns on the light.

You're very good-looking. But I'm sure you already know that. He studies his face in the mirror. Heavy, dark brows and brown eyes. A nose. A mouth. Right, everything there. His hair, clean and decently cut at last; his skin, clear. God, his skin *is* clear, when did that happen? How long has it been since he looked at himself? He turns on a foolish, fake smile. Another plus. Straight, even teeth. An outside chance. That she is right.

He turns off the light and goes to sit on the edge of the bed. The freak, the one-man side show answer no longer fits. So, what is the catch? Some danger he is not yet aware of? What will he have to pay for all of this, for thinking well of himself? He lies back on the bed, hands over his head, staring at the ceiling. Whatever the price, it is worth it. Even for ten minutes, it is worth it.

"So, then what happened?" Berger asks. "C'mon, I'm spellbound. You followed her home and she took you into her bed, right?"

"Not exactly."

He takes a bite of the sweet roll he has lifted from the bakery box on the floor next to him. "She drove away, and I went home. I told you not to get your hopes up."

Berger sits like a plump guru, legs folded under him. There are flecks of powdered sugar dotting the front of his sweater.

"Anyway," Conrad asks anxiously, "what d'you think? She's probably some woman who goes around saying stuff like that to guys all the time, huh?"

"Do *I* know?" Berger raises palms upward, flashing a sly smile. "She's probably some woman who goes around saying stuff like that to guys who are hideously ugly. You know, to make 'em feel better about themselves."

"Okay." He bangs his head smartly against the wall. "You won't take it serious, your loss."

"I take it serious! I want to know something else. What happened when you looked in the mirror? No censoring voices?"

"Not at first. Then, later on I heard, 'Conceited, fantasizing, delusions of grandeur,' stuff like that. I ignored it."

Berger laughs. "There's hope for you yet, kiddo."

He shifts position, brushing the sugar from his sweater. "So, how you feeling now? About Christmas. About the car."

"Better, I guess," he says. "I drive it, don't I?"

"You still think it commits you to something?"

"Sort of. Like a bribe. 'There, now be happy.' "

"So, what's the problem? Aren't you happy?"

"Yeah, but I don't want him depending on me for it. What if I can't live up to it? What if it's a temporary thing?"

"Ah, he doesn't seem like the type who asks for the impossible, kiddo. He doesn't expect you to be happy every minute of the day, does he? He'd probably settle for an hour or two a week. And maybe his big motive was a selfish one. You're his kid. He gets a kick out of giving you presents. No big contract, just Merry Christmas. Period."

"Yeah, maybe." He considers. "It takes a long time to get over the feeling that everybody's watching all the time." He clears his throat. His eyes are fixed on the desk in front of him. "Listen, there's something else I've been wanting to talk about." In a careful monotone, he relates the problem he has now, of female bodies; the fact that the world has suddenly become overpopulated with them and with their individual parts—breasts and legs and round-apple asses that he would like to fit his hands around. The day Lenore Phillips slid silkily into the desk beside his and he had gotten a hard-on that lasted halfway through the English period. Violent urges that entrap him each morning and each night and for which he knows only one cure. Afterward, he suffers the most intense spasms of raw and painful guilt.

"Is that it?" Berger asks. "Listen, I told you, it's a tension-reducer. And it's normal, don't worry about it. It's also a sign that you're waking up, so relax, will you? You know what I think you oughta do? Call somebody up. How about that girl you know from the hospital? The one who lives in Skokie?"

"Karen," he says. "No. I haven't seen her since November. She's got this ten-foot pole she'd like to keep me away with. It'd just bother her if I called her up."

"Baloney. It's gonna bother her—a good-looking guy like you wanting to see her? A guy that women proposition in library parking lots?"

He laughs. "I thought psychiatrists weren't supposed to give advice."

"Or how about the one in choir? She sounds like a nice girl—"

"The problem is," he says, "the only dates I ever had were the All-skate type. A bunch of us getting together and going to the show, or getting a pizza after a basketball game. Nobody was *with* anybody else. I don't know how to act, you know, with *A Girl*, one-to-one."

"Simple," Berger says, grinning. "Listen to the expert. It's just like skiing. The first few times, you close your eyes and fake it, hope for the best."

"That's crap. What do you know about skiing? Right from go, there are a million rules."

Berger sighs. "Rules, again. They oughta burn every rule book that's ever been written!"

"And where would we be?"

"Out of the box!" He shakes his fists at the ceiling, in a parody of rage.

"That box," he says. "I feel like I've been in it forever. Everybody looking in, to see how you're doing. Even when they're on your side, they're still looking in. Like, nobody can get in there with you."

"Yeah. Not much fun, is it?"

"No. But sometimes I can get out of it, now. And then, there's you." He clears his throat nervously. "I never saw you out there, you know? You, I always saw inside the box. With me." He laughs, suddenly embarrassed. His face is hot. He brings his gaze to the opposite wall, glaring at the books, daring them to move from the shelves, daring the windows to shatter. "What I'm saying . . . I guess I think of you as a friend."

127

There is movement at the edge of his eye. Berger, nodding.

"Well. I think of you as mine, too, kiddo."

"You don't have to say that."

"Right. I don't. So, I wouldn't."

They look at each other, and, abruptly, he relaxes, grinning.

"You understand, there weren't a helluva lot of people standing in line."

"Good," Berger says. "I hate competition."

17

He finishes tying the last bundle of newspapers; small, portable piles to be carried out to the street on Monday, garbage-pickup day. He gives the knot a yank; cuts off the ends evenly with a paring knife.

"Some birthday present," Conrad says, leaning on his broom. "Cleaning the garage." The dust settles around them.

"Come on, don't be a crybaby. How long did it take? An hour?"

"One whole hour out of my birthday, when I oughta be blowing out candles, opening presents—"

"Finish the sweeping, then tell me your sad story."

He goes inside to make lunch for the two of them; rummages in the refrigerator, pulling out salami, cheese, tomatoes, lettuce, mustard, mayonnaise. Two cans of beer.

Conrad comes in as he finishes assembling the goods on thick, dark slices of rye bread.

"No mayonnaise on mine, okay?"

"Oh, hell—"

"All right, forget it. I'll eat it." He grins. "Jesus, what a birthday!"

He sits at the table, drumming lightly on it with his fingers.

"Thought I heard you playing the guitar last night."

"Yeah. Am I rusty."

"Sounded good to me."

He laughs. "You were always easy to please."

"No, uh uh. Not me. Good guitar player, lousy garage cleaner, that's my opinion." He picks up his beer. "Happy birthday!"

"Thanks."

The beer slides, golden and cool, down the back of his throat. "I used to have to keep an eye on both of you, whenever we did that job," he says. "Couldn't give you anything to put away inside the house, or I'd never see you again. Buck, especially. He was a genius at getting out of work."

"Yeah, I remember."

"In fact, the only time he worked his tail off was when we finished the rec room. Remember the plastering job we did down there? You guys wrote dirty words on the wall, and then gave it away, laughing so hard—"

"They're still there," Conrad says.

"What?"

"They are! We put 'em all back when you went upstairs. Come on, I'll show you."

And they head for the basement, Conrad leading the way to the room that is Cal's pride; he had designed it all himself; the three of them had finished it together. Dark Tudor beams in the ceiling; flat boards in an X-pattern on the walls, and between it they had slapped on the thick, curling plaster with their hands. In a corner near the furnace room, Conrad shows Cal the upside-down obscenities, carefully printed and preserved. And, another memory slips out, then, of himself, lying on the sand at the beach while Buck and Con are building a sand sculpture. The sleek lines emerge and he sees the outline of a huge race car. When they leave, he goes to view it; sees, instead the flaring hips and generously mounded breasts of a giant woman, stretching seductively at his feet. "Sex!" he shouts.

"Maniacs!" and, behind him, the laughter becomes obligingly maniacal.

He straightens up, smiling. There is pressure behind his eyes, and the blood is beating in his head.

They go upstairs and finish eating lunch. Cal is busy, filling out this Saturday in his mind. A cake, a few presents, nothing fancy this time, nothing big. They will go to Howard and Ellen's because she makes a big deal over birthdays. She always has felt sorry for Con, as his comes so close to Christmas.

Conrad is whistling; drumming again on the table.

"You're in a good mood today," Cal observes. "You like being eighteen, do you?"

He laughs. "Yeah, I guess so."

"Tell me something," he says. "You and this Dr. Berger, what do you guys talk about?"

He shrugs; looks surprised. "Anything. I don't know. Why?"

"Just curious. What kinds of things?"

"Whatever we feel like. He's an easy guy to talk to. There's not a lot of jargon. Once in a while he gives a little lecture—" he leans back in the chair, hands on his thighs, in imitation: " 'Perspective, kiddo, that's the key word—' "

"What would you think," Cal said, "if I were to go and talk with him?"

"What for? About me, you mean?"

"No. Just—I don't know. To get a few things straight in my own mind."

Conrad sets his beer down; says with finality, "There's nothing wrong with you, Dad."

"Nice. How do you know?"

"You fishing? You want a grade? Okay, I give you a B plus."

"That's great," Cal says. "I buy you a new car, teach you everything I know—how to play tennis, how to clean a garage, I let you beat me at golf—and the best you can do is B plus, that's great."

Conrad laughs. "So, I'm a hard marker."

"Anyway it isn't important. Just an idea I had."

"See him if you want to, I don't care. It's okay with me."

But, do I want to? Why do I want to? What's happening? Nothing is happening, except that now he is imagining. A peculiar, stiff set to Conrad's shoulders when she speaks to him. But, does she speak to him? She issues directives: "Wear the sweater your grandparents gave you for Christmas," she says, walking out of the room without waiting for, without having any interest in his reply. And Conrad is cool to her, cool as he lowers his head in a mocking bow: "Yes, ma'am. No, ma'am." As for himself, he feels undercurrents at work: tremors in the earth.

Last night, when they made love (she opens to him only in darkness, only in sex), she let him hold her afterward, whispering against his shoulder: "You haven't been very friendly, lately."

"Friendly?" he said. "I'm always friendly."

"Please." A silky rush of breath against his face. "I need you to love me, Cal! Please promise!"

"I love you, Beth. God, you know that!" But he could not hold her tightly enough; she clung to him urgently as he stroked her hair, and he was obscurely frightened, because it was not like her, and because he felt beneath them a fault, imperceptibly widening, threatening.

Drifting into sleep, he lost his balance, tipping backward again into memory. A Saturday morning in October, when Jordan was thirteen. Michigan playing Northwestern. They had planned to go to the game with Nancy and Ray, and Jordan had broken his arm playing football on the front lawn. In the back seat of the car, on the way to the hospital, the two brothers had sat, side by side, and he had turned around to scold them. He had been annoyed at having to miss the game, at the prospect of spending his whole afternoon at the hospital while Buck got X-rays and a cast, and he had said, "I'm beginning to think you're accident-prone, you know it?" Beth had leveled a look at him: *Not now, you idiot!* Buck, his arm held awkwardly in front of him, asked, "How was I supposed to know the kid would fall on me?" "That's what tackle is, isn't it? I've told you kids a hundred times, that game's too rough without equipment! Touch, okay; but not tackle!" "Dad, we promise, we don't do it again." But it had been Conrad, shaken and scared who answered him, not Buck. Buck had never worried about anything.

"Coffee?"

"No, thanks."

He crosses his legs; uncrosses them, tries to relax. God, he has never been so nervous. He surveys the room: its windows are oil-streaked; cloudy with dirt. An overpowering air of disorder dominates, weighs him down. The bookcases are tightly packed with dark, musty-looking volumes.

The man sitting across from him has a wild look: Primitive Man. His hair is a dark and fuzzy halo about his head; his eyes, a sharp, stinging blue. All the jokes, the stereotypes of psychiatrists flood his mind: they are mad, their children are mad. He knew a boy at Michigan, studying psychiatry, who had gone berserk in the dorm one night and cut up all of his clothes, stabbed his mattress, screaming that Eisenhower had called him person-to-person from Washington, telling him to do it. An absurd memory. It has nothing to do with this man. Yet all of his reactors are at work—summing up, evaluating, rejecting. He shifts uneasily in the chair. "I don't really believe in psychiatrists," he says.

Berger laughs. "Okay. What do I do now? Disappear in a puff of smoke?"

"I didn't mean that. I meant that I don't believe in psychiatry. As a blanket. A panacea for everybody, you know?"

"Okay," Berger says. "Me neither."

Helpful. Trying to be friendly. Only, he is too strange, too alien. Cal stares at the overcrowded, sloping bookshelves, reminded suddenly of a professor that he had in law school, whose briefcase bulged with books, scraps of notes, impedimenta that spewed forth whenever he opened it in class. That first year, the briefcase haunted him; reminded him of the inner caverns of his own mind, adrift in terrible disorganization. "I'm not putting you down," he says. "Or what you've done for him. He's better, I can see that."

"Well, he's working at it, now."

He feels trapped and hot. "I knew something was wrong," he says. "Even before. But I always thought— I mean, he's very smart. He's been an all-A student since he started school. I just always thought that intelligent people could work out their own problems. . . ." He fixes the bookshelves with a stern look. "These books," he says, "are they all about treating people?"

"No. Not all."

He looked down at his hands, clenched into fists on his knees. "I wish," he says, "that I knew what the hell I was doing here."

"I could use an objective opinion on my coffee," Berger says. "Your son tells me it's lousy."

"Yes. All right."

He gets up and goes to the table in the corner. "I'm getting a feeling from you," he says, "of heavy guilt. About missing the signals. Am I right?"

"Yes," Cal says, "sure." It is easier now that Berger's back is to him. He hadn't realized it was the eyes that were making him nervous. "You don't have something like that happen and not feel the responsibility."

"Guilt."

"Guilt. Yes." He takes the cup Berger is holding out. "Well, I'm guilty. And lucky, too. I was there at the right time. I could have been at a meeting, we could have both been at meetings."

"Your wife was there, too?"

"Yes."

Banging on the door, begging to be let in, while Beth called for an ambulance: "He wouldn't, Cal, oh, he wouldn't!" "Just call!" he had directed her over his shoulder.

"So, you think of yourself as a lucky man."

"No, I wouldn't say so. Not any more. I used to, before—before the accident." Then his voice shifts, cuts through the film of the windows, through thousands of pages in hundreds of books, "Hell, all life is accident, every bit of it—who you fall in love with, what grabs you, and what you do with it. . . ."

"That sounds more like the philosophy of a drifter than a tax attorney from Lake Forest," Berger says.

"Okay, I'm a drifter," he says. "I'm drifting now. I can see myself—I see both of them, drifting away from me while I stand there, watching. And I don't know what to do about it."

"What do you want to do about it?"

"Nothing! I don't want to do anything but sit here on the fence. Until I fall off. On one side or the other."

Berger sips his coffee. "You see them on opposite sides of the fence, is that it?"

"Yes," he says. "No. I don't know."

Berger nods. He strokes his upper lip with the edge of his coffee cup.

"I see her," Cal says, "not being able to forgive him."

"For what?"

He shrugs. "For surviving, maybe. No, that's not it, for being too much like her. Hell, I don't know. She's like a watercolor. They're hard to look at, watercolors. You disappear in them sometimes. And after, you don't know where you've been, or what's happened—" Abruptly he snaps his gaze back inside the room. "I don't know what the hell I'm talking about. I'm not a drifter. I'm not on any fence.

I'm not any of those things. Except maybe a lousy husband and father."

"Ah." Berger nods. "Well, maybe rotten sons deserve lousy fathers. Yours tells me Tuesdays and Fridays what a rotten kid he is."

"He shouldn't. It isn't true."

"He comes by it honestly, though." The smile, open and friendly, invites him to relax, and he wants so much to do it.

He leans back in the chair, rubbing his face with his hands. "He used to call the hospital the Zoo. I asked him if coming to see you was like going to the Zoo, but he said no, it was more like the Circus."

Berger laughs. "That's either a compliment," he says, "or damn poor PR, I don't know which."

He takes a deep breath; the first since he has entered the office.

"I think I know why I came here. I think I really came to talk about myself."

"Okay," Berger says. "Why don't we do that?"

18

Exam week. The first day dawns, sunny and below zero. His car barely has time to warm up before he pulls it into the school parking lot. He leaves it unlocked. Someone might want to take a cigaret break in it, cry in it, who knows?

English. On Miss Mellon's desk is a stack of plain white paper, and next to it, the sheets of exam questions. She has written, in her spiky, up-and-down handwriting across the chalkboard: RELAX. NO BIG DEAL. Nice. She really is a nice person. He sits down near the door and glances out of the window. Shadows of trees, blue on the snow. Everything glittering out there. She has not been trying to smother him, after all; just trying to be nice. *Don't get distracted!* He looks around the room at the rest of the class: Joel Marks, Buzz Fayton, Neva Welles sitting dutifully hunched over their papers on three sides of him. The room is thick with the silence of concentration. He looks down at the sheet of questions:

1. Discuss Hardy's view of Man's control over his inner/outer environment, using *Jude the Obscure* as example.

2. Are the characters in *Of Human Bondage* people of great strength or great weakness? Support your theory.

3. What is Conrad's viewpoint, as illustrated in *Lord Jim*, concerning action and consequence?
   Suggested time limit: 40 minutes per question.

Automatically, he takes out a pencil, even though his mind has gone stubbornly, soddenly blank. Well, that's that. Three lousy questions to sum up one semester's work. What does he have to say about them? Nothing. He has read the books. Period. Miss Mellon passes by his desk, and her skirt brushes the edge of it lightly. During A lunch each day she sits with Mr. Provosky, the algebra teacher. They lean toward each other across the table. Miss Mellon's hands form neat, geometric shapes in the air when she talks. Probably explaining to him how Jude Fawley was powerless in the grip of circumstances. Yeah, probably. He keeps his head down. He needs his virtue intact this morning. She is one of the females whose bodies he imagines in various stages of undress. And other things. This is waking up? He shudders. Not today. Please. *Concentrate, damn you, Jarrett.* He has read the books. Okay, so he is no further behind, no less equipped than anybody else in here. "Relax," she says. *Okay. Okay.*

At his locker he collects the books he needs for his chemistry exam on Thursday. He notices, then is noticed by a group of girls at the end of the hall. Someone calls out, "Hi." He waves; out of the corner of his eye he sees them heading for the exit doors. All but one of them. Jeannine. She shrugs into her coat, tying a scarf firmly about her head. God, if she should come down this way! He has not spoken to her since they came back from Christmas vacation. He wonders now, why he ever put 7. *Girls* on the list. To frustrate himself, for sure. *Girl* would have been ambitious; *Girls* was ridiculous.

He takes another cautious look; she is gone. *Nice going kiddo. Another opportunity missed.* So easy, too. She was by herself; no one to see or hear him stammer around—Ha. No one but her. This is worse than any exam. He stares fixedly into his locker, wasting precious seconds; then he slams it closed, locking it in one lightning motion, and sprints down the hall.

He bursts through the first set of double doors, breathless.

She is standing in the tiny, overheated lobby, pulling on her gloves, her books balanced on the radiator.

"Hi." He sets his books next to hers as he zips his jacket.

"Hi." Cool and reserved.

And rightly so. Exactly what has he to offer someone like her? Someone with directions, goals, interests. "What did you have today?"

"History. You?"

"English," he says. "It wasn't too bad. How was yours?"

"Easy."

"Big, smart senior." He grins at her. She smiles.

He opens the door for her and the air hits them, a wall of piercing cold. She shivers, gripping her books tightly. " 'Bye. See you."

"Would you like a ride home?"

She hesitates; gives him a small, grateful smile. "Oh, that'd be nice. Thanks."

In the car he turns the radio up loud; it relieves him of the need to talk. Ragged piano blues. They listen intently. She sits, gloved hands in her lap, her books beside her on the seat.

"I didn't know you had a car," she says.

"Christmas present. My folks."

"It's nice."

Her voice is soft; he turns the radio down so he can hear her better.

"I live on Wisconsin," she says.

"Yeah, I know."

She looks over in surprise. "You do?"

"Yeah, you told me. Before Christmas. Remember?"

"Oh." She nods. "Well, it's that one, there." She points out a white frame house, with dark green shutters. He pulls to a stop in front, leaving the motor running. Her hand is on the door handle. "Thanks a lot."

"Welcome."

"I'd ask you to come in, but my mother—she's funny about that. She works—" She turns suddenly to face him. "There was something I wanted to say to you. That day we—I said a stupid thing that day. I didn't know about your brother, then. I'm sorry."

Stunned, he sits there, not moving. He had almost forgotten the incident. Now it rushes back to him. An embarrassed silence while they sit; he, staring out at her house, she, at her hands, lying limply in her lap.

He gives a small, brusque flick to his pants leg. "You know the rest of it, too? I mean, about me?"

"Yes."

Should have told her. Should have known someone would tell her. Sometime. Sure. Bring it up over a Coke, "Oh, by the way—" whip out the newspaper clippings. ". . . police chief . . . Lake Forest . . . reasonably certain . . . no drugs involved. . . ." No drugs. Part of the shame. Somehow it is not such a personal failure if you are on something anybody can do something crazy if he is stoned but crazy on your own time is much more serious damning in fact.

"There are worse things," Jeannine says, still looking at her hands. "People do worse things than that."

"Yeah." He wants to help her through the awkwardness of the moment, but it comes out rudely, as if he is cutting her off.

"Well," she says. Her hand moves quickly downward; the door swings open. "Thanks again for the ride. I would have frozen." And she is out of the car, safe on the sidewalk, turning away, hurrying up the steps and into the house.

He pulls into the driveway to turn around. *Nothing to be ashamed of. Maybe not. Nothing anybody particularly wants to be associated with either.*

The circular drive in front of the house is choked with cars, some of which he recognizes: Truan's mother's Mercedes; the Lazenbys' white Pontiac; Mrs. Genthe's Cadillac. He parks in front and walks up the driveway; lets himself in through the garage. As he enters the kitchen, the dining-room door swings open. "I thought I heard somebody trying to sneak in!"

Mrs. Lazenby confronts him. He smiles at her, awkwardly. "Hi, how're you?"

"I'm fine, you dreamer. Thinking you could get away with that! Up the back stairs without saying hello to anybody, huh?"

He grins. "That was the plan."

"Carole? Bring him in here!"

No way out. She takes his hand, leads him into the dining room. He is greeted by his mother's bridge club—Mrs. Cahill, Mrs. Genthe, Mrs. Leitch, Mrs. Truan, two other women he hasn't met; he nods, smiling politely during the introductions. His mother sits quietly through his ordeal.

"He's thin, Beth," Mrs. Truan says. "You should fatten him up."

She smiles. "How was your exam?"

"Not bad."

Mrs. Lazenby has cut him a piece of chocolate cake. She hands it to him, on a napkin. "Here. For being such a nice boy, humoring the old ladies. Where've you been, anyway? We miss you."

"I've been meaning to stop by," he lies. "I've been busy."

"Well, don't be so busy," she says sternly. "Come over some night, I'll make lasagna. Talk to Joey about it."

"I will," he says.

He escapes then, to his room, where he sits staring out of the window. The problem of connecting is partly that of fitting mood with opportunity. When he sees Lazenby's mother, he remembers their house, all warmth and friendliness; eating toast spread with peanut butter, playing catch in the back yard with Major, the fawn-colored boxer; he and Lazenby and Buck, each trying to kill the other in a game of Horse under the basketball net. If Lazenby were here. In the room, this minute. But, no. Passing each other each day in the hall doesn't do. The moment is wrong; the mood is wrong; too much clanging—of lockers, bells, echoes of other conversations. It wouldn't work anyway.

Likewise, Jeannine. But if there were a telephone number here on his desk pad. So that when the feeling hit, he could go directly to the telephone, without stopping to think or to collect himself; just dial the number and it would be done.

He gets up; goes to the telephone table in the hall, flipping through the telephone book. D. Pratt on Wisconsin. Carefully he notes it down. On the desk pad in front of him is another number, written months ago. 356-3340. Under it, in pencil: *Karen*. He looks at it for a long minute. Then, he gets up and goes again to the telephone.

The telephone is answered on the first ring. The voice is suspicious.

"You want Karen? Who is this?"

"It's—I'm a friend of hers. From Northville."

"Northville." The voice goes flat. "Well, she isn't home right now. She's at school. Don't you go to school?"

Her mother, of course. Nobody else would take the trouble to cross-file him, or to be so damn worried. *No ma'am, no school. No time. Too busy being crazy.*

"Yes," he says. "I do. But we're off this week. Exams. Would you tell her I called? My name is Conrad—"

"I'll give her the message."

The receiver bangs loudly in his ear.

"Thanks very much," he says politely to no one. Replacing the receiver, he goes to his room to fall, face upward on the bed, arms outstretched. Nice. A nice cool zero for the day. Well, she wouldn't have wanted to talk to him anyway. Why should she? Why would anybody? He tries again for the image of the woman outside the library, but it won't come. If she had stared, it was merely out of curiosity. Wondering why one of his eyes were set higher than the other, or if his head was too small for his body.

Anyway, a person who performs these joyless and ritualistic sex acts upon himself, this is what he deserves. He rolls onto his stomach, hands behind his neck. Downstairs, the laughter of women escapes the living room, finding its way up the stairs to lie beside him. *Fairy. Fag.*

He rises grimly from the bed. *Get it over with. Cross off both numbers in one afternoon why not?* He dials Jeannine's number.

"Hello?" Her soft voice, musical even over the telephone.

He clears his throat, nervously. "Hi. This is Conrad," he begins. "Jarrett."

"Oh," she says. "Oh, hi."

"Listen, I was wondering." *What Jarrett? What were you wondering?* "Would you be interested in going out sometime?"

A long pause. "You mean, with you? Like, on a date?"

Eyes closed, he grinds his forehead, slowly and deliberately against the wall, a bubble of laughter loose in his chest.

"Yeah," he says, "well, it wouldn't have to be a real date. We could fake it. See how it goes, sort of."

She giggles. "Okay, that was dumb, I agree. Just pretend I didn't say that. Start over."

He grins at the receiver; obligingly he clears his throat. "Hi," he says. "This is Conrad. Jarrett."

"I'd love to," she says. "When?"

19

"What we need," Ray says, "is a secretary."

"I thought we had one."

"No. A legal secretary. A widow, sixty years old, bad legs, good eyes, willing to work nights, willing to knock herself out for this goddamn job—"

"Gee, how come we can't find her?" Cal leans back in his chair. "Sounds like a terrific deal for her." He stretches, arms over his head, glancing at his wristwatch. Eleven-thirty.

"This is ridiculous," Ray says, rolling down his sleeves. "We are not accountants, we are lawyers goddammit. Why do we mess with these returns? Why don't we tell 'em all, 'Look, guys, we advise, that's all, we do not prepare tax returns, we do not do your busy work'—What're you laughing at?"

"I'm laughing because we have this same conversation every year. Here, give me those files. I'll take care of them."

"Nah, just leave 'em. Sandy'll do them in the morning."

"Sandy," Cal says, "is a lousy filer."

Their new secretary. Cherry has gone, but the new one has the same fake smile, the same wide-eyed,

145

over-made-up look and apologetic fluttering hands. And the file baskets are still overflowing. Business as usual.

Ray sighs. "She's an improvement, though, huh? Three letters this week, no errors. She doesn't crack gum in your face when she talks to you."

Her name is Sandra Farentino. She also has a boy friend who goes to Northwestern. A bad sign, he told Ray.

Ray said, "Well, that's what happens when you let your partner do the hiring, buddy."

They lock up; descend the smooth and silent elevator to the street. A hollow quiet fills the building, even though it is not empty tonight: there are lights behind many doors on their floor. The building glows as they walk away from it.

"Want to grab a sandwich?"

"Sure."

They walk the two blocks to the Carriage Grill, a fancy name for a dull spot, with its menu of pale, warmed-over food. A lawyers' hangout. Down the street, at the Orrington Hotel, are the accountants and data-processing men. Just the same as college, when groups of look-alikes had their own spots: fraternity men, independents, foreign students, med students, art students, the rich, the working (no poor students—just the rich or the working). So. Nothing has changed. Beside him, Ray complains over his coffee cup. ". . . said I gave her a raw deal, I was the villain because I overexpected, I was a narrow-minded, arrogant chauvinist—her exact words —Christ, I ask you, is it chauvinistic to expect six hours of work out of somebody, when you're paying for eight—"

"Cherry? She told you all that?"

"She wrote it in a letter. Addressed to me. You were innocent, I'm not sure why."

"I suppose," Cal says, "because I left it up to you to handle it. I'm sorry. I know I do that to you. Cop out. I never know how to tell somebody. 'Hey, you're just not making it.' I don't know why."

Ray shakes his head. "No problem, Cal. I don't mind that. It's just—well, I like to be let in on what's happening with you off and on, you know?"

"With me? What d'you mean?"

"You haven't been around the last couple of months, that's all."

"Around? What are you talking about?"

"Jesus, Cal, I've known you for over twenty years, you think I can't tell when something's wrong?" He looks down into his cup. "You're not yourself."

"I'm not myself," he says. "Okay, Howard, who am I, then?" But Ray doesn't answer. The waiter approaches with their corned-beef sandwiches. He refills their coffee cups.

"What do you want me to do?" Cal says. "Stop by your office, hum a few bars from *The Sound of Music* every day? Everything's fine, Ray. Nothing to worry about."

"Why are you worrying, then?"

He laughs. "I'm not. In fact, I've been thinking about taking a couple of days off in March to play in the lawyers' tournament in Dallas."

"Well, great. Why don't you do it?"

"The middle of the month—I'd be leaving you with all this crap—"

"Don't be dumb, I'd do it to you in a minute." He takes a bite of his sandwich. "Beth going with you?"

"Probably, yeah. We'll stay with her brother and his wife. They have a place in Richardson."

"I think that's good," Ray says. "I think it'd do you both good to get away for a few days. That's the answer."

The answer to what? Life, reduced to the simplest of terms. Formulas. Get away for a while. Everything works out for the best.

"Look, I'm sorry," Ray says. "It's none of my business. But, you worry too much. You've been on the

147

rack about him long enough. It's a habit, now. You got to let go sometime, buddy."

"Ray, I'm not on the rack about him."

"Thing is," Ray says, "in another year he'll be gone. Off to Michigan or Harvard or wherever the hell he gets it in his head he wants to go. Maybe he'll decide to take a tour of Europe for a year, not even go to school, who knows—"

"How come all of a sudden you know so much about him?"

"I don't. Look, I'm giving you the benefit of my experience."

"Thanks," he says drily.

"I mean, with Valerie, it's more than her living away from home. She's gone, Cal. She's got her own life, her own friends, she breezes in for a few days of vacation—maybe girls are different, I don't know. Or maybe she was too aware of the stuff that happened—I mean, between Nance and me. But they leave, Cal. And all that worrying doesn't amount to a hill of crap. Just wasted energy."

"I'm not worried about Con," he says.

"Who, then? Is it Beth? Is something wrong between Beth and you?"

"No!"

"You sure?"

"Yeah, I'm sure!"

He turns. Ray is wearing an uncomfortable look.

"Well, you gave me some advice a long time ago, on that business with Nancy, and you know what that lets you in for, don't you. Getting it all back someday, whether you want it or not. So, how do you want it?"

He gives a snort of laughter. "I don't want it."

No mistaking the look of discomfort, now. Ray has something on his mind. "Listen, Cal, Nance and Beth had lunch together, last week—" He breaks off, staring down into his coffee cup.

"Next time," Cal says, "try for more directness.

Make an appointment. What are you supposed to tell me?"

"I'm not supposed to tell you anything," Ray says unhappily. "I'm just telling you. They had lunch together. Beth is pretty upset. She thinks you're out of focus. She says you're obsessed with Con's problems. You can't think about anything else—"

"That's ridiculous," he snaps. "She can't think about them at all. Now what does that say to you?"

"It says nobody's normal," Ray says. "Nobody's got it together, not anybody in this frigging world. Look, I'm sure as hell not setting myself up as some example, Cal, I'm just—I just didn't know if you knew how she felt."

"I know."

He feels sorry for Ray. This is not a pleasant role. Counselor. He remembers that from seven years ago, wants to tell him he sympathizes, wants to ask, How are things with you and Nancy now? How would you describe your marriage, in terms of knowing each other? In terms of being friends? Of understanding that hopelessly intricate network of clash and resolution that has been woven over the last twenty years? Two separate, distinct personalities, not separate at all, but inextricably bound, soul and body and mind, to each other, how did we get so far apart so fast? How can she believe that? Is it true? She believes it, or she never would have said it to Nancy, and even saying it is unlike her; she has never given so much of herself away. God, he is wandering tonight, his mind dealing in irrelevance. It is always this way when he is overtired.

"Listen, forget it, will you." Ray takes a swallow of his coffee. "None of our business, anyway. And I'm feeling very existential tonight. People are born. Then they die. In between, they perform a lot of pathetic and more-or-less meaningless actions—"

"Ray, Jesus! You don't believe that."

He grins. "Oh, yeah, when I'm sober, I believe it

a lot." He looks at Cal. "How about you? What do you believe, buddy?"

"I believe I'll go to Dallas," Cal says. "Play some golf, maybe get blind one night with my crazy brother-in-law, and raise hell."

"Do it," Ray says. "My blessings."

On the subject of losing people, Ray is bitter. So much of the worrying you do, he tells Cal, is about losing your kids. And, in the end, you lose them, anyway. So, what's the point? He feels he has lost Valerie forever. But things change, situations change. She could come back. She probably will, someday, through a husband, some children.

The fear behind the fear of losing people is that there might have been something you could have done to prevent it. Last Christmas they had lost Con in Florida, at Miami International. Standing in the underground garage, the dirt and the oppressive heat surrounding them, the rental convertible parked at the curb, his heart had jolted in terror as he waited. Conrad had disappeared when they deplaned. He was gone for forty minutes, while Calvin Jarrett, world traveler, champion fence-sitter, had waited, finally getting hold of the Airport Police (how did you explain "losing" a sixteen-year-old in an airport?) and, as they were taking down a description, he had suddenly appeared, walking toward them from the escalator, and through the glass exit doors. He had gone to look for a men's room. He had gotten lost. End of explanation.

And then had come the telephone call from Howard, two days later. They had gone to play golf. They had left him on the beach with some kids he had met down there. Nice. He had found some friends. And, after they left, he had gone upstairs to the room, called Lake Forest to ask if his grandfather remembered how many strings of lights he and Buck had put on the outdoor tree in front of their house last year? The telephone had been ringing when they walked in. Howard was frantic. "Cal, don't do that again, don't leave him alone down there, something's wrong. I know it. You'd better have a talk with him."

And so he had. He went immediately next door, to the connecting room, and Conrad was lying on the bed in his bathing suit, reading a magazine, calm and relaxed. Yes, everything was fine. Yes, he had called them, to wish them a Merry Christmas, why?

And, for some reason, he had bought that, too. Even though, like a single frame of film, flicked on the mind-screen and off, it had been there that day. The knowledge of the thing that he would do to himself someday.

Out of focus, she said. Obsessed. Maybe she is right, maybe he is. One thing for sure, Ray is not right. Life is not a series of pathetic, meaningless actions. Some of them are so far from pathetic, so far from meaningless as to be beyond reason, maybe beyond forgiveness.

He looks around the dim interior, at the knots of heads, nodding purple flowers in the dark. How about it? Illusion versus reality? All those in favor. He could poll them, but they are not representative, they are a bunch of hotshot lawyers, what do they know?

20

Standing on the front porch of her house, he nervously shoves his hands in his pockets; pulls them out again. Too casual. Wouldn't want her mother to get the wrong impression. He takes a quick glance at his watch. Eight-thirty. He is right on time. Her mother is strict, she says. Maybe she has a rule about her not being out after midnight. He hopes so. A series of five-minute telephone calls over a two-week period does not establish much precedent for the evening that now stretches lengthily ahead. Too long between the asking and the actual event. Like having to think in advance about going to the dentist. But she had been busy that first Saturday, and Friday nights she works. What is the problem? No problem. He is in great shape for this event. He has just been cut down to once a week by his analyst. He finds on waking each morning no terrible urgency to escape his thoughts. They are harmless. They concern a report he has to write, a section of tenor melody he is learning, small goals to purify his days.

Berger yesterday had grinned lecherously at him over a sugar doughnut. "Psychiatry has its advantages. I expect to hear all about it on Tuesday."

He had laughed. "Yeah, well, I didn't hear all about how it went with my father, did I?"

"I've told you before, kiddo. I'm the doctor, you're the patient. Sooner or later all you cats start pulling out of line."

"What did he want anyway?"

"He wanted," Berger said, "the name of a good allergist. Listen, you want me to tell you what he wanted?"

He had thought it over briefly; decided he didn't want that, after all. Respect for privacy was what he wanted. He had let it drop. And now he is on a Tuesday only schedule. "Gee, coach, I hope I make it," he had said on his way out the door.

Berger had sighed. "And I just ordered a couch, how'm I gonna pay for it?"

With a start, he realizes he has forgotten to ring the doorbell *Nice beginning, Jarrett.* He rings and the door is opened seconds later by a pleasant-faced woman with red hair, a wide smile. Her eyes are on a level with his. She is much taller than Jeannine.

"Hi. C'mon in. You're Conrad, right? I'm Jen's mother."

She ushers him into the small, tidy living room, where a small boy sits, cross-legged on the couch, watching television.

"Mike, this is a friend of Jen's. Conrad . . .?" She looks at him.

"Jarrett," he supplies. "Hi, Mike."

"Hi." The eyes do not move from the screen.

"Sit down. Jen just got home from work. They asked her to stay late tonight. Let's see now, you're new here, aren't you?"

"Me? No. You mean to the city? No, we've lived here for about ten years."

"Oh." She is puzzled. "Aren't you the one that works at the music store in Lake Bluff?"

"No." He smiles.

"Well, then, did she meet you at the Evanston symphony concert?"

He shakes his head, wishing he could help her. How many are there anyway? "I go to Lake Forest," he says. "I gave her a ride home from school once."

"Oh, you're the tenor!" she says.

"I can't hear the TV," Mike says. "You guys are talking too loud."

Relieved that she has nailed him down at last, she feels free to go on with the more serious, motherly questions: Where does he live? What does his father do? Is that civil, or criminal? What grade is he in? A junior? And he's how old? Eighteen? He endures them in an agonizing fit of nervousness. He couldn't even think of the words "tax attorney," almost forgot the name of his own street. As for his age, let her think he is stupid, it is infinitely preferable to whatever else she might discover about him.

He gazes about the room. Plants everywhere—on tables, in the windows, in corners—one of them, a tall, slender tree, supports huge, fantail leaves, and is nearly touching the ceiling.

"You must like plants," he says. *Oh brilliant Jarrett. Brilliant.*

She laughs. "Well, they make nice pets. They don't bark, or jump up on you and tear your stockings." She jumps up herself. "I'll just hurry her along."

He is left with the small boy, who sits, scratching his leg, glancing over at him appraisingly. He is blond and thin. His voice is a low rasp.

"I'm gonna take guitar lessons."

"Are you? Good," Conrad says politely.

"But I might take karate instead. Ten lessons for four bucks. After school at the Community House."

"Sounds great."

He goes back to the TV, chewing a corner of his lip. The room is warm. Conrad takes off his jacket; holds it across his knees.

"I'll probably have to take the karate," Mike says. "because I don't got a guitar."

"You got a karate?" Conrad asks.

"Huh?"

He laughs. "Nothing. Just a dumb joke."

"What's your name?"

"Conrad."

"You look just like the guy who was here last Saturday."

"Yeah? What was his name?"

"I forget. There's too many."

Jeannine appears in the doorway. Behind her, from the end of the hall, the command is issued: "Don't be late!"

"I won't!"

She grabs her coat from the closet, on their way out. Settled beside him in the car, she sighs. "I heard her grilling you. I'm sorry. I tried to hurry."

"That's okay."

They drive in silence for a few minutes.

"I'd better warn you now," she says. "I'm a horrible bowler."

"That's okay."

"Well, it's not, really. You haven't seen me."

"Look, we don't have to go bowling if you'd rather not."

She glances quickly at him. "No, I'll go. If you want."

"What would you rather do?"

She shrugs.

"Do you want to go out at all?" he asks.

"Do *you?*"

"I asked you, didn't I?"

"You didn't talk to me all week in choir. I thought you might have changed your mind."

"I haven't changed my mind," he says. "Have you?"

Abruptly, she laughs. "This is dumb. I haven't changed my mind, I want to go, but I just hate to go and do something that'll make me look silly—"

"You won't look silly," he promises her. "I'm a great teacher, you'll look like you belong to a league in twenty minutes, okay?"

"Okay."

And it is all right after that. She is right, she's a lousy bowler but a good listener, a quick learner. He gives her all the tips he can, and she absorbs them easily, trying very hard. And besides she looks terrific up there, no matter what happens to the ball. He notices that she is wearing the blue skirt, the one she wore the first day he saw her at school. And he notices, how she sits with her legs tucked back, half on the seat, her hair a smooth river of silk.

"You were a natural," he tells her, across the table at McDonald's, afterward.

"Oh, sure. I'm also a gemini, so be careful."

"Why?"

"Because. We are two-faced and unpredictable. And what are you?"

"January tenth."

"Capricorn. Good. That's a good sign."

"Is it?"

"Sure. Dutiful. Responsible. Serious. Capable."

"Boring."

She grins. "Late-bloomers."

He laughs. "For sure." He looks around at the people, begins to play an old game: Instant History. "See that guy there? Divorced. That's his daughter with him. He gets to see her once a week. He'd like to take her someplace fancy—Diana's, The Red Carpet. She only likes McDonald's. Every week they come here for dinner—"

"Uh uh. That's not her daddy," Jeannine says. "Sugar daddy, maybe. Okay, my turn. There's a couple. It's their first date. She's afraid of getting fat, so she just has a burger, no roll, and a cup of coffee, but he's not, so he has two Big Macs—" she rolls her eyes "—what a pig! And he's been dying to ask her out. For months he put it off. Finally he got up his nerve.

156

He called her on the phone and said, 'Say, I was won-dering—' " She giggles.

"Oh, all right." He mimics her soft soprano. "And what did she say? 'Who, me? On a date? With you?' "

"Well, I was shocked," she says. "You took long enough."

"I thought I was pretty swift."

"September to February? Is swift?"

On the way home he allows his hand to slide across the seat, encounter hers, and hold it lightly while she talks: about her parents' divorce; about her father, who lives in Akron and manages a department store; about her mother, who is a nurse at a small, private hospital in Glenview.

"My uncle is on the staff there," she says. "He helped her to get the job. That's why we came here. And there were some other reasons, too." But she does not elaborate. They pass the library on the way to her house. It sits, hunched, waiting for him. So many things he does not know. His body, under touch from all stimulation tonight, leans toward it, yearning.

In front of her house, they talk some more, and he smooths his palm around and around the steering wheel, staring out at the street light, diffusing the yel-low bloom of its rays through the windshield.

"Well, what d'you think?" he asks. "Did this work out okay? You want to try it again?"

"Sure."

So they set up the following Saturday night. A re-turn engagement. And, as casually as the earth one day spun itself loose from the sun and off into whirl-ing space, he kisses her, his hand on her shoulders, her mouth under his, cool and firm. And an unexpected sensation, then, causing his groin to swell with warmth; her hand at the back of his neck.

Marvelous accident. Did he discover her in her blue skirt that day last September, in Lazenby's car?

If so, Berger is right: the body doesn't lie. He says against her cheek, "I'll call you tomorrow, okay?"

"Okay," she whispers. Her breath is warm against his ear. "Two phone calls in one week. You are swifter than I thought."

21

She looks up from the checks she is writing at her desk in the bedroom. "When would we go?"

"March thirteenth. It's a Friday. Tournament starts on Saturday, runs until Monday, the sixteenth."

"All right." She puts down her pen. "Would we stay with Ward and Audrey?"

"If you like."

"I'll write to them."

"Good."

Not a trip to Europe, but he can do this for her; take her to visit her brother. Ward Butler is big and loud, nothing like his sister, in looks or temperament. Married a woman just like himself. Easy people to like, and to be with. And she is as close to Ward as she is to anybody. *As close as she is to me?*

He wanders from the bedroom to the family room downstairs; makes himself a drink at the bar. A quiet Saturday night, for a change. Conrad is out for the evening. He didn't say where, only that he wouldn't be late. He flips idly through a stack of record albums on the stereo; pulls out "A London Symphony," by Vaughan Williams. The only symphony with which he has ever become familiar. He remembers the music lit course Beth was taking when they met; all those inane lyrics they put to the main themes to help her study for the exams.

The power of suggestion. That particular symphony does make him think of Europe, although not London specifically, just all the places they have been. Spain. Toledo, with its streets narrower than any alleys he has seen, and those outdoor stalls with seafood, fresh fruits, hand-knitted shawls, hand-tooled leather belts—those delicate carvings on the handles of swords and knives—what was it called? God, his memory failing again. Senility setting in.

The smell of boxwood. Granada. In the monastery where they stayed, Parador de San Francisco, the gardens were laid out so neatly, with fountains and stone benches, and stones inlaid on the walkways. So beautiful and unreal. And yet, with the unreality, and, considering the timing of it—Con still in the hospital, Jordan dead less than a year—they had been happy there. Away from home, away from all of it, everything seemed orderly and safe.

Safety and order. Definitely the priorities of his life. He is not a man inclined toward risk. There. A definition at last. *I'm a man who believes in safety.*

Christ, is that all? Is that why decisions are so difficult? No. He would have classed Arnold Bacon as a man who believed in order and in safety. Yet Arnold had no trouble with decisions. Arnold had written him off, without hesitation, when he had married Beth. He had been re-evaluated; found wanting. The subsidy was withdrawn, the offer of a future partnership in Arnold's firm disappearing with it. It seemed at the time a terrible misunderstanding. No way to put it right. Not with telephone calls or letters after the fact. And it was not the withdrawal of the subsidy; that meant nothing. The withdrawal of friendship. That was what had crushed him. After five years of looking up to someone, of thinking of him as a father.

"You had a goal, once," Arnold told him over the

telephone. "You were going to be the best tax attorney in the state, remember?"

"Sure. And once I wanted to be a fireman. Then I met you." He had been angry, then, but he hadn't really meant that his goals had changed. And, in vain, he argued that a man can have more than one goal at a time; that he had not abandoned one for the other. He just no longer wanted to think of himself as the kid from the Evangelical Home. He wanted a family, a wife. People to share his goals with him.

"Then you've made a bad choice," Bacon observed. "She is not a sharer, Calvin. It's you who will end up doing all the sharing."

Bitterness talking, he had understood that. There had been, on contact, instant hatred between Arnold and Beth. She had referred to him after the very first meeting as Arnold Fagin; had never missed an opportunity to point out the ways that Arnold worked to control him. To own him, she said. Between those two whom he loved, he had tried to wedge his own wants, his own needs, sitting nervously on the fence. It hadn't worked.

His eyes blur suddenly, and he blinks back tears, furious at himself. Since that visit with Berger, all manner of internal wheels have been set in motion, heaving up thoughts he has not encountered in years. Old stuff. Too late to do anything about it, and what could he have done? Gone to his funeral? What for? To pay his respects to a man who would have nothing to do with him for the last fifteen or so years of his life? No. All over. It had not been him, anyway, who made the decision. It had been Arnold. So maybe Beth had been right. Maybe people did use other people according to their own needs. It had not felt like ownership to him, but, afterward, what else could he call it? He had not lived up to his end of the bargain. Therefore, Arnold had cut him loose, gotten rid of him.

People use people according to their own needs.

Or don't use them. When a primary need is one of safety. Is that why he has never gotten involved? With a secretary, a girl in a bar, a client, a friend's wife? Is it because he loves her, or because he is afraid? Affairs. They are common knowledge, discussed, just as they say, in the locker rooms of the clubs he had belonged to. Women everywhere. Hundreds of opportunities. Thousands of attractions. Then why not him?

The closest he has ever come was nine—no, ten —years ago. A woman lawyer he knew. Molly Davis. Her client and his were considering a private merger; they had worked together on it for several weeks, and he felt the vibrations; they could have worked out a private merger of their own—so why didn't they? What had happened? So long ago, it is hard to remember. It seems that he had quietly and simply, one day, turned it off. Before it had gotten started. Priorities again. Safety and order. Infidelity is a dangerous business. People get hurt. And she does not forgive. She never forgave Arnold for—for what? For simply being Arnold.

No. Too easy, pushing it off on her. *Face it, you are not a hungry man; sexually or otherwise. You were content. You never looked.*

But, in any case, she would not have forgiven him. They had discussed it once, after Ray and Nancy.

"If I were her," she had said, "I would never come back. Not for a house in Glencoe, not for the children, not for anything. It is too humiliating."

"Why? She loves him. What does it matter?"

"It matters that we know about it," she said.

"Suppose nobody knew about it? Then would it be humiliating?"

"I would know," she said, "and you would know. That's enough."

A thrill of fear had touched him. Is it that some people are not given a capacity for forgiveness, just as some are cheated out of beauty by a pointed nose,

or not allowed the adequate amount of brain matter?
It is not in her nature to forgive.

No. That is absurd. Again, a reducing of the complicated dimensions of life to a formula that is more simple than sensible. It comes from too much thinking.

He rises in disgust, setting his glass down on the bar. Too much thinking merely causes him to feel vaguely that he is on the point of learning something, only to have the circuits blocked; the answers inaccessible.

22

On impulse, he attends a swim meet after school;
sits alone, behind a group of freshmen. Short boys;
tall girls. The air is moist and hot; coats and sweaters
are piled everywhere. The girls turn around to rear-
range clothes, to tuck scarves and gloves into coat
sleeves, to stare. The boys watch the meet. They voice
loud, unflattering opinions of the home team.

"Jesus, they stink!" one kid says in disgust, and
Conrad feels oddly hurt by the remark. Defensive.
But it is true. Their record: one win, four losses. They
should be better. Lazenby, a dependable breast-
stroker; plenty of talent in the free style; Truan the
best backstroker around, maybe even as good as Buck.
Still, they don't have it. For the first time, he feels a
twinge of regret. Maybe he could have helped. Watching Salan as he shouts encouragement to Bill Danoff,
his best in the two-hundred-meter free style, he wonders about Lazenby's remark that day in the hall.
No. Salan is a Man of his Word, actions have consequences, *Lord Jim* and all that.

Afterward he hangs around. The crowd thins out,
and he heads for the lower doors, passing the stairway that leads to the locker rooms. Laughter surges
upward from the stair well. He recognizes the voices.

"Come on, guys, move it, my goddamn ass is melting!" Lazenby pleads.

"Your goddamn ass could use it!" Genthe says.

He hesitates; then he moves on, toward the door, his books slung under his wrist, against his hip.

It is dark, and he has to pick his way around pools of half-melted snow in the parking lot. Warmed briefly this afternoon by the sun, the puddles are bubbled over now; thin sheets of ice that will not hold weight. Behind him the doors burst open. Shouts of laughter push outward.

". . . glad you can laugh about it, Genthe, it sure as hell wasn't funny—"

"Ah, come on, we weren't that bad—"

"—face it, we got waxed! We stunk!"

"—Truan, no kidding, I don't know how you can listen to that lecture one more time about Buck Jarrett, the all-time great swimmer of the world. Jesus, he bores the crap outa me when he does that—"

"—you think he's ever gonna quit kissing the guy's picture—"

An abrupt silence. It stabs deeper than the words. Someone says, "Shut the fuck up, will you?"

He continues across the parking lot, reaching into his back pocket for his keys, the blood thick behind his eyes, his throat tight. The lot is nearly empty of cars. It is slippery and wet. He misses one puddle, steps into another, and icy water oozes through the seam of his boot.

"Hey, Con." Lazenby comes up behind him.

He turns, gives him a blank smile.

"Could've used you today, buddy," Truan says.

"I don't think so."

Lazenby laughs. "He's right. Nobody could help us today."

"How's it goin', Jarrett?" Stillman materializes out of the darkness, checking out the LeMans, swift and professional. "Your old man's so loaded, how come he didn't get you a friggin' Eldorado?"

"I tried not to let it ruin my Christmas." His voice sounds wooden and expressionless in his ears. He is surprised when they laugh.

Truan says, "I heard you were going out with Pratt."

"No kidding," Lazenby says. "Since when?"

He cannot answer. The blood is still pounding. His throat is scratchy, hot.

Stillman flashes The Grin. "How ya doing? You in her pants yet?"

"Do me a favor," he says. "Try not to be such a prick. I know it won't be easy for you."

They stop walking and eye each other warily. Truan backs up, getting himself out of the way.

"Hey, you guys—" Lazenby says.

"Man," Stillman says, "you're the prick. Guys like you who walk around acting like you're King Shit, you give me a goddamn pain in the ass—"

Something explodes inside his head, the sound shattering the parking lot, the red brick wall of building behind him, the white doors, gray cement—all dissolving into broken bits of color, heading swiftly toward him as he slams his fist, hard, against that face —a sweet rush of mindless ecstasy washes out everything in perfect release and makes him whole again. The rough feel of cloth tearing in his hands as he holds on, shoving, pushing, and they go down together on the gravel. Stillman's arm is around his neck, his hand digging, punching at his back—"—goddamn you, Jarrett!"

He hits him again. Everything is bathed in yellow light now, faded, like an overexposed photograph, and again he hits him, as, miles away, someone calls his name: "—Con—Con—Connie—!" and he is grabbed suddenly from behind, swung roughly around. He hits out again.

"Cut it out!" someone says, "Cut it out!"

A second explosion in the pit of his stomach. He doubles over.

A solid wall of pain is packed into his lungs. There is no room for air. The passage is blocked, and he has lost the secret, the rhythm of breathing. He gasps, and the wall dissolves. Behind it, there is only a hole, filled with pain.

"You okay?"

It is Lazenby holding him up. He straightens slowly, looks at Stillman, lying on the ground, legs sprawled, and elbow crooked high over his face. Something white in his fist. A handkerchief. He is rocking slowly. Truan and Genthe bend over him, helping him up. He takes the handkerchief down; looks at it, moaning. Blood pours from his nose. The yellow light is receding; the photograph coming into focus. Rough gravel and slush underneath their feet. Truan, Genthe, Lazenby, Van Buren, two other guys he does not know who came to watch. There is sound, but it's garbled and he cannot understand it. He doesn't want to.

He walks away, brushing something wet from the front of his jacket. His knees are trembling; his body feels loose and watery. He gets into his car and sits, holding on to the steering wheel. His hands hurt. The knuckles are scraped raw, and he flexes them on the wheel. He reaches behind him, feeling for his keys in his back pocket. They are not there. They are somewhere out in the parking lot. Along with his books. He rests his forehead on the wheel, fatigue, and another feeling that he cannot identify, moving in, trying to overcome him.

The door on his right opens. His books are tossed in on the seat. Lazenby leans across and hands him his car keys.

"Thanks." He takes them without looking. The door stays open a minute, then Lazenby gets in, slams it closed behind him.

"I want to talk."

The darkness outside is dense; illuminated at intervals by a bluish glow from the parking lot lights. He stares at the dashboard, holding the keys lightly in his hand.

"The guy's a nothing," Lazenby says. "A zero upstairs. What d'you expect from somebody whose class votes him least likely to grow up? Listen, you used to know that about him, Connie. Since fourth grade you've known it."

"So?"

"So. You make yourself look stupid when you let him get to you like that."

"So, I look stupid," he says. "Is that the message?"

"No. No, it isn't." Lazenby looks away, staring out into the darkness. "What is it with you, man? We've been friends for a long time—"

"Laze," he says, "we're still friends."

"Are we?" Lazenby's voice is flat, strained. "Look, I don't know why you want to be alone in this, but I wouldn't shit you, man. I miss him, too."

A blow he is not expecting at all. He concentrates on the cold bunching of metal, his car keys under his hand, against his thigh. He looks out at the bare, black-limbed trees.

"I can't help it," he says. "It hurts too much to be around you."

The keys dig into his thigh. Next to him, Lazenby sits, elbow against the door, his hand propping his cheek. What he said is true. The three of them were always together, why does he think of it as only his grief? *Because damn it it is.* His room no longer shared, his heart torn and slammed against this solid wall of it, this hell of indifference. *It is. And there is no way to change it.* That is the hell.

His heart pounds painfully in his chest. He slows his breathing with an effort, staring out of the window at nothing.

"I've got to go."

Lazenby stirs, not looking at him. "Yeah. Okay."

The door opens and he is gone. Conrad waits until he has crossed the parking lot and gotten into the red

Mustang. He lets him pull out first, holding himself tight, control is all, he will not, will not. Not here. Not again.

He lets himself into the house with his key. Wednesday. His father is working late on tax returns; his mother is playing tennis. The house is quiet; empty. Good. He does not want to talk. He looks down at his jacket. Blood drying into the brown suède. He should try to get it off. It feels stiff under his fingers.

He sinks into a chair in the kitchen, staring wearily at the wall. He takes off the jacket. There is blood on his shirt; flecks all over it, as if he had slapped a loaded paintbrush against his hand. He strips to his undershirt, and works awhile at the stains on the jacket. The blood runs off into the sink, a pale brown that mixes with the water and looks like beef broth.

Carefully rinsing his hands, he lays the jacket on the counter. He takes the shirt into the laundry room. Maybe she won't notice. Or else she will think it is mud. No. He scrapes at the spots with a thumbnail. Pinpoints of brownish dye on the pale blue fabric. No, too definite. Mud would blur; rub out.

He holds the shirt under the faucet; runs water over it. The spots dissolve, washed away in the sink. He squeezes the water out of it and throws it in the dryer; spins the dial to ON. Since they were little, they have done this, getting rid of the evidence, Buck called it. He shivers suddenly. The house feels cold.

He heads for the kitchen again; searches the refrigerator for the TV dinners, bought for him for Wednesdays. Fried Chicken. Peas and carrots. Mashed potatoes. Apple slices. He turns on the oven. "Take the dinner out of the cardboard envelope, tear back foil to expose chicken, cook 35–40 minutes." Obey all rules and do as directed, punishment may be lessened.

Don't doubt that there will be punishment.

169

Punishment? Of course, for losing control. Always. One of life's unwritten laws.

He heats water in the teakettle; looks in the cupboard for the jar of instant coffee. Sees Stillman suddenly lying on the ground knees raised his mouth a round O of surprise his eyes widen the head snaps back *Goddamn you Jarrett!* A cold sensation in the pit of his stomach; his skin prickling with fear. *How many times did I hit him?*

He sits at the table to eat his dinner. No TV tonight. And no music. Each small punishment he inflicts could lessen the larger one *But it was no big deal just a stupid fight.*

The telephone rings, sharp and insistent, and his stomach knots. He lets it ring. Nine, ten, eleven times. It stops. His father, maybe. He sometimes calls on Wednesdays, to talk over the day, to have him pass a message to his mother. Surely it was him. Who else?

He looks down at his dinner, and quickly looks away. *Out of control. Don't doubt that there will be punishment.* It was Stillman's father, calling from the hospital. His nose is broken, his jaw is broken. And he sees them all again—Truan, Van Buren, Genthe—all watching; the parking lot a huge stage lit up and Mr. Knight telling his father they must expel him. He is dangerous, they cannot have these attacks occurring in the parking lot. No control, it is shameful, terrible—*Oh God I didn't mean to!*

He picks up his dinner, goes to the sink with it, and flushes it down the disposer. He stares out the window into the chill February darkness. *How many times did I hit him?* And how will he be punished? He doesn't want to think about it: he could punish himself first, but how? *You are always. Fucking up. You never mean to. Never mean to doesn't mean shit.*

He picks up his coffee cup and drinks the scalding liquid. It burns his mouth as he swallows it. A hot blur of pain in his throat, in his chest. He stands rigidly at attention, absorbing it, knowing that it is not enough. Not enough. *And it wasn't Stillman, anyway it wasn't even him but some other fucking bastard I didn't even know who said it the world is full of fucking bastards so it's all pointless you can't fight everybody and what goddamn difference would it make if you could?*

He goes to the laundry room, retrieving his shirt from the dryer. The spots are gone. It is clean, warm, and he slips it on and goes to sit on the couch in the den. He leans his head back. His body feels churned up; brutalized. He needs to move around, but he will not allow this, either; he will allow himself no comforts tonight. Waiting is part of the punishment. So he waits.

23

The distance between people. In miles. In time. In thought. Staggering, when you think about it. Here he is, driving on the Edens, and he catches a glimpse, in the lane to his left, of a passing car. The driver is raising an angry finger at him, behind the double space of window glass separating them. And he is amazed. What has he done to deserve this gesture of contempt? Of course. Glancing at his speedometer, he understands. Thirty miles an hour. You don't do this on the Edens, drive thirty in a fifty-mile zone, even at eleven-thirty at night: it can get you more than an obscenity, it can get you into an accident. No thanks. No more. The quota is all used up.

Well, he should catch up with the driver. Thank him for the reminder. Really, it was an act of kindness. Only the guy would not understand, would suspect him of playing some kind of game, of trying to get back at him.

Communication. The bridge between the distances. He passes a sign, high off the highway and to his left: *Are you on the right road?* In the shape of a cross, leaves and flowers entwined around it. That is not communication. That is alienation. Like the car he saw one day on I-94. A huge sign on top of it: *Re-*

pent! You can only wonder about the sign-carrier. Who the hell is he and what does he think he's doing?

So, can there be no communication without contamination? Without that peculiar message of *This is me telling you?* In the end that does more to separate people than unite them. People don't like to be told things. There has to be a way of getting a message across, without setting yourself up as a holy man. But, shouldn't the need to send the message be proof enough that you are not a holy man?

Doing it again, Jarrett, straighten up, no more circular thinking. Exhausted, disgusted with himself, he leaves the Edens to the faster drivers, turns off on Half-Day Road. He looks at his watch. Nearly twelve. He will be home in five minutes and he can go to bed. Leave the rest of the world to the faster drivers—that's what he ought to do tonight.

He pulls into the driveway, gets out of the car, and opens the garage door. Her car is there; Conrad's is parked on the circle in front of the house. Good. Everybody safely home and waiting for him. He pulls in, closes the door, lets himself in through the kitchen. The oven light is on; an eerie glow in the dark room. He switches it off and makes his way toward the den, where another light is burning.

Conrad is asleep on the couch, sitting up, his head back, hands in his lap. The television set is off. Cal stands a minute, looking down at him, his mind blank, thinking nothing, thinking only that he is very tired, so tried that he must get to bed immediately, or he will be flat with exhaustion again tomorrow. If he can help Ray clean up the worst of the work, he will not feel so guilty about leaving.

He sets his briefcase down and takes off his coat. He touches Conrad's shoulder, gently. "Hey."

He snaps upright, his eyes open; blinking. He rubs a hand over his mouth. "Wait," he says. "Wait a minute."

Cal smiles. "Okay."

But he is still not awake, staring vacantly ahead, confused and dazed. Waking up has always been a painful process for him, ever since he was a baby. A struggle. Sometimes he would spout gibberish, staring intently, the words formed from unknown syllables of a dark and primitive language. They would ask him questions: "What are you talking about? What do you want?" And he would answer, but not in any tongue they could understand. They would laugh and tease him about it the next day. He didn't believe it; never remembered anything. "What did I say?" he would ask. They would try to make the sounds, but it was a dialect known only to him, only at the edge of consciousness.

He is conscious now, shading his eyes with his hand against the light. "Time's it?"

"Twelve."

"You just get home?"

"Yeah. What're you doing down here?"

"I couldn't sleep."

Cal laughs. "I see that."

"Time's it?"

He turns away to hang up his coat. "I just told you. Twelve o'clock. Let's go to bed, okay? I'm bushed."

"Wait a minute," he says. "I need to talk to you."

A note of urgency in the voice. He turns back; drops his coat on the arm of the chair. *Oh, shit.* "What's the matter?"

He is wiping his hand nervously again across his mouth. He does not look at Cal directly. "Something happened today. At school. I got in a fight."

"A fight?" He sits down in the chair. "Who with?"

"Just a guy. You don't know him. Kevin Stillman."

"Sure I know him. Diver on the swim team, isn't he?"

"Yeah. I forgot. You'd remember him, yeah."

"What was the fight about?"

"Nothing. I don't know. He's just a jerk, but I

174

didn't—I shouldn't have—I know that's no excuse . . ."

"What happened?" Cal asks. "Did you get hurt?"

He looks up, then. "Me? No." He takes a breath and lets it out nervously. "I think I hurt him, though."

"What makes you think so?"

"I don't know, there was a lot of blood. His nose—"

"Was he on his feet?"

"Yeah. I mean, not at first, but he was when I left. Lazenby took him home, I think."

"Joe was there?"

"Everybody was there," he says. "Everybody from the swim team. I stayed to watch the meet. Then I hung around for a while. They were all coming out of the locker room. That's when it happened."

"And it wasn't about anything?"

He shrugs. "I guess it was about how he bugs the shit out of me, and I bug the shit out of him."

"Well, now you know it," Cal says. "Maybe you won't have to fight about it any more, huh?" He rubs the back of his neck with his hands. "I called you around seven. You weren't here. I wondered where you were."

"I was here."

"Why didn't you answer?"

"I don't know." He looks at the floor, his hands folded between his knees. Cal sees the start of a small mouse under his left eye. "I thought it might be somebody else."

"Who?"

He won't look up, won't say what he is thinking.

"Relax," Cal says. "He's all right."

"How do you know?"

"I know," he says. "It was just a fight. Guys have been getting in fights since school was invented. Think about it. Think about the last fight you were in."

"I was never in one," he says.

"What?"

"I wasn't. This is it. The first one."

"You're kidding. I can't believe that."

He shakes his head.

Cal looks at him, thinking hard. "Listen, a bloody nose is nothing. I'm telling you, he'll be there tomorrow. Nothing to worry about. Once, I broke my finger in a fight, knuckling a guy on the head. Doctor told me next time to use a baseball bat." He laughs, remembering, and Conrad looks up at last, grins faintly.

"You're not mad, then?"

"Mad? No," he says.

"I shouldn't have gone out of control like that," he says. "I shouldn't have blown up."

"You never blow up," Cal says; then corrects himself. "Hardly ever. I can count the times you've blown up. You owed yourself. So, forget it."

Not just to comfort, it is the truth. A disposition like an angel's, Ellen used to say. Sunny and sweet, he never got mad. And that wasn't good. Everybody has resentments, everybody has anger. He was one who kept everything inside. Cal has learned a thing or two from Crawford: razoring is anger; self-mutilation is anger. So this is a good sign; he is turning his anger outward at last. But something bothers him still. "You don't want to tell me what it was about?"

Conrad shrugs. "I told him he was a crappy diver. The guy's got no sense of humor."

He undresses in the dark, listening to the silky rush of her breathing. Regular and smooth. She falls asleep in seconds. Another thing to be layered protectively over with logical reasons, so as not to come upon it in an unguarded moment: she did not stop in the den on her way to bed. Maybe she assumed the light had been left on for him. She must not have looked in his room, either; or she would have noticed that he was not in bed. He had asked on their way upstairs, "Did you hear your mother come in?" Conrad had said no.

Wouldn't she think it strange, him sleeping on the couch at whatever time she had come in? Wouldn't she have wakened him to ask—at least— *What the hell is wrong with her?*

24

"Okay, I guess we're off. You've got the number, haven't you?"

He helps his father load the last of the suitcases into the trunk; slams the lid down. "Yeah. Have fun. Play good."

"I'll try." His father reaches for his wallet. "Let me give you some money."

"You already did. This morning, remember?"

"You sure that'll be enough?"

"Plenty."

His mother comes out of the house, carrying her coat. She is wearing a dark green dress, banded with white at the throat and wrists. Her hair falls loosely, hiding her face, but he knows the expression she is wearing: a look reserved for airports and other public places—remote; responding only to inner sounds today. They are a complete contrast in attitudes: his father jokes with ticket agents, starts conversations with other passengers. On the plane he will talk to the stewardesses, ask them where they are from, how they like their work. His mother will remain cool and aloof, as if she is alone on the plane. It is not her fault. She can't help it if she is afraid of strangers.

"Good-by, Mother," he says.

"Good-by," she answers. "Be nice to your grand-mother."

She gets in the car, shutting the door. Sun glints off the side window, obscuring her from his view. That's it. She is afraid of strangers. Why hasn't it ever registered before?

"The flight gets in Wednesday at four. You wait here, okay? We'll go out for dinner."

"Okay."

His father smiles at him. "Listen, don't let her push you around too much. Five days, you can stand it for that long, can't you?"

"Right."

He looks at his watch. "You heading over there pretty soon?"

"As soon as you get out of the driveway."

His father gives him a helpless grin. He can't resist organizing. Likes things nice and neat. "You got plans for this weekend?" he asks.

"I thought I'd cruise through town, run a few red lights, smoke some hash, get a couple girls in trouble, nothing special, why?" He smiles. "Quit worrying. You're making me nervous."

"I'm not worrying. Just take care, okay?"

"I will. See you Wednesday."

He waves them out of the driveway, then goes upstairs to his bedroom to get his own suitcase, thinking with longing of the comfortable silence of the empty house, of playing the stereo in his room and eating salami sandwiches, drinking beer, coming and going as he pleases but this wouldn't work. His father wouldn't go under those conditions and he had told him no, he wouldn't mind staying with his grandmother and grandfather, in that house on Green Bay Road that reeks with the too-sweet smell of her perfume, so that even the walls seem coated with it. It will cling to his clothing when he leaves. He loves his grandmother, but talking to her is like being on a loaded quiz show; her questions defy answering. "Have you completely lost your senses?" is one of her favorites. She uses it on his grandfather like a weapon; a whip to keep him in line. With him, the words are gentler, but the technique is the same. Maybe that is where his mother learned that there is danger in revealing too much; in giving his grandmother ammunition.

Seated across from him at dinner, she eyes him sternly. "You're letting your hair grow, aren't you?"

"I don't let it, Grandmother, it just does it. All on its own."

"Well, I hope you're not turning into one of those hippie freaks. Howard, he needs some more meat."

"No, thanks. I've had plenty. No more." Hippie freaks. She is ten years behind the times. On everything. In fourth grade she wondered why they didn't wear short pants to school; in junior high, why they had abandoned rubber boots and raincoats.

"Where's your appetite?" she demands. "How can you put on weight, eating like that? At least have more potatoes and gravy."

He allows her to refill his plate, even though he is full, doesn't really mind her bossing him around. Last year, when the hole was closing over his head, there were no lectures, no words of criticism from anyone. He reads this as a statement of his good health. Today he is capable of improvement.

"How were your grades last semester?" she asks. He answers with his mouth full, a feeble attempt to assert himself. "Not bad. Two C's, a B, and an A."

She clicks her tongue against her teeth, shaking her head.

His grandfather says. "Ellie, please. Let him eat."

"I'm wondering," she says, "what ever happened to all those A's? I remember you getting all A's and at the same time you were playing golf, swimming, taking guitar lessons, tennis lessons—"

"Sounds like I was overprogramed."

180

She sniffs. "Overprogramed. What's that? Keeping busy is not being overprogramed, Conrad. What are you doing with all your time?"

"Nothing much," he says.

"Ellie, for pete's sake—" his grandfather says. Too late. She is already launched into the lecture of the Easy Life and he half-listens, as he pushes the peas and carrots around his plate.

". . . and you have absolutely no worries whatsoever about food, or clothing, or shelter. You are so protected, you can't even imagine what it was like in the old days, I mean, you should just thank your lucky stars every night—"

"My what?" he asks. "My lucky what?"

She stares him down. "You heard me. I don't believe you properly appreciate your advantages, Conrad. Being born into a good family. Having a head on your shoulders—"

"Is it fair to count that? Everybody's got one, Grandmother."

Her lips fold in. "All right. Make fun. It's the thing you do best anyway."

He grins, coaxing a smile from her at last. "Thanks. It's nice to be good at something."

That night he picks Jeannine up at work. The sign in the bakery shop window says CLOSED, but the woman behind the register smiles and motions him to come inside. He remembers what Jeannine told him the first time he came to pick her up: that the woman warned the rest of the girls to keep an eye on him while she got to a telephone. She thought he was planning to stick up the place. "He has a furtive look," she had said.

He liked that image of himself as the bakery rip-off man: the girls cowering behind the counter, in front of the neat, brown loaves of bread, the sticky-sweet cinnamon buns. Everything waiting for his greedy hands. "Okay, girlie, get those danish twists off the counter and into the bag, no funny business!"

181

Jeannine waves from the back room. "Be right out."

"How about a cookie?" the woman asks.

"Sure. Thanks."

He takes it, even though he is not hungry; he is stuffed, from dinner. Still, it is rude to refuse. Like refusing her friendship, her trust.

"Want the rest of this?" he asks in the car.

"Ugh. No. I don't think I'll eat another cookie as long as I live. Your parents get off all right?"

"Yeah, they left."

"How is it going?"

"Oh, fine. I got real tough with the old lady right away."

"I'll bet." She slides over closer to him, squeezing his arm.

"What'll we do? Good movie in Lake Bluff. Starts at nine-fifty."

"I should go home first. Just to let her know."

They ride the rest of the way to her house in silence, her hand on his arm, the soft purr of the heater backing up the music on the radio. As they round the corner, she suddenly sits up very straight in the seat. "Damn," she says. "Oh, damn."

A black Buick is parked in the driveway.

"Looks like you've got company."

She gets out of the car the instant he pulls it to the curb. He reads in the light from the street lamp the car's Ohio license plates.

"Is it your father?"

"No," she says. "Not my father."

The porch light is on. The door opens as they come up the walk.

"Hi, honey." Her mother stands in the doorway. "You remember Mr. Ferrier, don't you?"

The man is light-haired and heavy-set, with a rough, outdoor look about him. He reaches out to take Conrad's hand, smiling broadly.

"Jen, you're prettier than ever. Nice to meet you,

Conrad. Jarrett, you say? Any relation to the Jarretts who own the drugstores in Akron?"

"No, I don't think so." He smiles at the man. He always admires these take-charge guys, they make awkward situations, like meeting people, fast and simple. He glances at Jeannine. She is not smiling.

Mrs. Pratt says, "Paul and I were thinking about going to get a quick bite to eat. Honey, would you mind keeping an eye on Mike?"

"I don't know," Jeannine says stiffly. "We were going to the show."

Her mother laughs nervously. "Honey, Paul's on a business trip. He's only here for tonight. He's leaving tomorrow for Minneapolis."

"I'll bring her back early, Mother," the man says, winking at Conrad. "Don't worry."

"It's up to Con."

"I don't mind," he says. He looks swiftly from mother to daughter.

"Good, then," Paul says. He gathers Mrs. Pratt's coat from the arm of a chair. "See you later. See you, tiger." He reaches around the couch to ruffle Mike's hair, and they are gone, out the door. It slams behind them.

Mike peers over the back of the couch. "Can we have popcorn tonight? Mom said."

Jeannine doesn't answer; she stands, staring at the television screen, her hands at her sides, lips pressed tightly together.

Conrad waits, feeling awkward, as if he has come in on a movie in the middle. He peels out of his jacket and drops it on a chair. "Let's make popcorn," he says.

She looks at him. "I'll make it, you stay here. Mike, turn down the TV. It's too loud."

She disappears into the kitchen and Conrad sits beside Mike on the couch.

"What're you watching?"

"Nothin'. Friday night stinks. Hey, you wanna hear me play the guitar?"

"Hey, yeah. When did you start?"

"Couple weeks ago. Mom bought me a guitar. She says if I do good, she'll buy me a better one for my birthday."

He listens to the chords: C and G, D and A. E minor. A minor. After each chord change, Mike looks up, expectantly.

"Fantastic." He rewards him. "Terrific."

"Nah. But I don't think it'll take me long to get good, do you?"

"Nope. Anyway, you got time. You've got your whole life, right?"

Mike hands him the guitar. "Now you play something," he orders.

He entertains him with a Simon and Garfunkel tune he still remembers, then some James Taylor, John Denver, a little Eric Clapton, for good measure.

"Hey, you're really good, you know?"

Way to go Jarrett can't resist can you? You sure can impress the hell out of those eleven-year-olds.

He hands the guitar back. "It's not hard," he says. "You keep working at it. You'll be able to do it in a while."

In the kitchen, a cupboard door bangs.

"I'll go check on the popcorn," he says.

She has her back to him, all business.

"Jen, what's the matter?"

"Nothing. Never mind. I'm acting dopey tonight. Just forget it, ignore it, okay?"

"Okay," he says. "He seemed like a nice enough guy to me."

"Well, he's not!" she snaps. "A man who dates a married woman, in my opinion, is not a nice guy."

"I thought your parents were divorced."

"They are! Now they are! They weren't before he came along. He was a friend of my father's—" She

184

stops abruptly. "I'm sorry, this is all very boring for you."

"I'm not bored."

"Well, you should be. I am. And I don't like acting like this over it. And especially I don't like it, in front of you."

"Why, in front of me?"

He moves across the kitchen, toward her, and she quickly turns her head away. She is crying. "Oh, damn!" she says, "I'm sorry, I can't help it, oh, damn."

He puts his arms around her. "It's all right," he soothes. "It'll work out all right."

"I don't think so." Her voice is husky. "I kept hoping something would happen, I kept thinking they would decide to get back together, and I know, *I know* that's just stupid! It's stupid even to think about it! They don't love each other. They just don't and that's that, so why do I make such a big deal of it?" She pulls in her breath, and her arms are around his waist, her head on his chest. He stands, holding her; tests the feeling of someone leaning on him, looking to him for support. He feels as if he could stand here holding her forever. Her lashes are wet, golden in the harsh overhead light. He lifts her chin with his hand and kisses her. Her face is tear-streaked, her mouth loose under his, turned slightly down. He has never felt so strong, so needed.

25

Audrey pours him a cup of coffee.

"Not much to celebrate with, is it?" She smiles at him. "Ward's going to stop for beer on his way back. He and Beth went riding. He's been dying to show her that horse."

He leans back, relaxed. "That's okay, I can wait. I'll just sail along on this high for a while."

"Seventy-one, that's really good, isn't it? I'm not much of a golfer."

"It's the best I'll do in this thing, I'm sure. I was playing over my head today. God, it was beautiful out there, too. Summer comes early around her, doesn't it?"

"Oh, no, take my word, Cal. This isn't summer! Summer is absolutely *unbearable!*"

"Where are the boys?" he asks.

"They're right outside. In the pool."

"Gee, they look great. They're getting so big, I hardly recognized them."

"I know. I can almost see them growing myself."

Their two sons, Charlie and Kerry, are ten and seven, now. Lively and wild, streaking through the house, snapping towels at each other's bottoms and thighs. They are built like Ward, plump and square, and they are large for their ages. Blond, with Audrey's wide blue eyes.

"Charlie's such a daredevil," she says. "He wants to do everything Ward does, and *now*. Kerry's more cautious."

Like his own. Buck was the one he had to watch. Conrad had all the common sense that his children, together, were allotted.

She puts a bowl of fruit on the table, and sits down across from him.

"How is Con?" she asks.

"Pretty good."

"I thought he must be. Ellen writes, but she doesn't tell me much. Her letters are: 'Hi, how are you, how are things? We're fine, everything's fine.' Not too informative. And I tried to talk to Beth last night. She made me feel like it was off limits, sort of. Then I started to worry a little."

"No, he's fine." A lot of subjects are becoming off limits, these days. On the flight down here, he had attempted a discussion of their summer plans. Would she like to go to London? Dubrovnik? Did she have something else in mind? She met his questions with polite indifference. Whatever he would like to do was fine with her. He took it as delayed punishment for Christmas. Okay, fair enough. But his try for a talk about the conversation he had with Ray in the bar was greeted with stony silence. She definitely did not want to hear any of that. She did not want to explain what she had meant in her talk with Nancy.

"If you don't know, Cal, it's hopeless for me to try to tell you."

"Oh, great, it's hopeless," he said. "Terrific, it's hopeless."

And she had twisted toward him in the seat, saying, "Please! Can't we just go and have a good time for these few days? Is that what you got me up here for, so you could make me say what you want me to say? Please, let's just not have any big discussions, let's just relax and have fun for a change."

So, okay, he blamed himself. He had come on too strong, maybe. He would relax. He would have fun. He would quite nagging her to confide in him.

"You're always so *sincere*," she said bitterly, "and so *pushy*."

But it surprises him that she would be as reserved with Audrey. She likes Audrey. And it was an honest question. And honest interest, not like Marty Genthe's. Why duck it? He is in the process of making a discovery: that he never knows how to read her, and she offers him no clues. There are fewer and fewer openings into the vast obscurity of her nature. He is on the outside, looking in, all the time. Has he always been?

"I know," Audrey says, "that you have to be careful with Beth. I mean, emotion is her enemy. She wants everything to go smoothly, to go right. You know. The way she's planned it."

Is it that obvious? Is it even true? He remembers Carole Lazenby's words at lunch that day. "She's a perfectionist. . . . She never lets herself get trapped . . ." Oh God, that is not true, not true at all, once she was trapped and she knew it. She knew it, then. A night in August, hot and sticky. She had gone out for a walk. Alone. He sat, alone, in the living room, thinking about the set of her shoulders as she walked away from the house; she had looked so small, so sad. And he had gotten up, gone after her, found her in the back yard, weeping, and trying not to weep. Those dry, tight sobs. It was the only time he saw her cry. She had not cried at the funeral. Not at all. He had cried. Howard and Ellen had cried. But she and Con had been stony and calm throughout. The scene in the garden had come later, much later. After Con. After the other thing. She had crouched on the ground with him beside her, crying over and over, "How did this happen? How did it happen?" and nothing he said could reach her. She was grieving. He had thought it a good thing. At last. She had not been able to before. Now she could.

They had neither of them cried that night on the dock. Too awesome, too catastrophic for tears. That murderous, lead-colored moon. The sky, wispy with cloud-strings. The black water all around them, indistinguishable from the black sky. The people who didn't know who they were, only that something terrible had happened: "Those kids never should have been out there without power." A man next to him had answered, "Doesn't make any difference. The lake whips up like that and it doesn't make any difference, power or not." And the radioed message from the cruiser: "We found her, sir. She's dismasted. Only one on board. Sorry."

"They'll find him," she had said, gripping his arm. "They'll find them both." Her hand had felt small and childlike in his. What had it been like out there? he had often wondered. Impressive. Enough to rob them of happiness, of security, of the easy peace of mind that is nothing but lucky accident. Enough to put Con in the hospital for eight months. They had not found them both. They had not been able to find Buck for two days.

Morbid thoughts. He looks across the table at Audrey, who is frowning slightly at him.

"Is something wrong, Cal? I mean, something else?"

"No," he says. "What could be wrong? Here I sit with my lovely sister-in-law, a seventy-one' under my belt, on the way to winning the first tournament of my career, what could be wrong?"

A car has pulled up in the drive, and Ward's voice, booming through the door, greets him: "Hey, you big-city dude, how'd you make out?"

"I made out great!" he says.

"What did you shoot?"

She follows Ward into the kitchen, looking like a

sixteen-year-old, in jeans and a red-checked shirt, her hair in pigtails.

"Seventy-one." Audrey says.

"Seventy-one! Oh, Cal, that's marvelous! That's just great! Oh, you *are* going to win it this year, you really are!"

"Hey," he says, "you'll jinx me."

"Nobody did better, did they?"

"Not today. Still two days to go, though."

Ward sets down the case of beer in the middle of the kitchen. "What you need," he says, "is an early ride tomorrow, to set you up."

He laughs, looking at Beth. Her eyes are alive, her cheeks burned from the sun. She is freeing her hair from the braids, tossing it back over her shoulders.

"Listen, I had her on the biggest damn horse you ever saw today, and she was beautiful! She's got great hands—"

"Oh, shut up, Ward!" She looks at him, laughing.

"Buy her a big Appaloosa, keep it in your back yard over there in leafy Lake Forest—"

"Why is it that Texans always confuse 'big' with 'best'?" Cal teases. "Just like that crazy airport, Jesus, I thought O'Hare was bad!"

"Whaddya mean, that's a great airport! It's the ultimate! Ten thousand acres of concrete!"

"And ask a security guard where the baggage is, and he tells you, 'I have no idea.' "

They all laugh.

"Well, we got a few problems to iron out, yet," Ward says. He has turned, over the past five years, into a native Texan, with the drawl, the handlebar mustache, the hat, the boots, the works. He does not look like a computer-company executive, but that is what he is. The image he prefers to project, however, is pure cowboy.

"Hey, let's break out the Coors, we'll celebrate the company, and the beautiful day, and a big seventy-one tomorrow!"

"Little seventy-one," Beth corrects him. "What are we doing for dinner tonight? I'm starved!"

"Let's just throw some steaks on the grill, how's that? Aud can whip up a salad, we'll be in business." He ruffles his sister's hair affectionately. "Hey, I'm glad to see you so cheerful, Sissie. Things going good for you again, huh?"

A pause; a half-step off the beat. She does not look at Cal. "Yes," she says. "Things are going fine."

"Good. I'm glad you could come. Mom and Dad wrote and said Con was staying with them, huh?"

"Yes," she says.

"So, what's the status? How's he doing? Everything okay?"

"Everything's fine, Ward."

He does not catch the slight frown.

"He seeing anybody? I hear you do that, sometimes. You know, like an outpatient sort of thing."

"He's seeing a doctor in Evanston," Cal says. "Twice a week. No, once a week, now. He's coming along."

"Twice a week!" Ward lets out a low whistle. "That must have kept you pretty busy at the office, huh, Cal?"

"It was worth it."

Beth is studying her wristwatch intently. A platinum watch, set with diamonds. His gift to her on their fifteenth anniversary. In April they will have been married twenty-one years.

"Listen, I'm not kidding," Ward says. "Tomorrow morning, before you tee off, just a good, brisk ride. It'll do great things for you!"

He laughs. "No, thanks. I'll stick to my sport. You two go ahead."

"Did I tell you not to marry a dude, Sissie? Hey, this sister of mine rides better than anybody around here, so you do well tomorrow, or we'll send you back east by yourself!"

26

On Sunday, at breakfast, his grandmother asks, "What time did you get in?"

He knows that she knows. The light was on in their bedroom when he pulled into the drive; off, as he came up the stairs.

"I don't know. Twelve? Twelve-thirty?"

"One-thirty," she says.

"One-thirty, then." He nods amiably, helping himself to the toast she has kept warm for him in the oven. The small breakfast nook is washed in sunlight. Sun glints off the jar of honey sitting on the table, filtering through the pale yellow curtains at the window. His head sings with an intricate, melodic line— Telemann? Marais? John Bull? He cannot remember, but he loves those fresh and unfamiliar instruments, the recorder, the harpsichord; their simple statements of truth. He wonders what the weather is like in Dallas. Sunny, he hopes. Warm.

"How can you expect to get a decent night's sleep, coming in at that hour?" She is frowning across the table at him.

"I give up. How can I?"

She sighs. "Everything's a joke with you, isn't it?"

"Grandmother, you know something, I'm nuts about you," he says cheerfully. "You're always agitating, I think it's great. You oughta run for President. No kidding."

He gets to his feet, pushing the chair back.

"Where are you going?"

"Outside to wash my car."

"Well, don't get chilled. It's not summer, you know."

"I know, I know!"

It is a perfect day. The temperature is in the fifties. It threatens to break a record. And tonight he will go to Jeannine's to study. Seven-thirty. Thinking about it makes his skin ripple pleasantly, his stomach pull. A feeling you get going up in an elevator. *Shouldn't plan ahead like this shouldn't expect minutes hours and the elevator comes down you could hit the ground but what a trip.* Last night, he took her out, again: the old Saturday-Night-Show Date. Afterward, at Lombardi's they had run into Phil Truan and Shirley Day. Phil had talked about the four of them going bowling sometime and Jen had said, "Oh, I'm a terrible bowler, ask Con." And Phil had said, "Hey, so am I, ask Con," and suddenly he was the authority figure, although he does not remember Truan being a bad bowler; he was probably just being nice, making him feel important.

Truan is a nice guy. That is the truth. He would like to do something with him again. He liked the look of Jeannine and Shirley, leaning toward each other acoss the table, the peach-silk river flowing toward Shirley's dark curls. Everything looks washed and new this morning. The concrete, wet from melting snow, smells clean; the soap, sharply pungent; the water, cold as it runs over his hands.

And another truth. That there are no secret passages to strength, no magic words. It is just something you know about yourself. Since last night—no, before last night—it is as if he knew it all along. He is strong, he is able, *because he is.*

193

After dinner he and his grandfather sit in the living room, reading the Sunday paper, while, in the kitchen, his grandmother does the dishes. He listens to the comforting sound of her bustling about, the cupboard doors banging loudly, the water going on and off with that peculiar, groaning wail as the pipes protest. Another memory that belongs to this old and comforting house. He waits patiently for the sports section. His grandfather reads every article, chuckling, rattling the paper at the stuff he likes; grumbling and crossing his legs when something annoys him. He leafs through his section casually, reading a dull article on riverfront-housing investments from beginning to end, testing his memory. He checks out his horoscope: *home, family, your life-style are spotlighted. Taurus and Libra individuals figure prominently*. He wonders about his life-style—what is it? He is becoming, Berger says.

An article, halfway down on page three suddenly leaps out at him. *Girl Takes Own Life*. Oh, God. He skips to the middle of it. ". . . carbon monoxide poisoning . . . nineteen-year-old Skokie girl . . . dead in her car early Saturday morning. She had been reported missing the night before by her father, Raymond Aldrich. . . ." He goes back to the beginning of the article. "Karen Susan Aldrich of 3133 Celeste, Skokie, Illinois . . . dead on arrival at Skokie General Hospital . . . hose attached to the car's exhaust pipe was drawn through a rear window. . . ."

His body is suddenly numb. The words thicken and swim before his eyes. *Oh God. Oh no. Oh God*. His head fills with strange sounds—a tuneless humming, like violin strings. His body trembles. I ". . . we are in shock . . . father told reporters . . . everything going so well, I can't believe . . . I don't believe it. . . ."

He folds the newspaper carefully, holds it carefully on his lap, rocking slowly. He is dizzy and sick at his stomach.

"Conrad? What's the matter?"

His grandfather stands over him, the newspaper in his hand. "Are you all right?"

"I'm all right," he says. He can hardly hear himself, the sounds inside his head are so loud. His grandmother is there and there is more talking; broken pieces of conversation that he cannot follow. Her hand is on his forehead.

"You don't feel hot to me. Is it a headache?"

"A headache, yes," he says, getting up. "I need to go to bed. I'm tired."

"Let me get you some aspirin. You see? You don't get enough sleep, and then you work outside and get chilled and overtired."

"You're going to bed?" his grandfather asks. "At seven o'clock?"

"I'll get you the aspirin," she says.

"Never mind. I don't need it."

He heads for the stairway, holding himself stiffly upright. In his mind he sees himself putting his feet, one before the other, on the steps, carrying himself upward. His body feels nothing.

Fully awake, he lies on his side in the bed, memorizing the lines of the desktop, and above it, the half-inch ridge of desk pad, the chair beside the desk, the precise angles of his schoolbooks piled upon the chair. His eyelids feel dry and scratchy.

So safe so safe floating in the the calmest of seas what happened? What happened? A stone bench outside the hospital where they sat for hours soaking up spring and its sunshine Leo with them laughing and joking Karen's legs swinging back and forth back and forth and the blue cotton dress clings to her slim body her hair long and black freshly washed shines flatly against her skull smiling at him a dimple appears in her cheek what happened? "What happened?" Crawford you liar you promised you said you were never wrong oh Jesus God please I don't want to think about this let me sleep God let me sleep.

195

Eyes closed a knee in his back hand at his neck forcing his face into the floor of the elevator rough under his cheek smell of vomit and matted fur "God don't hurt me" struggles against the indignity his pajamas pulled down around his knees a needle sunk deep into his thigh twists moans and all of it loose like water flowing salt tickles inner edges of his eyes into his mouth twists onto his back arms over his head raw wails of anguish break off in pieces hurt his ears "Baby, it's okay" Leo is over him lifts coaxing "Let's get up off the floor huh?" arm around his waist sags heavy his wrist aches where Leo holds him dragged along the watery dark he rolls off Leo's shoulder to the bed eyes closed hands folded in prayer between his legs can't look "God don't hurt me. Please."

Shock. His mind egg-shaped gray loose tracings of paths over it rat scratchings white hospital gown gentle Leo helps him into it never hurries him old friends in the steel-and-white room greet him with smiles "Here he is just lie back and relax head on the pillow that's it" get him ready shoot him up so he can't move can't get away Leo smiles down at him his face is purple in the light his teeth glitter "Easy now you know it doesn't hurt" no but afterward exhaustion fatigue that moves outward from the center of him flowing like warm oil in his veins can't lift arms or legs his ears ring his head light and empty all rat scratchings erased and Leo feeds him "Atta baby eat some peaches."

His body jerks awake. His hand reaches for the lamp. He turns it on; lies motionless in the sudden, bright light. He is in the narrow, twin bed in his grandmother's spare bedroom. Blue bedspread, blue-and-white-striped wallpaper, blue-and-white rag rug on the floor, everything in order. No good. No good to think about it. About anything. It will not change. Just as before, it is done. He wills his mind to drop him under; to let him pass through into dreamless sleep.

Sits against the wall cool at his back in only his shorts the door locked testing only testing tension of skin sharpness of blade thin threads of blood well up from scratches his legs his arms have no feeling in them draws the blade down into his left wrist a deep vertical cut the artery bubbles up like a river widens does it again to his right arm warmth and color floods the room he is free at last comforted it crosses his mind to compose himself for dying awkward there is nowhere to put his hands the blood makes everything slippery lies on his side using one arm as a pillow he sleeps and then arms tied his jaw aches something hard pinches his mouth between his teeth "to keep him from swallowing his tongue" they say he knows better it is how they punish you for failure here and someone crying crying "Lord, what has he done? What has he done to himself?"

He awakens to fear again; his mouth dry. For terror-filled seconds he doesn't know if it is happening all over again. Or worse, that time has tipped backward and it is happening still. Numb with fear, he scrambles out of bed, pulling his clothes on over his pajamas.

The house is dark. It hovers around him as he fumbles for the stairway, fumbles for his jacket in the downstairs hall closet, quietly feeling for the handle of the front door, to let himself out.

He walks swiftly, without direction. To calm himself. To get away from dreams, because there are worse ones and he doesn't want to remember them, doesn't want to think at all, less intense, less intense, but how to do it? To concentrate on that is to at once accomplish the opposite. A phrase attaches itself to his mind: ". . . Why a kid would want to hurt himself . . ." a swift, sinking feeling in the pit of his stomach as he remembers another newspaper article. About him. The police chief was quoted. He couldn't understand why a kid would want to hurt himself like that. Crawford had let him read it afterward. He had tried to explain that he had not been trying to hurt himself, he had merely been trying to die.

No. You do not slash yourself in a dozen places if you are merely trying to die. Nor do you overlook the full bottle of Valium beside the razor blades in the medicine chest. Not for him that quiet, dream-drifted road outward on sleeping pills. Too easy. And too neat. *Oh, God, why, then?*

He stops walking. The sidewalk is shadowy; the air around him still and cold. Stiff, black limbs arch over his head. The black houses crouch, ready to spring. He is shivering, his skin clammy and wet underneath his pajama top, down his back, under his armpits. Freezing out here.

Ahead of him, a car approaches. It pulls to the curb opposite him. Police car. The door opens, and he has a sudden urge to run; swiftly he puts it down. He stands still, shoving his hands into his jacket pockets as the cop crosses the street.

"Where you headed?"

"Nowhere." He wets his lips nervously. "Just taking a walk."

"Pretty late, isn't it? After two. Where do you live?"

"Fourteen-thirty Heron Drive." He is surprised at how calm, how normal his voice sounds.

The cop frowns. "Long way from home, aren't you?"

He has given his home address. He takes his hands out of his jacket pockets; lets them hang limp at his sides. *See? I'm harmless. I'm okay.* "I'm staying with my grandparents. On Green Bay Road."

"Where do they live?"

For a moment, he panics. He cannot remember

the number, and he stumbles over the words: "It's a gray house with black shutters. On the corner of Green Bay and Booth. Fifty-one thirty-five—"

"What's the name?"

"Butler. Howard Butler."

"Yeah, okay." The cop smiles, then. "I know the house. They know you're out?"

He shakes his head. His hands are sweating. His wallet is back on the dresser, in the bedroom. Suppose they should ask him to prove who he is. Will they take him to the station? Call his grandparents?

"What's your name?"

"Jarrett. Conrad Jarrett."

"Well, listen, Conrad, I wouldn't walk around here this late. Too many nuts in the world, these days. You want a ride back?"

"No, that's okay."

"You'd better head back, then. They might wake up. Be worried about you."

"Yeah, I will."

They drive off. He lets his breath out slowly, even manages a wave as they signal to him from the car window. *Too many nuts.* Meaning you aren't one of them. All the outer signs must be right, then: hair cut to the right length, polite answers, expensive suède jacket made in Mexico. *You're all right kid. Ordinary.* And this event, walking the streets at two o'clock is ordinary, too, but something is wrong about it, something not normal, what is it? He cannot remember. He is shivering again. He wipes his hands on his pants, zips his jacket up tight; turning, he follows the disappearing taillights, two red eyes in the darkness.

The door is unlatched, as he left it. He slips quietly inside; goes to the kitchen, to the sink, where he hunts in darkness for the faucet and a glass. He drinks greedily, then lets the cold water run over his hands. Still in the dark, he makes his way to the den at the back of the house. No lights. He doesn't want to wake them. No going back to bed, either. Not safe there. He sits upright in the chair beside the door, his arms along the armrests, not leaning back.

Unforgivable. It is unforgivable. They wrestle with the boat together, the sails snapping like rifle cracks in the wind "Get it down! Get the goddamn sail down!" grabbing at gray a billowing mass sticky and wet against his face it smothers him with its weight a loud crack and the terrible rolling begins everything out from under the water closing over his head he fights his way back to the surface screaming emptied of everything but fear "Buck! Buck!" in front of him a hand stretching out an arm along the upturned hull water crashing against him pushing them apart Buck yells "Kick off your shoes!" mindless he obeys chokes as water closes him off again from the moon from everything they collide in the water Buck grabs his shirt "Hang on, I'm gonna go under, have a look!" he screams at him "Don't go Don't go!" and the wind takes it throws it back into his face Buck is already gone and above him the sky lumpy with clouds black it is painful to breathe terrifying he must turn his head away from the dark shape of hull from safety to do it Buck surfaces beside him shaking hair from his eyes gasping "We screwed up this time, buddy! He's gonna haul ass over this!" They stare at each other and Buck breaks into a grin "Well? You got any ideas?" he shakes his head biting his lips to keep back the terror "Always thinking, aren't you?" and he finds his voice then "It's not so goddamn funny, Buck!" he soothes him "Okay, okay. They'll be looking for us, they're looking now, for sure, just hang on, don't get tired, promise?" He says "Don't you either!" and they stop talking then address themselves to the dull, dogged task of enduring and the clouds level out it starts to rain hours into the night they hang two fish caught and strung off the sides of the boat arms straining hands numb with cold the water is icy laced with foam like root beer *"How long you think it's been? I dunno. An hour? Two hours? Oh, hell, longer than that, don't you think?"*

When did it happen? When did they stop calling to one another from opposite sides of the stern where they hung for better more even balance did he think it was over?

——*"Man, why'd you let go?"*

——*"Because I got tired."*

——*"The hell! You never get tired, not before me, you don't! You tell me not to get tired, you tell me to hang on, and then you let go!"*

——*"I couldn't help it."*

——*"Well, screw you, then!"*

Unforgivable and his grandmother crying at the funeral "Poor Jordan, poor baby, he didn't want to do it, he didn't want to leave us like this!" and he had answered her saying coldly "Why did he let go, then? Why didn't he hang on to the boat?"

And he was punished for that because afterward everything make him ill. Food and the sound of people eating it crushing breaking slurping. Smells. He would lift a glass of orange juice to his mouth inhale the acrid odor of dirt and dying flowers even to think about eating made him gag and for weeks afterward not being able to sleep that was punishment too being forced to submit over and over to a hopeless rerun of that day to what could have been done to make the sum of it different. Nothing. That is the nature of hell, that it cannot be changed; that it is unalterable and forever.

Was it painful? He cannot believe so if it was he would have cried out he would have known it and he could have stopped him he could have said "Buck take me with you I don't want to do this alone."

He is awake again. *No more. No more.* He gets up quickly; goes to turn on the television set, kneeling beside it as it warms up. An old set; the images are snowy. The brightness hurts his eyes. He tunes the sound down and goes back to the chair, focusing his eyes in concentration on the screen. His hands smooth the worn denim of his jeans methodically as tears fill his eyes, run down his cheeks. He feels the sudden, chill prick as they drop from his chin on to his jacket. Nearly morning now. Outside the window he can see faint streaks of light, separating the trees from their background of sky. Six-thirty already. On the television, a *Sunrise Semester* course in astronomy. Soon the light inside the room will match the grayness on the screen.

He gets up again, to go to the bathroom, taking a leak, washing his hands, staring at himself in the mirror. He can barely make out the contours of his face. His heart is pounding slow and full, keeping time with the cracking headache that has ignited behind his eyes. He leaves the bathroom, going to sit in the hallway, beside the telephone. It will be seven soon. People get up, then. It is not too early to call.

He looks up the number in the book: on Judson Avenue in Evanston, his home number. Waiting, he stares at the faded wallpaper, a pattern of eagles and stars in gold and blue and dull red. As he traces it with his eyes another pattern emerges. Wings and talons, a sideways stripe across the wall. It begins to move and his stomach heaves. He quickly dials the number.

It is Berger's voice at the other end: "Hullo."

"This is Conrad," he says. Tears blind him. His throat closes up.

"Conrad? Are you there?"

"I need to see you," he whispers.

"Yes. Okay. Can you make it to the office in half an hour? Come in through the back. The front doesn't open up until eight. I'll prop it for you."

"All right."

He replaces the receiver; goes upstairs for his wallet and his keys. He scribbles a note to his grandparents, leaving it on the telephone stand. *Had to leave early. See you tonight after school.* The writing looks stiff and jerky to him.

Nearly light as he gets into the car. He wipes his eyes, wipes his hands on his pants again. *This is how people get in accidents keep calm keep calm.* He grips the wheel tightly, his wrists aching, his head throbbing as the grayness around him washes away to chilly March sunshine. It is thin, without power. A huge truck, gears grinding, lurches past on the Edens and he fights the panic that engulfs him, trying to think of nothing but the mechanics of driving. *Now a red light, now stop, now watch the car in front of you turning left.* It feels like the very first time he has been behind the wheel. He tries to stay in his own lane, tries not to swerve, to keep his foot on the gas constant and even. He focuses his eyes carefully on nothing but the road ahead.

27

The light is on, and he pushes the door open. He stands a moment in the waiting room.

"You made good time."

He moves to the doorway. Berger is in the corner, filling the coffeepot. He says, over his shoulder, "You gonna come in and sit down?"

Outside the window, down below, a truck rattles slowly up the street. He is fumbling for the zipper on his jacket, but he cannot find it. There are pockets of tears behind his eyes. His throat aches. He stands, motionless in the doorway.

"It might help if you just let it out, Con."

Not the words but the use of his name that releases him, and he comes slowly forward to sit in front of the desk. The tears roll down his cheeks.

"I need something—"

"Okay," Berger says. "Tell me."

But old and powerful voices slam into him. He covers his face. *He is back in the hospital again back in B Ward the night of the burning Robbie Clay his friend a bachelor certified public accountant the joker always laughing his sister had committed him "First I was a certified public now I am publicly certified!" that night no jokes no laughter*

*but an agony of sound the roaring of a bull Robbie
had burned himself with matches a rag tied around
his waist soaked in alcohol where had he gotten it?
Nobody knew they knew only that he had hurled
himself into the void it could happen to any of them
it lay like a disease over the floor the nurses walking by talking late that night they passed his room
he heard the words "penis, scrotum and thigh" and
a wave of dizziness nausea sweeping over him he
had gone to stand facing the corner of his room
hands on the wall and Leo had found him "Baby
he's okay you don't have to worry about Robbie" he
had snarled "Stay the hell away from me!" but Leo
would not he was the only one who could get close
when he was begging loudest to be left alone laid
his hand on his back "It isn't bad he's gonna be fine"
but of course he wasn't fine moved that night up to
Three and never seen again. Buck. Robbie. Karen.
Everyone he touches he has a sudden vision of
himself naked tied down on a table his penis scrotum and thigh cut away*

"I can't!" he cries. "I can't!" He drops his head
on his arms. "You keep at me, make me talk about
things I can't talk about, I can't!"

"Is that what you came here to tell me?"

He lifts his head, holding himself tight. Control.
Control is all. He tries to clamp his throat shut over
it, to stifle the sound, but he cannot and he begins
to sob, a high, helpless coughing sound. There is no
control any more, everything is lost, and his body
heaves, drowning. His head is on his arms again, the
smell of old wood is in his nostrils, the warmth of
his own breath against his face.

"Ah, God, I don't know. I don't know, it just keeps
coming, I can't make it stop!"

"Don't, then."

"I can't! I can't get through this! It's all hanging
over my head!"

"What's hanging over your head?"

"I don't know!" He looks up, dazed, drawing a deep breath. "I need something, I want something —I want to get off the hook!"

"For what?"

He begins to cry again. "For killing him, don't you know that? For letting him drown!"

"And how did you do that?" Berger asks.

But it is coming from some part of him that is separate and unknown. He is helpless against it, hits his fist hard against the desktop. "I don't know, I just know that I did!" Head cradled on his arms again, he sobs. Cannot think, cannot think, no way out of this endless turning and twisting. Hopeless.

"You were on opposite sides of the boat," Berger says, "so you couldn't even see each other. Right?"

He nods his head as he sits up. He scratches his cheek, staring at Berger through the slits of his eyes. The itching creeps downward, under his pajama top.

"And he was a better swimmer than you. He was stronger, he had more endurance."

"Yes."

"So, what is it you think you could have done to keep him from drowning?"

Tears flood his eyes again. He wipes them roughly away with his hand.

"I don't know. Something."

It is always this way. His mind shuts down. He cannot get by this burden, so overpowering that it is useless to look for a source, a beginning point. There is none.

"You don't understand," he says. "It has to be somebody's fault. Or what was the whole goddamn point of it?"

"The point of it," Berger says, "is that it happened."

"No! That's not it! That is too simple—"

"Kiddo, let me tell you a story," Berger says. "A very simple story. About this perfect kid who had a

206

younger brother. A not-so-perfect kid. And all the time they were growing up, this not-so-perfect kid tried to model himself after his brother, the perfect kid. It worked, too. After all, they were a lot alike, and the not-so-perfect kid was a very good actor. Then, along came this sailing accident, and the impossible happened. The not-so-perfect kid makes it. The other kid, the one he has patterned his whole life after, isn't so lucky. So, where is the sense in that, huh? Where is the justice?"

"There isn't any," he says dully.

Berger holds up his hand. "Wait a second, let me finish. The justice, obviously, is for the not-so-perfect kid to become that other, perfect kid. For everybody. For his parents and his grandparents, his friends, and most of all, himself. Only, that is one hell of a burden, see? So, finally, he decides he can't carry it. But how to set it down? No way. A problem without a solution. And so, because he can't figure out how to solve the problem, he decides to destroy it." Berger leans forward. "Does any of this make sense to you?"

"I don't know," he says. "I don't know."

"It is a very far-out act of self-preservation, do you get that, Con? And you were right. Nobody needs you to be Buck. It's okay to just be you."

"I don't know who that is any more!" he cries.

"Yeah, you do," Berger says. "You do. Con, that guy is trying so hard to get out, and he's never gonna be the one to hurt you, believe me. Let him talk. Let him tell you what you did that was so bad. Listen, you know what you did? You hung on, kiddo. That's it. That's your guilt. You can live with that, can't you?"

He cannot answer, does not have an answer. He leans back against the chair. He feels as if he is seeing Berger through a curtain of mist. The air shimmers between them. He is lightheaded, his bones fragile, without substance, like scraps of paper.

"The thing that hurts you," Berger says, "is sitting on yourself. Not letting yourself connect with your own feelings. It is screwing you up, leading you off on chases that don't go anywhere. You get any sleep last night?"

He shakes his head.

"How about food? You had anything to eat since yesterday?"

"No—" He starts to say that he is not hungry, that he is too tired to eat, but Berger is on his feet and heading for the door, and he stumbles along behind him, unable to voice a protest, down the stairway and out into the street, dragged along by the force and flow of Berger's monologue.

"Geez, if I could get through to you, kiddo, that depression is not sobbing and crying and *giving vent,* it is plain and simple *reduction of feeling.* Reduction, see? Of all feeling. People who keep stiff upper lips find that it's damn hard to smile."

The restaurant is called Nick's. The lettering is spread, in red, block letters, across the front window. It has a dirty, neglected look about it, but inside it is clean and warm and cheerful. Berger picks out a table by the window. He pushes back the blue-and-white checked curtains so they can look out on the street. He orders for them both: orange juice, toast, bacon and eggs, coffee. He spreads his napkin across his lap, looking around, smiling at everyone—the two plump, dark-haired waitresses, Nick in the kitchen, a table of burly Greeks.

Conrad sits in the chair, hands between his legs. He is exhausted, his eyes swollen and tight. He looks down at his hands, at his fingernails, bitten to the quick again. He doesn't remember doing that. Narrowing his eyes, he blends everything to gray—the curtains, the walls painted with huge, atomic grapevines and leaves, the dark, gorilla-like man across the table from him.

"The little girl in Skokie is what started all this, am I right?" Berger asks quietly. "Crawford called me last night. He was pretty shook, too."

"Oh God," he says.

Berger hands him his handkerchief.

"Kiddo, you know the statistics. Out of every hundred, fifty are gonna try it again. Fifteen eventually make it."

He had thought himself empty of tears, but without warning they start up again. He covers his face with his hands. "Don't," he says.

The waitress brings their breakfast, and he blows his nose, then props his elbows on the table. "She was okay," he says. "She was fine. Into everything at school, and happy. She told me to—to be less intense, and relax and enjoy life. Shit, it isn't fair!"

"You're right. It isn't fair," Berger says. "I'm sorry. I'm damn sorry for her, the poor kid. Crazy world. Or maybe it's just the crazy view we have of it, looking through a crack in the door, never being able to see the whole room, the whole picture, I don't know." He runs his hands through his hair. "Listen, eat," he says. "You'll feel better once you eat."

But he is too exhausted to eat; he takes a few tentative bites of the eggs; pushes the plate from him. No go. Too risky.

"Come on," Berger urges.

"I can't," he says. His legs feel as if they were weighted to the floor. "I don't know what I would have done if I couldn't have gotten you this morning. I felt so shaky."

"And now?"

He closes his eyes. "Still shaky."

Berger laughs. "That's what I like about you, kiddo. You got style. Listen, what happened this morning was that you let yourself feel some pain. Feeling is not selective, I keep telling you that. You can't feel pain, you aren't gonna feel anything else, either. And the world is full of pain. Also joy. Evil. Goodness. Horror and love. You name it, it's there. Sealing yourself off is just going through the motions, get it?"

He opens his eyes to study the ceiling, too tired to comment, even to think of a comment.

"Go home and get some sleep. You look whipped."

"I can't. My grandmother would hassle me all day. I can't take the flak. She might even call my father and tell him I cut school."

"So, go to your own house. You've got a key, haven't you?"

He sits up. "Yeah, I do. I should have thought of that."

Berger laughs again. "You would have. When are your parents due back?"

"Not until Wednesday."

"Okay, go home, rest up, eat something, hear?"

"Should I come tomorrow? For my appointment?"

"Sure."

"It's okay for me to go, you think?"

"What d'you mean?"

"You don't think I'll do anything crazy?"

"Like what?" Berger asks. "Give yourself a haircut or something? You're a big boy. You're not gonna punish yourself for something you didn't do."

"All right."

"And anyway, punishment doesn't do a damn thing for the guilt, does it? It doesn't make it go away. And it doesn't earn you any forgiveness."

"No," he says wearily.

"So, what's the point of it, then?"

Berger walks him to the car. As he gets in, tears well up again behind his eyelids. For so long he has shielded himself from hurt, not letting it be inflicted upon him. Suddenly he is naked, unprotected, and the air is full of flying glass. All his senses are raw, open to wounding.

He wipes his eyes. "I'll see you tomorrow."

"Drive carefully."

He lets himself in through the kitchen. The air inside is heavy with the sweetish odor of too ripe fruit. Or furniture polish? He goes upstairs to his bedroom, laying his keys and his wallet on the dresser, opening the window, slightly.

He turns on the shower and strips down, leaving his clothes in a pile on the floor. He gets in; adjusts the water to as hot as he can stand it. He does his best thinking in here. The heat relaxes the clots inside his brain, making the juices flow, and he leans his forehead against the wall, hands behind his back, as the warmth spreads downward from his neck to his shoulders, his buttocks, the backs of his knees.

He closes his eyes, sees Berger, a confident, sly gorilla riding a unicycle in a red felt jacket, eating a banana. Berger smiles and waves. Gorillas don't ride unicycles, though. The only one he has ever seen sat inside a huge truck tire suspended from a chain in his cage at the zoo. He rocked back and forth, sticking his tongue out at the world. Making judgments. He and Buck pondered the primitive intelligence of this gesture: *People laugh but maybe he knows something,* Buck said. *We wouldn't laugh if he gave us the finger, would we?*

Guilt. Is not punishment Berger said. Guilt is simply guilt. A run-in he and Buck had years ago, with a clerk in a drugstore. He said they had not paid for two comic books, wouldn't believe them. He had threatened to call their father and expose them to the world as liars and thieves. *Go ahead* Buck said with scorn *My dad knows we don't lie and he knows we don't take things. What do I care what you think?* But he, Conrad, had cared desperately, and had felt, even as he knew he was innocent, guilty and shamed by it. Why?

Because it has always been easier to believe himself capable of evil than to accept evil in others. But that doesn't make sense. The clerk in the drugstore wasn't evil, just mistaken. Bad judgment doesn't make you evil—can he only see these two opposites—good and evil? Innocence and guilt? Is it necessary to believe others guilty in order for himself to be proved innocent? There is a way through this, an opening, if only he can find it. He stands very still, letting water sluice over his shoulders and river into the creases of his stomach to his crotch.

"——*C'mon!*"

"——*No. I changed my mind.*"

"——*C'mon, you promised!*"

"——*Why do I always have to go first?*"

They are eight and nine the leader and the follower as always in the garage that day with the door closed stuffy and hot in here and Buck is abruptly disgusted with him.

"——*Ah, forget it, big-ass baby! I said you could do it to me after!*"

Buck turns away tossing the clothesline to the floor, and as always with freedom in sight he opts for prison it is easier to face than Buck's cool contempt he stands obediently still as Buck ties his hands behind his back sits then as the rope is lashed around his ankles Buck pulls a handkerchief from his pocket "How can you make me talk if you gag me?" and Buck considers "First we torture you. Then we make you talk" but he is no longer sure turns his head just as Buck discovers you don't need permission when you have the power forces him back against the cement floor sprawls across him while he ties the handkerchief around his mouth it is clean and smells faintly of his father abruptly for him the game is over terrified he struggles to free himself fights the gag choking a peculiar hollow clonging sound the garage door opening a shadow falls across them a cool breeze entering "What the hell is this?" he is pulled to his feet the ropes roughly loosened the gag snatched from his mouth not relief but horror as he sees Buck's pants jerked down to his knees his father's hand cracking across the bare ass Buck howls in protest while he stands in helpless terror waiting for his punishment only a game but they had both been playing it and then his father's anger is mysteriously spent and he kneels on the garage floor, an arm around Buck's shoulders Buck is sobbing his head down "Don't you ever do a thing like that again, Bucky, you understand?"

"——But I wasn't gonna hurt him, Daddy——"

"——People get hurt without anyone meaning it, don't you see?"

For some inexplicable reason he was left out of this. Passed over. His shame and guilt ignored. It must have been too monstrous to mention. His crime, his part in it, and so he had to suffer alone. But what for? There is no evil there, after all. Just a boy's game, dangerous maybe, but not evil, and not Buck's fault, not his either. Nobody's fault. It happened, that's all. Not so frightening, is it? To believe them both innocent *Oh God*. His sinuses are packed with a spongy material. Tears leak out from beneath his eyelids. Resigned, he lets them come as he soaps himself carefully: his arms, his shoulders, and his back; his legs, between his legs. He stands and lets the water run over his head, washing his hair. When he is finished, he gets out, towels himself dry. Slowly and carefully he turns his arms up to look at the insides of his wrists.

In grade school a girl named Sally Willet sat next to him. She had taken his hand in hers one day, those strong, brown fingers tracing the creases in his palm, showing him his lifeline, curving beside the heel of his hand almost to his wrist: a deep and definite mark. He draws a ragged breath, wondering about Karen, about her lifeline. Was it a long one, too?

Tears of grief this time *Not fair not fair!* no, but life is not fair always, or sane, or good, or anything. It just *is*.

He hangs up the towels in the bathroom and turns off the light. He puts on clean underwear, picking up his dirty clothes, throwing them down the clothes chute. All the while the hot oily liquid seeps out from beneath his eyelids. He continues to blink it back, to wipe it away.

Reduction of feeling. At least he is not guilty of that today. He sets the alarm on his clock-radio, stripping back the covers on his bed. He climbs in and cleanliness surrounds him, its smell cool and seductive. He rolls to his face and, without a sound, without a thought, he sleeps.

28

The air is balmy and fresh as they sit on the patio, watching the boys swim. It is cool this evening for the adults, and, besides, Cal is content to sip his martini, savoring the sharp, juniper smell of it as it mixes with the heavier perfume of the surrounding air. Magnolia. Around the pool the stiff, strawlike grass gives off a mossy odor.

Ward raises his glass. "To your low total the first day."

"No," Audrey says. "To that thirty-foot putt on the fifteenth hole. I was poking everybody around me. 'Hey, that's my brother-in-law!' "

"You did look good, Cal," Beth says.

He grins. "At isolated moments."

"Well, you didn't really expect to win," Ward says.

"Hell, no!"

But that is the funny part, or maybe not so funny. After Saturday, when he saw that he could do it, that he had a good chance of doing it, he had tightened up. Those three double bogeys on easy holes. If he could have dropped a few more lucky putts like the one on the fifteenth. *You didn't expect to win.* Maybe that's it. You get what you expect.

"Why don't we go out and celebrate anyway?" Ward asks. "How about it, you both like Mexican food? Or we could go to the Captain's Table, whatever you want."

"That'd be nice," Audrey says. "Let's go there."

"I'll check to see if we need reservations. What time? Nine? Ten?"

"Whenever you say."

Audrey gets up, too. "I'll put some hamburgers on for the boys. Keep an eye on them, will you?"

Beth nods, and they are left alone on the patio, as Charlie and Kerry splash and shout under the diving board at the opposite end of the pool.

"Having fun?" he asks her.

She smiles. "Yes. Are you?"

"Sure."

"I'm sorry you didn't win."

"Me too."

"But third place is good, Cal."

"Third place," he says, sipping his drink, "is third place."

"I've been thinking," she says, "that we should play more golf together. Maybe our next vacation should be strictly golf. We could go to Pinehurst, or Myrtle Beach."

"Sounds great," Cal says. "I bet he'd like that, too."

A short silence. Then, "Do you do that deliberately? Or is it a reflex action? I'm curious."

"Do what?"

"Insert him into the conversation. Whenever I mention you and I doing something together."

"I'm sorry," he says. "You said vacation. I guess I assumed that you meant him, too."

"I'm surprised that you haven't felt the need to call him since we've been here."

"I was going to do it tonight."

She laughs. "It must be hard to grow up when your father is breathing down your neck all the time. I think I would hate it."

He gets up; goes to stand near the edge of the pool, watching Charlie tip himself off the end of the board, backward, arms outstretched, screaming; the drowning-man bit. He gazes then at the magnolia tree, those pink knots of petals glowing eerily in the dusk. Behind him he hears the patio door slide open. Ward says, "Everything all set. Nine-thirty. We've got time for one more round, folks."

"I don't think I'll have another," Beth says. "I'm going to dress."

"Nothing fancy, Sissie. You look fine just the way you are."

The best time of year to be here. Everything fresh and green. Later on, Audrey told him, the sun, the heat bakes everything, people and plants, to a hard, nut-brown, and you have to stay in out of it; you live the air-conditioned life. Pure and perfect and artificial.

He turns and hands his glass to Ward, who has come up beside him. "I'll have one. Light on the vermouth, okay?"

"Always, always."

And again, he lets himself drink too much, not out of boredom this time. Out of anger at her, maybe. Out of fear. Out of whatever it is that is happening to them, that he does not want to see, and doesn't see when he is high and feeling good.

"One more!" Ward is gay, when they arrive home, clinking bottles at the bar, he and Audrey giggling together as if they didn't know how they had been used tonight. Intermediaries. She would not look at him all night. They skirted the edges of conversations, shielding themselves from each other, letting Ward and Audrey do the work. Without speaking now, without looking at each other, they sit on opposite sides of the small, cosy living room, the silence between them far from empty. It is hostile. Full of unspoken words. From tonight, from before tonight, from who knows how far back? He doesn't. He is sure she doesn't, either. But he is sick of the brooding, sick of *dwelling,* nothing gets spoken, nothing resolved, circles and more circles.

"There's a bottle in the garage," Ward is saying. "Honey, would I let us run out of Tía Maria, knowing how you love it?"

"Yes, you would!"

"I wouldn't! I bought it, I swear, this afternoon, only I set it on the workbench—"

"Well, get it!"

"You come on with me."

"No."

"Come on, I've got something else to show you—"

"Ward, you're rotten!"

But she goes with him and they are left with the silence. Beth picks up a magazine and leafs through it, and his anger ignites.

"Why don't we finish it?" he asks.

She looks up. "Finish what?"

"What you started out there tonight."

"I started? How did I start it? By suggesting we go away together on a vacation? And I didn't stop it, either, you did. You were the one who walked away from me, remember?"

"What the hell was I supposed to say to that? The old song and dance, I overprotect, I breathe down his neck."

"You do."

"It's a matter of opinion."

"Right. So there's no point in discussing it further. We never agree."

"I think there's a point."

"Why are you so obsessed?" she snaps. "God, I am sick of talking, talking, talking about *him!* He controls you, even when he's not around, even when he's two thousand miles away."

"Oh, stop it. We haven't exchanged a dozen words

about him in months—that isn't the problem. *He* isn't the problem."

"Isn't he?"

"No! So let's talk about what's really bothering you."

"Oh, no, let's talk about what's bothering *you!* That's what you want, isn't it? That's why you go around moping and depressed—just the way you used to! As if it helped, being half-alive, dragging everybody else down with you!"

"What the hell are you talking about?"

"I'm talking about last year! Last spring, when you couldn't answer the phone, couldn't open your mail without wondering if it would be the hospital with more bad news."

"Goddammit, sure I was depressed! But I wasn't too depressed to go to Europe, was I? I wasn't too depressed to take you to Spain and Portugal—"

"Goddamn Spain. And *goddamn* Portugal. If you're going to quote him, then quote him!"

"I am not quoting him! I am quoting myself! I am . . ." He struggles for control, his senses blurred. Important. This is important, don't screw it up, don't get off on old songs, old dances. "I am asking you to tell me," he says slowly, "what I've done that's made you so angry with me."

"It's not what you've done," she says. "It's what you think I've done."

"What you've done." He lets the words sink in, trying to get the message. There is no message, nothing coming through. "I don't know what you mean, I don't think you've done anything."

"Oh, you liar," she says bitterly. "You do, and you know it. You blame me for the whole thing."

"For what whole thing?"

"That whole vicious thing! He made it as vicious, as sickening as he could! The blood—all that blood! Oh, I will never forgive him for it! He wanted it to kill me, too!"

And suddenly she is crying. Painful, desperate sobs that shake her shoulders. Her hands are over her face, her head bent to her knees. Bewildered and frightened, he goes to her, kneeling beside her chair, trying to put his arm around her, but she will not permit it.

"Leave me alone! You got what you wanted, leave me alone, I don't want any of your *goddamn* false sympathy!"

"I got—I didn't—Beth, I love you, honey, please, let me help." He fumbles stupidly at her side, and her head jerks up. She looks at him stiffly, her eyes hard.

"Help? What do you mean, help? I don't need it. Not your kind of help. I can help myself."

Carefully she wipes her eyes. Ward and Audrey are standing in the doorway.

"Hey," Ward says softly, "I'm sorry about this. We don't want to butt in."

"You're not butting in!" Beth says. She starts to cry again, and Cal stands up, turning away from her, close to tears, himself. He goes to the window, looking out at the pool, at the shadows of trees and bushes on the cement.

"Don't you understand what he was saying?" she asks. "He was saying, 'Look! Look what you made me do!' "

"Why?" he asks. "Why was he saying that?"

"I don't know! I wish I knew!" She sobs, and then her voice is calm, more subdued, and she speaks slowly. "I just know how people try to manipulate other people."

"Oh God, Beth, I don't believe that! I don't believe he went all that way to try to manipulate us! What happened—what he did—he did it to him*self!* Can't you see anything except in terms of how it affects you?"

"No! Neither can you! Neither does anybody else! Only, maybe I'm more honest than the rest of you, maybe I'm more willing to recognize that I do it.

You're right," she says, her voice low and strained, "he didn't do it to you. He only did it to me. I don't know what he wants from me, and I've never known! Does he want me to throw my arms around him when he passes a chemistry exam? I can't do it! I can't respond, when someone says, 'Here, I just did this great thing, so love me for it!' I can't!"

"I don't think he wants that," Cal says. "I think he just wants to know that you don't hate him."

"Hate him? How could I hate him? Mothers don't hate their sons! I don't hate him! But he makes *demands* on me! He tries to blackmail me!" She looks up at him. "Where did you get that? About my hating him? Did he tell you that about me? Is that what he told you up in his room?"

"Beth—"

"And you let him say that to you?" Her voice is trembling. "You see? How you accept his feelings without question? But you can't do the same for me, can you?"

Ward moves toward her. "Honey."

"I don't know what you want from me any more, Cal. I don't know what anybody wants from me!"

"Honey, nobody wants anything from you," Ward says. "We all just want—Cal and Con and everybody, we all just want you to be happy."

"Happy!" She looks at him. "Oh, Ward! You give us all the definition, will you? But first you'd better check on those kids. Every day, to make sure they're good and safe, that nobody's fallen off a horse, or gotten hit by a car, or drowned in that swimming pool you're so proud of!"

"Beth!" Audrey says, turning her back, her hands to her face.

"And then you come and tell me how to be happy."

He closes his eyes, not listening any more, letting blackness surround him, blackness into last year, when he stood outside the bathroom door, begging to be let in. No sound, the silence was screaming at him.

He didn't want to know, didn't want to believe it was happening *Con, open the door! Let me in!* His shoulder bouncing, crashing against the door, the jamb splintering, giving way to the nightmare of blood, the towels soaked with it, leaking their overflow onto the rug, the floor. His arm curved, hiding his face. A sea-fan of dried blood on the wall behind his head.

And in the hospital. *Let me die.* His eyes bright with the drugs they had given him, strapped down in the high, criblike bed, his face pale against the green emergency-room sheets. *I want to die.*

In shock, watching the bottle, upside down in its rack as it drained healing liquid into that arm. In shock, unable to think, already broken by the note they had found on his desk: *I wish I knew why but I just don't.*

After the accident, after they had towed the boat in, on the way from the dock to the hospital, he had moaned over and over, "Mama, I'm sorry! Dad, I'm sorry, I'm sorry!"

That second time. There had been no apology. A bloody, vicious thing. She is right. It hasn't killed her, but it has done something to her; something terrible. Circles and more circles, where does it end? How can it end?

29

The moon scuds from behind a cloud, a flat, pale slice of light. The air smells of darkness, of endless space, as he stands on the porch, an extension of it, and Beth, inside reading, Conrad upstairs doing his homework, all, all extensions of it. Space. And time. These dimensions that embrace him, control him.

This afternoon on the plane, Beth sat, fragile and untouchable beside him, and he had left her alone at last, knowing that if he tried to approach her, she would simply move her seat. *Let her move her seat, let her believe what she believes, you cannot change her anyway, you are not God, you do not know and you are not in control, so let go.*

He has finished the work he promised Ray he would have done by tomorrow.

Conrad teased him when he saw him seated in the den, his books and papers piled around him. "The indispensable man, huh?"

It had made him flinch. Another illusion hits the dirt. This feeling that he has existed *in order to* understand, to control, to predict. This idea that he was *necessary.* To organizations, to his family, to his wife. To life. All these things, including himself—they exist all right, but not *because of anything.*

Then, are no decisions required? Is there nothing to be done? No action to be taken?

Right. Sit tight. *Never confuse movement with action,* says Hemingway. She had been reading him one day. She told him that, declaring her agreement with his statement. Maybe she won't then. Confuse movement with action. *Lie back. Don't be hasty. Haste makes waste.* He is inundated with Howardisms suddenly; all true, those old and wrinkled maxims, proverbs, clichés. *A rolling stone gathers no moss.* Well, who needs moss anyway? *Oh, hell.* He is abruptly disgusted with himself. *Do not clutch so at things, it is useless, useless. And do not be paralyzed. It is better to move than to be unable to move, because you fear loss so much: loss of order, loss of security, loss of predictability.*

Better sometimes not to know what to expect. Like tonight at dinner. She was perfect, The perfect wife, the perfect mother, the perfect hostess. Conrad picked the restaurant—Naroff's—the small Italian place in Highwood. And Conrad did all the talking, while she and Cal listened, quietly attentive. Once she reached out to pull the collar of his shirt from under the neck of Conrad's black pullover, and he sat, not moving under her touch, but drinking in every ounce of her attention, knowing that, mysteriously, he had done something right tonight, maybe just walking in the door and being glad to see them, or maybe it was his description of the impromptu picnic on the school lawn in thirty-degree weather, to celebrate the coming of spring.

"—and we damn near froze our asses off!"

And, when he refused dessert, even her correcting his table manners seemed right and proper: "You don't need to say, 'I'm full.' Just 'No, thanks' is sufficient."

"Sure. Okay. Wait, let me write that down, will you?"

"You've got a mind, haven't you? Just retain it."

"—I've told you fifty times!" he teased her.

Now he stands on the stairs, as Cal comes back inside.

"I'm going to bed," he says. "See you in the morning."

"All through studying?" Cal asks.

He nods. "It's just a quiz in trig. Shouldn't be hard. I'm tired. It was sort of a rough week."

"What happened?" he asks. "Your grandmother give you a hard time?"

"No. Nothing like that. She was fine. I'm just—I'm glad you're back, that's all."

And he goes to *her*, then, without any hesitation; it is what he has come downstairs for, obviously. He bends his head, puts an arm around her in a quick, clumsy embrace.

"G'night." His voice is thick. He exits swiftly, his face turned away.

She sits on the couch, her legs curled under her, the book in her lap, just as he has left her. She is staring off into space. Then, after a moment, her head drops over her book again, her hair spilling over her shoulder. Her face is hidden from Cal, also.

30

"Already I'm thinking about next fall," Jeannine says. "Isn't that dumb? I don't want to go away now."

They are sitting on the floor in her living room, their backs against the couch, as Conrad picks out chords on Mike's guitar. Conrad has Mike's cowboy hat on, pulled low over his eyes.

"I don't want you to go, either," he says.

"Don't you?" She reaches up to snatch the hat from his head, but he grabs her wrist.

"Ah, ah, no you don't—" He settles the hat more firmly on his head. "Why don't you hang around here for another year? Wait for me?"

"I can't," she says.

"You can't."

"No. Did you write that, Con? It's beautiful. Play it again."

"It's not anything special. Just note patterns. Fooling around. Here's a good one." And he plays her the song he has composed upstairs in his bedroom over the past week. He loves doing this; the mathematics of it, organizing the notes into definite pictures. She sits watching him, elbows on her knees, chin in her hands.

"I love it. Let's notate it, okay? I've got some paper. Here, play it again. It's so lovely and clean—"

He laughs. "I've got some dirty ones, too."

"No, I mean it's neat. Pleasant and orderly and neat."

"Those are horrible adjectives. Rapturous. Passionate. Use those. Pleasant and neat do not make it."

He fingers the chords, one at a time, and she copies them briskly on staff paper.

"You should write words for this one."

"I'm not too good at that."

"You used to write poetry, didn't you?"

"Who told you that?" he asks. "Lazenby?"

She nods. "Are you mad?"

"No. Surprised, though. How did he happen to tell you?"

She smiles at him. "How do you think? I asked him. I said, 'Tell me everything you know about Conrad Jarrett.' So he did."

He laughs. "The hell you did!"

"The hell I didn't," she says calmly. "You were the mysterious figure. I wanted to know about you."

"Mysterious? I was just scared, that's all."

"I saw Suzanne in school today."

"—Suzanne—"

"—Mosely. She asked me if I was still going out with you. I said yes. Then she asked me if I was 'serious,' or was I just having a good time?"

He looks at her from under the hat. "What did you say?"

"I said 'both.' She's crazy about you, Con."

"I'm sure!"

"She is. She told me she was. She told me that you were the only nice boy in the whole school, and she would be very disappointed in me if I were just fooling around with you."

"I can't believe she said that. She never even talks to me—"

"She's shy. She has a terrific inferiority complex."

"Tell her to join the club."

"You tell her."

He snorts. "That is not my style."

"Oh? And what is your style?"

He grins at her. "Well, on Friday nights, I perform bakery B and E's and babysit with some twerpy eleven-year-old and his sister."

"That's a joke, isn't it? You performing a B and E, I mean. You, who couldn't even say hello in the hall, unless I said it first."

"Hey, that's not true. There were always guys around you, what was I supposed to do?"

"Oh, sure. Well, at least they were friendly, they paid some attention."

"I paid attention," he says. "I paid a lot of attention in my mind. I used to sneak looks all the time in choir. I like to look at you." To illustrate, he pulls the cowboy hat lower over his eyes. They sit, side by side, he playing and she notating, until he is tired of it, and stretches his arm back over his head to drop the guitar on the couch.

"Enough."

"If you don't write them down, you'll forget them."

"If I forget 'em, they weren't worth writing down anyway."

"That isn't true. You certainly don't have a very clear idea of what you do well," she says, "and what you don't do well."

"I don't?" He tilts the hat back to look at her. "What don't I do well?"

She laughs. "I knew you'd say that. Okay. You don't accept compliments gracefully. Like, when I told you how much my mother likes you—"

"I'm just waiting for the rest of it, that's all. My mother likes you, my brother likes you, thanks for everything and I'll see you around."

"Oh, you're hopeless, you really are."

But she is not laughing. Instead she is looking at him with a solemn, wide open expression. His mouth is suddenly dry, his head feels queerly light. A highway is moving toward him and he is on it, traveling with such force and speed, all his senses open again. He turns toward her, puts his arms around her gently. Her mouth opens under his, her breath is sweet-smelling, like apples, her eyes closed. The eyelids are small, delicate curves that he touches with his lips, his fingertips. Her tongue in his mouth, exploring. He cannot concentrate any more, gathers her against him tightly as his groin hardens, spreads warmth through his whole body. His face in the hollow of her neck, he rocks her slowly, gently in his arms.

They lie drugged and submerged, facing each other on the bed. Conrad's head is on his arm, one hand curved around her breast, eyes closed, shielding himself from the shining look of her; smooth, pale peach skin glowing in the light from the hall. His heart floats inside his chest. His skin feels branded everywhere that she has touched him, with fingers as light as bird wings. Comfortably and perfectly tired, yet his mind is engaged, recording bits and pieces. Data for assimilation, but later, later. She moves, drawing closer to him, drawing her arms inside his, her hands against his chest. He opens his eyes to look at her.

"Cold?" he whispers.

She nods and he reaches down to the foot of the bed to pull the blankets over them. Gently he asks her, because now he is her protector against the world, "Did I hurt you?" and, with his fingertips caresses again the rounded curve of her breast.

"No." She shifts her body slightly, and her knees bump against his. "I want to tell you something, Con. I'm not—you know—a virgin."

"Okay." His hand travels over her back; soft angles of shoulder blades, a hollow between.

"Do you care?"

"No."

"Do you want me to tell you?"

"You want to?"

"Maybe. I think I would feel better. It's no one I

knew here. It was a boy in Akron. We did things—"
Her voice sinks to a whisper and he must stop his hand
moving on her shoulder in order to hear her.

"After my father moved out. I felt so awful, like it
was me who was losing everyone. It was happening to
me. Not to them. My father tried to talk to me about
it, but I made up excuses, reasons for not listening to
him, I didn't want to get involved, I didn't want to
take sides. But I had already taken sides against them
both. And I wouldn't talk about it, so finally everybody just left me alone, and that hurt, too. Only I just
pretended that I didn't care a damn, not about them
or anything else. That's when it happened."

She stops to take a breath and he strokes her gently,
again. "Don't be too nice to me, okay?" she whispers.

"Okay," he says. "Why?"

"Becuse. It's not nice, the rest of it."

"Don't tell me, if you don't want to. You don't have
to, Jen."

"No, I want to. I started hanging around. You
know, with kids my parents were afraid of. They were
wild, I guess. Only not really, they were just stupid.
And I was stupid. And I started doing a lot of stupid
things with them." She sighs, her voice tired and flat.
"Nothing interesting. Nothing even unusual, just the
same old stuff. We smoked, we took pills, we junked
around. Sometimes we needed money and kids stole
stuff. I had enough money. My dad felt so bad about
me by then he was keeping me well supplied, but I
would go with them and steal, just for kicks. And then
one time we got caught. The manager of the store was
going to prosecute. He was furious, he'd had it. He
called our parents, got them down to the store—and,
Con, he knew my father. It was awful. My father
talked and talked to him, and finally he talked him
out of taking us to court. I don't know how he did it.
The man said he thought that he might be making a
mistake, letting us off, but he was doing it anyway,
and we were to stay the hell out of his store, period.

And my father cried——" She stops, suddenly, her hand over her face. He holds her tenderly against him.

"Anyway," she says, "at first I was just so relieved to have gotten out of it that I didn't think about anything else. But then I started to feel sick about myself. About what I was doing to myself. Not my mom, or my dad, but *me*. *I* did it. Why? Why did I want to hurt myself like that? So stupid, so stupid. I shouldn't be telling you this."

"Why not?"

"Because. What you must think."

"I don't think anything," he says.

"I'm so ashamed, I'm still so ashamed. That's why we moved here, you know. My mother thought it was Akron. But it wasn't Akron, it was me."

He shifts his position slightly, to ease the pressure of her body across his arm. He kisses her hair, her eyelids, tastes salt, wetness. It makes him want her again, but it is too soon, too feeble. He doesn't want to dilute that first powerful moment, wants to lie still, thinking about it. As if she reads his mind, she whispers, "Let's just talk, okay?"

And they sit up, then, with the sheet pulled up, their backs against the headboard of her bed, holding hands. She turns his arm up. The fingertips of her other hand brush lightly against the scar on his wrist.

"Did it hurt?"

"No," he says. "I don't think so. I don't remember."

"Would you rather not talk about it?"

"I don't know. I've never talked about it. To doctors, but not to anyone else."

Her fingers on the scar send out strange vibrations from nerve endings that are not completely healed. He wonders if they will ever be.

"Why did you do it?"

"I don't know. It was like falling into a hole and it keeps getting bigger and bigger, you can't get out. And then all of a sudden it's inside you, it *is* you, and you're trapped, and it's all over."

"I know," she says, "I know that feeling." She holds his hand lightly. "It seems right at the time. What is it that makes hurting yourself seem like the right thing to do?"

"I don't know," he says. "I don't even know why I don't feel that way any more."

"Listen," she says, "I was counting on you for some answers."

"Can't help you, sorry." Leaning away from her, he reaches down beside the bed, fumbling for the cowboy hat he has dropped there. He squeezes its soft crown; presses the hat low over his eyes. "These same questions I ask myself, over and over," he drawls. "And then I answer myself. I say, 'How the fuck do I know?'"

She laughs. "Why won't you take anything seriously?"

He lies down flat, the hat over his face. "No sense taking the questions seriously, if there aren't any answers."

"Con. Do you believe people are punished for the things they do?"

"Punished? You mean by God?"

"Yes."

"I don't believe in God," he says.

She lifts the hat up off his face. "Not at all?"

"It isn't a question of degree, I don't think. Either you do or you don't."

They are silent for a moment. "I believe in God," she says.

"Okay."

She turns toward him, and the ends of her hair fall lightly against his chest. "What do you believe in?"

"Oh, tennis courts, wallpaper," he says, "Florsheim shoes, Miami Beach——"

"Liar," she says, her arms sliding around his neck.

"——you," he says, kissing her.

"Liar again, but that's nice."

And he squeezes her tightly, feeling the sense of

calm, of peace slowly gathering, spreading itself within him. He is in touch for good, with hope, with himself, no matter what. Berger is right, the body never lies.

31

She left the telling of it up to him.

"You're the expert in human relations. You handle it."

Said calmly, as she was packing. He had felt the accusation behind it. When they talk now it is to hurl accusation and contradiction at each other. Rebuke. Revelation. But it all falls between them. No bridges are formed. The water gets muddier. Solutions do not surface.

"I don't understand why you're leaving!" he says.

"Because I can't stand the way you look at me. I can't stand that 'Poor Beth, poor old you' expression on your face."

"I don't believe you. I don't believe that's it. I'm not looking at you any differently—"

"When you suggested a counselor," she says, "that's when I knew."

"Counseling! I said counseling, for both of us."

"No! You're the one who isn't happy any more, can't you see that? You haven't been for a long time, Cal. You go and see a counselor, if you want. You do what you need to do."

"What I need," he says, "is for us to talk to each other! I want to talk to you, Beth, but when I try you freeze me out."

"Well, what do you expect from an emotional cripple?" she blazes. "That's what you've been trying to tell me, isn't it? That's what you really think of me. I won't have it, Cal. I won't have you wringing your hands over me, the way you have over him."

And there are too many rooms to which he has no access; too much that he doesn't understand any more. If he could know what he used to know! But what did he really know? There is addiction here: to secrecy; to a private core within herself that is so much deeper than he ever imagined it to be. He has no such core; at least, he cannot find it, if it is there. Is it fair to deny her the right to keep it, because he hasn't this space? This need?

Nightly they argue. Daily she gets up, spending hours at Onwentsia, organizing, supervising, putting plans into operation for the nationally advertised tennis tournament the club is sponsoring. Over there, they think of her as a marvelous miracle.

"That wife of yours!" Sara Murray said to him. "I don't know how she does it! Everything organized, down to the last detail. It's marvelous, really!"

Marvelous miracle, his wife, and they have come this far, this far, and no further. In spite of love. He knows there is love, but what good is it? It cannot help them any more. He had grabbed her roughly in an argument, wanting to hit her, to knock the stubbornness out of her; him! The Clark Kent of Samuel Mumford High School, the model of gentleness as he had courted her, he would never even presume to lay an indecorous hand on her breast in those days (Ah, innocence! Ah, ignorance!), and now, what was he trying to do? Brutalize her, violate her thoughts, interject, by force if necessary, his own notions of what was right, what was *practical*. For he sees something else here: that her outer life is deceiving; that she gives the appearance of orderliness, of a cash-register practicality about herself; but inside, what he has glimpsed is not order, but chaos;

not practicality at all, but stubborn, incredible impulse.

The night he had grabbed her, he had shouted in her face, "Do you love me, Beth?"

"Stop it!" she said.

"Tell me! I want to know!"

"I feel the same way about you," she said, "that I have always felt! You are the one! You are the one who's changed!"

Howard and Ellen are thunderstruck, bewildered. And Ray said flatly, "I can't believe it, Cal. I mean, Christ, that's a fairy-tale marriage. Nancy's been holding you two up as a goddamn example for years!" So, that is the mystery of it, as others see it. Two intelligent people, why can't they understand each other? Why can't they work out their differences?

The point is that it has nothing to do with intelligence. Or understanding.

He sits this morning across the breakfast table from his son, who has made breakfast for them both, while outside the sun is shining thinly. Spring is slow in gaining strength this year. The middle of May already. The mornings are still chilly, like fall.

"Want to go outside?" Conrad asks.

"Sure." Although he really doesn't want to, shivers in the thin pullover sweater as he sits, his hands around his coffee cup, on the stone steps of the patio. Conrad, in jeans and a T-shirt, remarks about how warm it is. Also remarks that the lilacs are in bloom, and isn't this the time they usually fertilize the lawn? Not that he is looking for a job, he would much rather play tennis, but he was just curious.

A good opportunity. Start slow; start with the house. They will not be fertilizing this year; they are planning to sell the house; it is too big for them, that's obvious.

"It's always been too big, hasn't it?" Conrad asks.

Right. Only now there are other things to spend money on—college expenses next year, some investments he and Ray have been contemplating. The trip that Beth is taking.

"What trip?"

"You mother's going away for a while."

"What d'you mean? You mean, not with you?"

"No. I can't get away right now—"

"Right now?"

"She's been wanting to go for some time."

"I don't get it. Who's she going with?"

"No one," he says. "She's going to your Uncle Ward's for a week or so, and then leaving for Europe. She wants to go to Greece. Maybe to Italy."

"What is this, Dad?" he asks abruptly. "Has something happened?"

"No." Nothing has. There is nothing definite, no talk of divorce, and to say the words could make it so, could force something into existence, isn't that true? Absurd. Whatever is happening has already happened, maybe years ago, the seeds planted in their separate natures, their backgrounds, because all you can do is, finally and simply, what you can do.

"I've rented a house. In Evanston. Down by Centennial Park, near the lake."

"What does she think about that? That doesn't sound like anything she'd even like."

There is an uncomfortable pause. "The thing is, this trip could last for a while. I'm not sure how long she'll be gone." Beautiful. Beautiful story. Just a couple of holes in it so big you could put your fist through them.

"What're you saying?" he asks. "What's the deal? When is she planning on leaving?"

"She's left," he says. Stupid, stupid idea. He should not have allowed her to do it. *And since when do you allow, and not allow?* "She left this morning, before you were up."

"Why did she do that? Was she in such a damn hurry she couldn't even say good-by?" His voice is bitter. "Never mind. I know why."

"No, you don't—"

"Yeah, I do. And I see your problem, too. You can't just come out with it, can you? First you have to check around, make sure there aren't any razor blades—"

"That's not funny! You think that's funny?"

An ugly silence, while they look at each other. Then Conrad looks away. "No," he says, "I'm sorry."

"You want the truth? I don't know why she left. And neither do you, because a lot of things happen in this—this world, goddamn it!—and people don't always know the answers! I'm no authority on her! You're no authority, either!"

Conrad stares at him, stricken.

In despair, he hears himself go on: "You're no authority, period. You just think you are. You make the judgments, don't you? But nobody's supposed to make a judgment on you! Do you think that's fair?"

"No," he whispers, his eyes fixed on Cal's face.

"I don't want you to say anything like that to me again," Cal says. "I don't like jokes about it."

"Dad, I'm sorry. I really am. I mean it."

And abruptly the anger recedes, swept away in the familiar, paternal desire to blanket and protect; when he was small, and he felt that he had been wrongly accused, he would go to the hall and stand on his head at the top of the stairs: "I didn't! I didn't!" and Buck would holler, "Dad, he's gonna do it, he's gonna stand on his head on the stairs again, make him quit it!" Maybe he should do it now. Such a funny, weird little kid he was—

There is movement in the grass. He can almost feel the diamond-shafts of green pushing upward, displacing the wet, trampled earth.

"No. I'm sorry. I don't know what I'm yelling at you for."

"No," Conrad says. "That's right. You were right. You ought to do that more often."

He gives a short laugh. "Oh, yeah?"

"No, really. Haul my ass a little, tell me to shape up." A slight pause; a key change: "The way you used to do with him."

He looks up in surprise. "He needed it. You didn't. You were always so hard on yourself, I never had the heart. Besides," he says, "you were the good kid. The easy one to raise."

"Ah, Dad, don't."

"It's the truth. You were the one I never worried about. That was the problem. I should have been worrying. I wasn't even listening."

The ground is wet, and smells of smoke; it feels soft and spongy to his touch.

"I don't think I was putting out many signals, then," Conrad says carefully. "You couldn't have done anything."

"Maybe not." He gets up and walks to the edge of the patio, hands in his pockets.

Behind him, Conrad sighs. "Well, so much for what I know," he says. "I thought that things were getting better. I thought they seemed great."

"They haven't been great," he says, "for some time."

"What happened, Dad? How did everything fall apart like this? Was it Buck?" And, another change of key; "Was it me? Dad, is it me, now?"

"No," he says wearily. "It's nobody. It's nobody's fault." Over and over this same lesson to be learned; it is the way things are.

"Listen" Conrad says, "it's not—it isn't something like—somebody else?"

God, he is young, I forget sometimes how young he is. Why else do husbands and wives separate?

"No," he says. "Nothing like that." And he comes back; sits beside him on the steps again. "I told you the truth," he says. "She wanted to go away for a while. Beyond that, I don't know."

It seems to him that she is like a child who cries for

the moon; she wants things to be the way they used to be, only she will not say it, and he cannot. So whose fault is it? And what difference would it make, if they could each voice their dreads, their suspicions?

Beside him, Conrad says, "You know I used to figure you for a handle on everything. You knew it all, even though you grew up alone, with nobody looking after you—"

"I was looked after," he says. "Where'd you get that idea?"

"Yeah, but nobody was responsible," he insists. "Nobody helped you with the decisions—I've thought a lot about that. I really admired you for it. I still do."

"Well, don't admire people too much," he says, tossing the remains of his coffee into the bushes. "They disappoint you sometimes."

"I'm not disappointed," Conrad says. "I love you, man."

He winces, and his throat is tight, his eyes filled with sudden tears.

"I love you, too."

It is awkward, having all this between them; it bumps clumsily against the sentences, pushing them out of meaning, out of order. Painful, the problem he has with these particular words; they threaten to overpower him, cut off his breathing. He hooks an arm around his son's neck and is at once caught in a fierce embrace. He smooths the dark head wedged against his shoulder, brushes the hair aside at the back of his neck to touch bare skin.

Conrad pulls away, straightening himself, arms on his knees, head down. "You think she'll be back soon?"

"I don't know," he says.

"You think she's coming back at all?"

"Yeah, of course!" Of course she is. *At all, God!* That is not a thought he needs to handle today. And he will not, that's that.

"She'd better," Conrad says. He wipes his hand swiftly over his eyes. "I'm a lousy cook."

No need for any more words. The sun is warm on his back. He could fall asleep here, maybe he will, waiting for whatever comes next.

Epilogue

The house looks the same to him; the red maple, tinged
from a late-August frost, its branches extending across
the drive, is the same size as he remembered it. Somehow, he has expected change. He parks underneath the
tree and gets out of the car. Nervous. Now that he is
here. He said his good-byes to Berger today; maybe
this is too much of a good thing.

Berger had raised his arms in the familiar gesture of
confusion and benediction: "Listen, you're my prize
pupil, you know that? How about if I use you in one of
my ads?"

"Hey, don't start depending on me," he warned.

Berger just laughed. "If I ever go to mange, you be
sure to get me to a good dermatologist, you hear?"
His sweater bagging and flapping about his hips; his
hair floating. He has never known what to expect of
the guy.

He had tried, then, to thank him properly. "I want
you to know," he said, "that I revised my original
opinion, and gave you a nine."

"My lucky day," Berger said. "Remember the rip-
off man? The guy who messed up my office? I heard
from him, too. He gave me a seven."

They laughed, and Conrad issued the invitation:

"The house is only six or seven blocks from here. You ought to stop. I mean, if you do that."

"What, visit friends? Yeah, I do it occasionally. Hey, you can do the same, you know."

And right then he had gotten grabbed, missing him already. He had taken off fast, before he acted like some goddamn six-year-old who just fell off his bike or something.

Now, standing on Lazenby's front porch, he has that same, funny feeling in the pit of his stomach. He half-hopes he won't be home. He probably won't. It has been so long, he has no idea what Lazenby is doing with himself these days.

A tall, blond girl answers his ring. Here is change, at last; Lazenby's sister, Katy, all grown up. "Yes?" she asks. Then, "Connie! Oh my gosh, Ma! Guess who's here?"

They beam at him, Katy and her mother, and he is suddenly overcome with shyness.

"Joe around?"

"He's out in back, I think," Mrs. Lazenby says. "At least he was a few minutes ago."

"I'll go see."

He moves off of the porch and around the house to the back yard. Lazenby is practicing chip shots into a tree hole.

"Forward press," Conrad advises.

Lazenby looks up. Then he lowers his head, steadying himself, dropping the shot neatly into the hole.

"How's it goin'?" Conrad asks.

"Okay. Fine." He leans the nine-iron against a tree. "How about you?"

"Good."

"I heard from Jen that you moved."

"Yeah. To Evanston."

"You like it?"

"It's different. You lock your bike in your bedroom with you at night." Then, he laughs. "No, I'm kidding.

243

I like it fine. We've got a house over near the big U. In case you want to drop by sometime."

"Yeah, maybe I will." He scratches an arm contemplatively. "So where will you go to school this fall?"

"Evanston Township. I took some courses this summer. I'll be through in January."

"That's good."

They look at each other.

Conrad says, "I've been thinking."

"Good." Lazenby nods approval.

"I'm thinking I'd like to beat your ass again at golf."

"That's interesting," Lazenby says, "considering you haven't beaten it yet. What makes you think you can?"

"That swing I just saw."

Lazenby laughs. There is a sudden, awkward silence.

"So," Conrad says. "How about it? You want to play?"

"I don't know," Lazenby says. "Ma's got a pile of things lined up for me to do today."

"Okay." He backs off at once. "Next week, maybe. Call me. Or I can call you."

"You don't want me to try and get out of 'em, huh? I mean, shit, it's worth asking."

He grins. "Yeah, ask."

He waits in the back yard, while Lazenby goes inside. He studies the shades of green in the back yard, light and shadow that edge the lawn; those sharp, precise measurements, signifying order. And other things that make him feel good: the clean flight of the ball on a good drive, the graceful blue-and-orange swallows that dip and swerve across the fairways. Gestures. He is learning to interpret them now. In a letter that she wrote to his grandmother she said, "The Aegean is bluer than the Atlantic, and rough and bumpy. It looks just the way the boys drew it on those funny school maps." For she had saved them all—the maps and papers and a construction-paper valentine trimmed with Kleenex-lace that he had made for her—and packed them away in a box he had made for her—and packed

244

when they had moved out. Do you save stuff like that if it means nothing to you?

Last year. Another time dimension. He had often punished her, in his mind. *They tortured us, you know, just for being there. Mostly at night with boiling water from the ceiling. I always slept with the covers over my head.* Casual and deliberate lies, to ease his own hurt.

A window opens behind him, and Lazenby says, "Ma says it's okay. She says first you got to come in, have some peanut-butter toast. She wants to rap to you."

He looks up at the window, as Lazenby rolls his eyes: *Mothers.*

He grins. "Be right there."

He will see her when she comes home, maybe drive over to his grandmother's house some morning, and say hello. Just hello, nothing important. No point in it anyway, because she knows it all, knows just as he does that it is love, imperfect and unordered, that keeps them apart, even as it holds them somehow together; knows also that there was no boiling water; no rats, either.

He follows the sound of Lazenby's voice: "Hey, anybody seen my golf hat? Katy, you seen my golf hat, damn it?" He picks up the nine-iron, swinging it lightly through the grass as he walks toward the house.

The best
in modern fiction from
BALLANTINE